T0402299

Therefore, my friends, I want you to
know that through Jesus the forgiveness
of sins is proclaimed to you.

—ACTS 13:38 (NIV)

A HEART
SET FREE

AMY CLIPSTON

G Guideposts

A Heart Set Free is a trademark of Guideposts.

Published by Guideposts
100 Reserve Road, Suite E200, Danbury, CT 06810
Guideposts.org

Cover and interior design by Müllerhaus
Cover illustration by Dede Putra at Illustration Online LLC.
Typeset by Aptara, Inc.

ISBN 978-1-965859-37-7 (softcover)
ISBN 978-1-965859-38-4 (epub)

Printed and bound in the United States of America
$PrintCode

For my wonderful Amish friend.

Thank you for always answering my
questions, no matter how small or silly.

Your friendship is a blessing!

Glossary

ach • oh

aenti • aunt

appeditlich • delicious

bedauerlich • sad

boppli/bopplin • baby/babies

bruder • brother

bruderskind/bruderskinner • niece(s)/nephew(s)

daed • father

danki • thank you

dat • dad

daadi • grandfather

daadihaus • grandfather's house

dochder • daughter

dummkopp • moron

Englisher • a non-Amish person

fraa • wife

gern gschehne • you're welcome

Gott • God

Gude mariye • Good morning

gut • good

Gut nacht • Good night

haus • house

Ich liebe dich • I love you

kaffi • coffee

kapp • prayer covering or cap

kichlin • cookies

kinner • children

kuche • cake

liewe • love, a term of endearment

mamm • mom

mammi • grandma

mei • my

narrisch • crazy

nee • no

onkel • uncle

rumspringa • the time before a young Amish person officially joins the church

schee • pretty

schmaert • smart

schweschder • sister

sohn • son

Was iss letz? • What's wrong?

Wie geht's • How do you do? or Good day!

wunderbaar • wonderful

ya • yes

zwillingbopplin • twins

Cast of Characters

Anna Byler • Renee's best friend

Autumn Martin • new English driver in Bird-in-Hand

Belinda Walker • Realtor

Delilah & Harvey Graber • parents of Jeannie and Jerome

Emmanuel Mast • Renee's biological father, deceased

Jeannie Graber • daughter of Delilah and Harvey, Jerome's fraternal twin

Jerome Graber • son of Delilah and Harvey, Jeannie's fraternal twin

Lovina & Isaac (Ike) Gingerich • mother and stepfather of Renee

Lucy, Maribeth, Mary, & Sarah • friends of Jeannie

Martha & Abner Mast • parents of Emmanuel, deceased

Murray Robertson • Martha's loner Englisher neighbor

Renee Mast • daughter of Lovina and Emmanuel, stepdaughter of Ike

Tim • Jerome's best friend

Cast of Characters

Note to the Reader

While this novel is set against the real backdrop of Lancaster County, Pennsylvania, and Holmes County, Ohio, the characters are fictional. There is no intended resemblance between the characters in this book and any real members of the Amish community. As with any work of fiction, I've taken license in some areas of research as a means of creating the necessary circumstances for my characters. My research was thorough; however, it would be impossible to be completely accurate in details and description since each and every community differs. Therefore, any inaccuracies in the Amish lifestyle portrayed in this book are completely due to fictional license.

Chapter One

Holmes County, Ohio
Saturday, April 5

A knock sounded on the front door.

"I'll get it!" Renee Mast called to her mother as she dashed down the steps from the upstairs to where the postal carrier, a middle-aged man with brushy gray eyebrows, peered in the screen door. She pushed the door open. "Hi."

"Good afternoon. Are you Renee Mast?"

"*Ya.*"

The man held out an envelope. "I need you to sign for this letter."

Renee signed a clipboard and then took the letter, along with the rest of the mail. "Thank you."

The man nodded before heading down their long, dirt lane toward the road.

Renee opened the mysterious envelope, which was addressed to her and listed a return address of Becker & Associates in Lancaster, Pennsylvania. She unfolded the letter and read.

Dear Ms. Mast,

I am writing to inform you that your paternal grandmother, Martha Mast, has named you in her last will and testament. As per her will, you will inherit her personal possessions, including her farm.

Please call my office to schedule a time to visit Pennsylvania to file the proper paperwork.

Yours truly,

Robert M. Becker, Esquire

Renee examined the letter, reading it over and over again and trying to make heads or tails of it. Her grandmother in Pennsylvania, whom she hadn't seen in twenty years, had passed away and left her...*everything?*

How could this be?

Renee's head started to spin.

"Who was that?" *Mamm's* question broke through her confusion.

Turning, Renee found her mother standing in the doorway leading to the kitchen. "I had to sign for this letter." She held it up. "It's from a lawyer, and it says *mei mammi* died and left me her farm in Pennsylvania."

"Martha passed away?" *Mamm's* words were barely audible as her dark brows drew together. She took the letter, and after skimming it, her brown eyes met Renee's. Then she frowned. "You need to give the land up." She pointed toward the door. "Take the horse and buggy to town and call the lawyer's office now to tell them that you don't want it. They can send you paperwork so that you can surrender. Maybe donate it to the nearest Amish community."

Renee's mouth worked, but no words came out for a moment. "Why?"

"Because we need to leave the past in the past." Mamm set the letter on the table next to the front door and traipsed toward the kitchen.

Renee trailed her. "Wait. I never understood why we don't talk about Mammi." She entered the kitchen, where Mamm stood at the counter beside their wood-burning stove.

"Let it go, Renee." Mamm's dark eyes focused on a cookbook, but her hand quivered while she turned the page.

"Mamm, please look at me." Renee paused to gather her words. She was never disrespectful to her parents, and she didn't plan to start behaving badly today. Still, she had questions about her grandmother that gnawed at her heart. When Mamm finally turned toward her, Renee moved her fingers along the hem of her apron. "Why did *Dat* leave Pennsylvania and turn his back on his parents?"

Mamm shook her head. "Your *daed* didn't want you to go into the past." She hesitated and took a deep breath. "I made a promise to your daed that I would keep what happened a secret. I can't break that promise. I need you to tell the lawyer that you don't want the land."

"But Mamm—"

"The discussion is over," Mamm said, interrupting her. "Ike will be in from the barn soon. I have to start supper, and you need to finish cleaning upstairs."

Renee's spirits sank. "*Ya*, Mamm." She would do what she was told, like she always did. It was their custom.

3

She scooted up the stairs, where she continued sweeping and dusting the bedrooms. While she worked, her mind twirled with questions about her father and his past, which had always been a mystery to her. No one would discuss why he had whisked Renee and her mother away from Pennsylvania twenty years ago when Renee was five. When they settled in Ohio, they built a new life in a new and more conservative community and never looked back. Her father had taken the secret of why they'd left Pennsylvania to his grave when he passed away eight years ago, and her mother never discussed it.

But the curiosity had always haunted Renee, and receiving the news that her grandmother, whom she barely remembered, had passed away tugged at her heart and also brought those questions back to the surface.

She stopped dusting and bowed her head in prayer. "Help me be a dutiful and respectful *dochder, Gott,* but also lead me to the truth about my family's past," she whispered while she worked.

Later, Renee sat in her usual spot at the table between her mother and stepfather. After a silent prayer, they began eating the stew and bread that she had helped Mamm prepare.

Renee lost herself in more curiosity about her late grandmother while she ate the filling meal. When she heard someone say her name, she peeked up from her supper and found her stepfather watching her.

"I'm sorry." Renee sat up straight. "Did you say something?"

Ike's kind hazel eyes showed loving concern. Renee had been so thankful that God had brought Ike into her and Mamm's life soon after Dat passed away. At sixty-four, Ike had salt-and-pepper hair and a matching beard. He was eleven years older than Mamm, and his six children were grown and had families of their own. He and Mamm were kindred spirits since both lost their spouses to cancer. He was a patient and loving man who rarely raised his voice and was always ready to listen, and he and Mamm had been married for seven years now.

"You look like something's troubling you," Ike said. "*Was iss letz?*"

Renee forced her lips to curl up in a smile. "Nothing's wrong." She moved her spoon around on her plate. "I received an unexpected letter today." She glanced over at her mother, who gave her a hesitant expression and then nodded as if giving Renee permission to share the news. "It was from a lawyer in Pennsylvania."

"What did it say?" Ike wiped his mouth with a napkin.

"Mei mammi passed away, and she left me her farm in Bird-in-Hand."

Ike turned to Mamm. "Your parents are gone, Lovina, so it was Emmanuel's mamm who died?"

"Ya. Martha would've been close to eighty now, I suppose." Mamm pinned Renee with a look. "And it's best that Renee does not go to Pennsylvania and dredge up the past. I told her that she should call the lawyer, tell him that she surrenders the land, and donate it to the Amish community." She hesitated. "Or she can sell the farm and use the money for her future."

Renee let that thought roll around in her head. If she sold the farm, she could help her parents. They depended on the baskets she and her mother made, along with her stepfather's small farm, to provide a living for them. Selling the farm would relieve some of their worries. Depending upon how much money the sale would bring, she might be able to help other families in her community as well.

She turned toward Ike. She wanted her stepfather to weigh in on the decision to give up her inheritance, but she couldn't bring herself to speak against her mother. Instead, she gripped the table and waited for Ike to speak his mind.

Ike took a bite of bread, and his eyes focused on his stew, looking as if he were deep in thought.

While her mother peppered Ike with questions about his day, Renee ate her supper and tried to dismiss her questions about her grandmother from her mind.

Later that night, Renee removed her prayer covering and changed into her nightgown. She sat on the edge of her bed and brushed her waist-length, dark brown hair while she studied the candle flickering on her nightstand.

As she moved the brush through her hair, she considered her life on the small farm with her mother and her stepfather. She had always imagined that she'd be married and starting a family of her own by the age of twenty-five, but although she'd been out on a few dates with young men in her community, none of them had seemed to warm her heart the way she'd hoped her future husband would. She supposed that Gott hadn't sent her the husband He'd chosen for her yet, and she hadn't given up hope that she'd meet that man someday soon.

Once again she contemplated her grandmother, and suddenly memories unlocked from the deep recesses of her mind. She stopped brushing her hair as the vision came into clear focus. She was around five years old, and she stood on a porch, holding her mother's hand as an elderly man and woman swiped away tears while her father spoke to them. She couldn't remember what her father said, but he was angry. His voice was so loud that she'd hid behind her mother's gray skirt.

Renee gasped. Had that been the day that she and her parents left Bird-in-Hand?

Then another memory overtook her mind's eye. She played on a swing set with a boy and girl. They were laughing.

"Jeannie and Jerome Graber," she whispered, and then she grinned. How had she remembered their names after all this time?

They were twins and her frequent playmates since Mamm was good friends with their mother. Her heart warmed as more memories of time spent with them passed through her mind—going to the park, eating grilled cheese sandwiches in a bright kitchen, digging in a sandbox.

Renee set her brush on her dresser and picked up the letter from the lawyer. She studied it as she felt a mixture of sadness and confusion. She wouldn't dream of disobeying her mother or Ike, who was a good and kind stepfather to her. Her parents loved her, and she loved them as well, but she still wondered what life would've been like if she'd grown up in Pennsylvania.

Would she have been close to her grandmother—spending time cooking and baking with her, sharing secrets, and getting to know her? And after all this time, why had her grandmother left everything to the granddaughter she'd never had a chance to know? And what had caused her father to turn his back on his parents and his community?

Aside from that, what had become of Jeannie and Jerome?

Renee padded over to her hope chest, where she stowed the letter. She would have to somehow put her curiosity about Pennsylvania behind her.

But as she climbed into bed, she wondered if she could convince her mother and Ike to allow her to go to Pennsylvania to see the farm before she signed it over to the lawyer.

Closing her eyes, she sent another prayer up to God.

Lord, if it's Your will, then please help me find a way to visit Pennsylvania and find out the truth about my family.

Then she rolled over onto her side and tried to silence her racing thoughts.

Bird-in-Hand, Pennsylvania
Sunday, April 6

Jerome Graber awoke with a gasp, and a cold sweat clung to his clammy skin.

Rubbing the heels of his hands into his eye sockets, he tried to shake off the frequent nightmares that had plagued him for the past two years. They haunted him at least three nights every week.

A banging sounded from somewhere beyond his bedroom. He turned toward the battery-operated clock on his nightstand and read the time. It was after eight.

He'd overslept! Had he forgotten to set his alarm last night? Today was a Sunday morning without a church service, but he still had to take care of the animals.

Banging echoed through his small house again.

"Just a minute!" he growled as he pushed himself out of bed and pulled on a pair of trousers, gray shirt, socks, and shoes. Then he tunneled his hand through his hair before limping toward the front door.

The limp and the nightmares were God's constant reminder of his mistakes, and he deserved them both.

Jerome pushed the front door open and found his twin, Jeannie, grinning at him while holding a casserole dish. Their parents stood behind Jeannie, and the delectable scents of bacon, eggs, and cheese whipped over him, causing his empty stomach to growl.

"*Gude mariye!*" Jeannie beamed. "It's a *schee* day that the Lord has made! We're bringing you your favorite breakfast." She indicated the casserole dish in her hands.

His twin always reminded him of sunshine, and it wasn't only due to her blond hair and bright blue eyes. It was her constant positive outlook, which had become the opposite of his after the accident.

Jerome grunted and opened the door wide.

She set the casserole dish on the table. "Let's enjoy this beautiful day together, Jerome."

He remained silent while Mamm and Dat filed into the house. Jeannie flipped on the propane oven, and Mamm began setting the table for breakfast.

Dat came to stand beside Jerome.

"I told Jeannie it was too early, but she insisted you'd be up tending to the animals," Dat said.

Jerome scratched the stubble on his neck. He wasn't going to share that he'd tossed and turned most of the night due to those recurring nightmares, or that he'd overslept. No one knew about the nightmares, and he planned to keep it that way. But he was certain his family could tell by his disheveled appearance that he hadn't been up before they arrived. "I was going to get up...soon."

Jeannie laughed while Mamm shook her head, causing the ties on her prayer covering to swish over her slight shoulders.

"We need to warm the casserole up a bit, so why don't you take care of the animals now?" Mamm suggested.

Dat patted Jerome's shoulder. "Ya. Let's go. We can feed them now. We can't linger too long over breakfast, but the cows will be okay waiting an extra hour to be milked."

Jerome grabbed his straw hat before he and his father trudged out into the bright, early April morning. A cool breeze moved over Jerome on his way to the barn. He scanned the farm—the home where Martha Mast had lived until she'd passed away a couple of weeks ago, along with the large barn, pasture, garden in desperate need of attention, and the small house where Jerome had come to live when he'd accepted the job as Martha's farmhand.

They entered the barn, and the smell of animals mixed with wet hay greeted Jerome. While Dat fed the horses, Jerome took care of the cows.

After they were finished, they returned to the house, where the small table was set and the casserole sat at its center. The delicious scent of the casserole and hot coffee filled the kitchen. Jerome and Dat washed their hands at the sink before sitting at the table and bowing their heads in silent prayer.

Jerome took a long drink of coffee before forking up some of his sister's hearty breakfast.

"It's difficult to believe Martha's been gone almost two weeks now," Mamm said.

"Ya," Jeannie chimed in. "What's going to happen to the farm now that she's gone?"

Jerome swallowed another bite of casserole. "I'm not sure. From what Martha told me, her granddaughter Renee is her only living relative. Her *sohn* died several years ago."

"Renee." Jeannie's already bright face somehow became more radiant with a big smile. "We used to play with her when we were *kinner*. Do you remember her, Jerome?"

Fuzzy memories flashed through his mind—giggling in a sandbox with a small brunette and his sister and then chasing them around the yard while playing tag. He shrugged. "Vaguely."

Jeannie turned her attention back to Mamm. "You were friends with her mamm, right?"

Mamm nodded. "Ya, Lovina and I grew up together and went to school together." She shook her head. "I was devastated when Emmanuel insisted that they move to Ohio."

"It was sudden, wasn't it, Delilah?" Dat asked.

Mamm's expression became grave. "Ya, it was, Harvey. Lovina was upset, but she insisted that she had to do what Emmanuel said. She told me that it broke her heart to leave her *schweschder* here in Pennsylvania, who was her only family left. Lovina's parents had passed away years earlier."

"That's sad," Jeannie said before turning her attention to Jerome. "Since Martha's gone, will you have to leave the farm and find another job?"

11

Jerome's stomach clenched. He'd become comfortable here on Martha's farm, and he was thankful God gave him the opportunity after the accident had destroyed his plans for the future. He'd once hoped to become an apprentice in his uncle's plumbing business, but working as Martha's farmhand made sense after all he'd been through. He was grateful that Martha had been looking for a new farmhand since her previous helper at the time was moving to Indiana with his new wife. Jerome appreciated working alone, along with Martha's easy friendship. They had eaten meals together and talked about their days, but Martha never pressured him to share about the accident or everything that Jerome had lost that night. Here on Martha's farm he had the ability to simply go through the motions of life, working, attending church, and living on his own in the *daadihaus* on Martha's farm. If he lost this job, he had no idea what he'd do.

"Martha left me a few months' pay, and the lawyer said I can stay here until Martha's survivors make a decision about the farm. As far as I know, the lawyer was trying to track down Renee."

"Well, that's *gut*," Jeannie said. "So, Mamm, I've been working on a new quilt for the mud sale. I'll need to get more fabric from the store."

Jerome lost himself in thoughts of his uncertain future and focused his eyes on his meal while Jeannie droned on about the quilts she was creating for an upcoming mud sale, and Dat talked about the fabric store they owned.

Soon their plates were empty, and the women were cleaning up the table.

"*Danki* for breakfast." Jermone started for the door. "I need to get to milking."

Jeannie spun from the sink to face him. "Wait," she said. "Are you coming out to youth group?" His twin's face glowed with hope.

"*Nee*," he said, repeating the same answer he gave when she asked him every single week since the day that changed everything nearly two years ago. He had to give it to his twin—she was relentless and never gave up hope in him, even when he didn't deserve it.

When his twin's smile wobbled, guilt tangled up his insides. Although he hated disappointing his sister, dating was the furthest thing from his mind. What Amish woman in her right mind would want a damaged man like him?

"You should come, Jerome," Jeannie insisted.

Mamm's expression nearly mirrored his twin's. "Your schweschder is right, Jerome. You have to start living again. Gott wants that for you."

Jerome swallowed his sigh. He knew his mother and sister meant well, but he was tired of their repetitive lectures. He nodded and headed for the door.

"Oh, Jerome," Jeannie said. "I meant to tell you that there's a new driver in the community. She just started offering rides." She pulled a piece of paper from her apron and set it on the table. "When you need a ride, you can give her a call."

"I will." He continued toward the door.

Dat was close behind him. "Let's go do the milking," he said before they headed out the door to the barn.

Chapter Two

Holmes County, Ohio
Monday, April 7

G ude mariye," Renee sang as her best friend, Anna Byler, walked into the basket shop, which was a small, cinderblock building located on the dirt lane that led to Renee's parents' farm. Renee and her mother made the baskets and sold them in the building located in front of their house. She was grateful that Anna frequently came to visit her while she ran the store.

Anna shook her head and groaned. "I thought I'd never make it over here. I couldn't get the kinner to get ready for school. I feel like I chased them around the *haus* for most of the morning."

"*Ach* nee," Renee said while trying to mask her grin. As the oldest girl of seven siblings, Anna always shared the best stories about corralling her younger brothers and sisters. Renee enjoyed living vicariously through her friend's colorful anecdotes. She was so thankful that Anna and her family lived next door. Renee had always considered Anna the sister she'd never had.

"They all thought it would be funny to run around screaming instead of eating breakfast since Mamm and Dat had left for an appointment with the midwife." Anna rubbed her wrinkled forehead. "It's just going to get crazier when Mamm has her eighth *boppli*, but kinner are the Lord's blessing, ya?"

Anna perched on a stool beside a display of baskets that Renee and her mother had made last week. She straightened her prayer covering on her blond hair, crossed her legs, and focused her pretty green eyes on Renee. "What's new?"

Renee looked out toward the road and then back at Anna. "I need to tell you about the letter I received yesterday."

"This sounds juicy!" Anna rested her elbow on her thigh and her chin on her hand. "I'm ready. Tell me."

Renee chuckled. "I had to sign for it. It was from a lawyer in Pennsylvania, and it says mei mammi passed away and left me everything, including her farm."

Anna blinked and then blinked again. "You inherited a farm in Pennsylvania?"

"Ya." Renee nodded. "Isn't that *narrisch*?"

"That *is* crazy! What are you going to do?"

Renee sat on the stool beside her best friend. "Unfortunately, I can't do anything. Mei mamm wants me to call the lawyer and tell him that I don't want it. She says I should surrender the land to the Amish community out there. She also suggested selling it and using the money toward my future."

"Don't you want to at least see it before you surrender it?" Anna's nose scrunched.

Renee moved her finger over a picnic basket. "Mei mamm says we need to leave the past in the past, which is what mei dat wanted, but I want to go to Pennsylvania."

"You have questions."

Renee sighed. "I have a lot of questions. The only thing I remember about my life in Pennsylvania are vague memories like playing with friends. I think I remember my grandparents crying the day we left for Ohio." She folded her arms over her black apron. "I want to know the truth about why my family left and never spoke to my grandparents again. And I want to see mei mammi's farm." Her throat thickened. "She never forgot me, and I feel like I owe it to her to visit the farm."

Anna reached over and touched Renee's hand. "That makes perfect sense, Renee. You should go."

"But I can't disobey mei mamm."

"I'm not saying you should disobey her. I'm just saying you need to convince her that you need to visit."

"How?"

Anna tilted her head. "What did Ike say about the letter?"

"Nothing." Renee shrugged. "I told him about it, and he just went back to eating supper."

"He hasn't forbidden you from going?"

Renee shook her head.

"That's gut!" Anna exclaimed. "Talk to both of your parents. Tell them how you feel. Explain that you want to visit and promise that you'll be back." Her smile faded. "And promise *me* you'll come back."

"You know I will."

"Gut, because you need to be in my wedding," Anna said.

Renee gasped. "Did Noah propose?"

"Not yet, but it's coming soon. I can feel it." Anna gave her a knowing look. "What about you? We're both twenty-five. We need to get married and start having *bopplin* before we're too old."

"I guess we'll see what Gott has in store for me."

Later that afternoon, Renee started up the short path from the store to the farmhouse. A bird tweeted nearby, and she stopped and turned toward the tree where the little bird sang. She smiled and hugged her arms to her middle while she listened to its song.

She glanced up at the cloudless sky and another memory flashed through her mind. She was standing in her grandmother's kitchen in Pennsylvania, and her grandmother was pouring tea from a beautiful teapot decorated with colorful flowers. Her grandmother's face was bright with a beautiful smile.

Go to Pennsylvania, Renee.

The thought took her by surprise, and Renee gasped. It was as though Gott had whispered in her ear! A chill raced up her spine, and she shivered.

She needed to go and see her grandmother's farm. She could feel it in her bones.

Now she just had to convince her parents to give her their blessing.

Renee's hands trembled later that evening while she carried a pan of goulash to the table at suppertime. She placed a bowl of pasta beside the goulash and then added a basket of bread before taking a seat and bowing her head in silent prayer.

"Did you sell a lot of baskets today?" Ike asked after the prayers were over.

"Three," Renee said.

"Gut," Ike said before swallowing a bite of supper. "This is *appeditlich*."

"Ya, it is delicious," Mamm agreed. "Renee insisted on making supper tonight," she told Ike before looking at Renee. "What's the occasion?"

Renee divided a look between her parents. "I was hoping to have a chance to speak to you both." She folded her shaky hands and prayed she looked more confident than she felt.

Both of her parents watched her with curiosity.

"I've been thinking about the letter I received from the lawyer, and I want to go to Pennsylvania." She managed to say the words and then waited for the protest.

Mamm's face clouded with a deep frown. "Nee."

"Wait, Lovina." Ike set his hand on her mother's back. "Let's hear her out." Then he gave Renee an easy expression. "Go on."

Relief settled over Renee. *Danki, Ike!* "I feel that if mei mammi remembered me after all these years, then I owe it to her to go to the farm." She paused and worked to recall the speech she had practiced in her mind all day. "I don't expect you to pay for the trip. I've been saving my money from the basket sales, and I'm sure I have enough to cover the trip and all of my expenses." She moved her fingers over the edge of the table. "I know you depend on the income I make selling the baskets since we always split the profits, and I don't want to make this difficult for you. I can ask Anna to help you make baskets and also in the store while I'm gone, and she can split the income with you like I do."

Silence billowed over the kitchen, and the only sound came from the hand pump dripping into the sink. Renee's heartbeat pounded in her ears. She had to find a way to convince her parents to agree to let her go.

"Please," she said, pleading with them. "Mei mammi left me the farm for a reason, and I feel Gott leading me to Pennsylvania to find out why." She folded her hands as if saying a prayer while dividing another look between them. "I really need your blessing for this. I promise I'll be home by Christmas."

"Christmas?" Mamm's voice squeaked. "It's only April! That's too long."

Ike held a hand up. "Okay. Let's compromise then. What if Renee promises to be home by August? That way she's here for the harvest to help prepare for winter."

Mamm hesitated, and Renee pressed her lips together.

"Please, Mamm." Renee's voice was thick with emotion. "I need to do this, and I need you to understand why."

A few more moments ticked by, and Renee almost gave up.

Finally, Mamm moved her head in a nearly imperceptible nod. But the tears in her brown eyes squeezed Renee's heart. "Fine," she said, sounding resigned. "I'll agree to it if you're home by fall."

Renee blew out the breath she hadn't realized she'd been holding. "Danki."

"Gut." Ike covered Mamm's hand with his. "Renee will have a chance to visit Pennsylvania and take care of her mammi's will."

Mamm nodded. "Ya." Then she paused. "I won't be breaking my promise to Emmanuel if you go to Pennsylvania and find out the truth yourself, Renee."

Renee touched her mother's hand. "Danki, Mamm."

"I'm glad we've found a compromise." Ike looked at Renee again. "After supper you can take the horse and buggy to town to call the lawyer and check the bus schedule."

"Danki, Ike." Renee felt the knots in her shoulders ease slightly. "I'll make sure my chores are done before I leave."

Relief ballooned inside her. Maybe she'd finally find out the truth about why her father left Pennsylvania. From what she remembered, her grandparents were crushed when her father took her and Mamm away. She could envision her grandparents' tears the day that they left. Both of them were heartbroken. The news she uncovered may be heartbreaking, but she was prepared to face that. She just needed to know why they left, and perhaps she could somehow pick up the broken pieces that her father had left behind.

Later that evening Renee guided Ike's horse up the dirt lane leading to Anna's family's house. She'd already gone to town to call the lawyer's office and leave a message, as well as to check the bus schedule, and she felt the urge to stop to see her best friend on her way home. She found candles flickering in the front windows, and the murmur of voices became louder as she ascended the front steps.

She knocked on the storm door and waited. Footfalls sounded, and voices became louder before the front door opened, and Milton, one of Anna's little brothers, stood staring at her. At eight he mirrored his siblings with their blond hair and eyes the color of the lush pastures in the summer.

"You're Renee," he announced.

"That's right." She smiled. "Is Anna around?"

"Ya." He turned. "Anna!" he bellowed. "Renee's here!" Then he scampered back into the house, the storm door slamming shut in his wake.

Renee bit back a laugh. Anna's siblings were always full of mischief. She sat on a plastic chair and hugged her sweater closer to her body as the sun began to set, sending a kaleidoscope of colors across the sky. Her leg bounced, and she looked toward the front door. She'd been anxious to share her news with her friend ever since she'd returned from town.

The door opened with a squeak, and Anna hurried out. "Renee! *Wie geht's?*"

"Anna. I have a lot to tell you." Renee jumped up to her feet. "I'm leaving Thursday for Pennsylvania, and hopefully I'm going to finally find out why mei dat brought mei mamm and me here and took us away from our family." She pulled her friend in for a hug. "Danki for encouraging me to talk to my parents."

Anna gave her a squeeze and then stepped away. "Oh, Renee. I'm so glad it worked out for you." Then her smile faded. "You're coming back, right?"

"Ya. I had to promise to be back by August, and actually, I need to ask you a favor. I'll need your help."

"Sure. What can I do?"

Renee paused and licked her lips. "Could you possibly help mei mamm make and sell the baskets? I know you're busy with your siblings, but if you have time while they're in school, you and mei mamm can split the profits."

Anna smiled. "I'd be happy to help." She leaned against the porch railing. "So, you leave Thursday?"

"Ya, bright and early. It's going to take me almost twenty-four hours to get there with the layovers and bus changes, so I won't arrive until Friday." She started to pace. "I have so much to do before I leave."

Renee spun to face her friend's unreadable expression. "I promise I'll write you. I picked up stationery and stamps while I was in town." She laughed. "I'm so excited that my thoughts are a jumbled mess." Her smile flattened as she studied Anna's frown. "Are you okay?"

"Ya." Anna touched Renee's arm. "I'm really happy for you. I know you've had questions for a long time, and this is really important to you. I'm just surprised that you're going so soon." Her lips curled up in a faint smile. "Now, don't go there and fall in love and not come home."

Renee scoffed. "That's the furthest thing from my mind."

"You never know what Gott has in store for you," Anna said.

Renee nodded. She knew that was true. Whatever happened in Pennsylvania had to have been heartbreaking for her father to insist that her mother not only leave but also keep the reason for their departure a secret. Renee had no idea what she was going to face, but she was going to be strong—with the Lord's help.

Renee hugged her. "I'm going to miss you."

"And I'm going to miss you too."

Chapter Three

Bird-in-Hand, Pennsylvania
Friday, April 11

"Thank you." Renee handed the taxi driver a handful of bills before the car backed out of the driveway and motored down the street.

She stood on the driveway and studied the small, white house while unexpected memories of when she was little rushed over her. She recalled riding in a buggy to the house, where an elderly couple met her on the porch and engulfed her in hugs. She could almost taste the delicious meals she'd eaten in her grandparents' home. And she remembered playing in the fields, chasing the barn cats, helping her grandfather with the animals in the barn, helping her grandmother bake...and being happy here.

"Why are all of these memories coming back to me now?" she whispered. "Is that You, Gott? Are You sending me these memories as a way to—"

She stopped speaking when an uneasy feeling crept over her skin. She turned toward a gray two-story house across the street, and she found a stocky man with dark hair and large glasses staring at her. He was dressed in jeans and a T-shirt, indicating that he was an *Englisher*. The angry expression on his face sent a chill racing up her spine. The hair on her neck stood on end.

The man disappeared from the window, but the unpleasant feeling clung to her. She shook it off before lifting her suitcase and trudging up the driveway, her black sneakers crunching on the crushed rocks. When she reached the top of the driveway, she glanced around the property, finding a spacious red barn, along with a large pasture that she recalled had been dotted with cows. She turned to the right and was surprised to see a small house, presumably a daadihaus, which was where her grandmother would have eventually lived if her parents had taken over the farm. Why had Mammi built a daadihaus after Dat had whisked Renee and her mother off to Ohio?

To her left she found a row of birdhouses hanging from tree branches above an overgrown garden, which had once overflowed with colorful flowers while bees buzzed around them.

Above her, the sky darkened, and a cool breeze moved over her, bringing with it the scent of moist earth and animals. An ache radiated along her spine after the nearly twenty-four-hour trip, thanks to the multiple connections at different bus stations between Ohio and Lancaster. She'd endured hours of sitting in uncomfortable bus seats and trying to sleep, which she'd only managed to do in short spurts. She'd been nervous traveling alone, but she was grateful for the gracious and pleasant drivers and employees at the bus stations who had helped her find her way. The other passengers hadn't stared at her attire too much, but she'd grown used to the curious looks she encountered when she ventured to town back home. And despite the fairly smooth trip, exhaustion covered her like a heavy blanket. She craved a warm cup of tea, a hot bath, and a warm bed.

A yawn overtook her as she plodded up the back steps to a small porch. When she reached the door, she froze. Although she told the lawyer that she'd meet with him on Monday, she hadn't asked where to find a key for the house.

Well, maybe it was unlocked. Many Amish folks didn't bother locking their doors. Renee rested her hand on the cool knob and then attempted to turn it. But the knob didn't budge.

Ach, nee!

Now what would she do? It was Friday night, and surely the lawyer's office was closed. She recalled that her grandmother had a phone shanty near the barn. She remembered following her grandmother to it once when she was checking messages. Hopefully the phone was still there, and if so, perhaps she could find a number for a taxi and ask if a driver could take her to a hotel. Then she could meet with the lawyer and pick up the keys on Monday.

"Wie geht's?" a deep male voice called. "Can I help you?"

Renee spun as a tall Amish man limped toward her from the direction of the barn. Some of her anxiety drained out of her. Perhaps he was a farmhand and worked here. But the lawyer hadn't mentioned employees. Yet someone had to take care of Mammi's animals until the property was sold.

She lifted her hand in a wave. "I'm Renee Mast."

The man continued toward her, and although his lips were turned down in a frown, she was intrigued by his intelligent blue eyes. Blond hair stuck out from under his straw hat, and his shoulders and arms were muscular as if he spent his days performing difficult manual labor. And if he was the farmhand, he most certainly did hard work.

For a moment he seemed familiar. But she had left Bird-in-Hand when she was five. How could anyone that she'd last seen twenty years ago be familiar to her?

"I was wondering if you'd get here," he grumbled, coming to stand beside her. "You're Martha's only relative." He slipped past her and pulled a set of keys from his pocket.

She gazed up at him. He was several inches taller than her own height of five-foot-six. "Who are you?" she asked.

"Jerome Graber," he muttered. "I ran the farm for Martha. Still do, for now." He unlocked the door.

"Jerome! I thought you were familiar." Another yawn overtook her, and she cupped her hand to her mouth. "Excuse me. I've been traveling for more than twenty-four hours."

"Let's get you settled." He held the door open wide and then picked up her suitcase.

Renee stepped into the house and more memories doused her as she glanced around at the family room with its worn brown sofa, matching end table and coffee table, and propane lamps. She recalled sitting on the floor and playing with a doll while her parents spoke to her grandparents.

Jerome set her suitcase in the den while she wandered into the kitchen, where she remembered baking with her grandmother. She moved her finger over the counter as the memories flooded her mind. When she turned, she found Jerome standing in the doorway, watching her with an indiscernible expression.

Suddenly her stomach growled, and heat crawled up her neck to her cheeks. "I haven't eaten since lunchtime." She turned toward the clock on the wall. "That was almost six hours ago."

"There's no food in this haus." He pointed toward the kitchen. "I cleaned it out after your mammi..." His deep voice trailed off.

"Right." She glanced around the kitchen and then toward a hallway leading to the bathroom and three bedrooms while an awkward silence stretched between them. She considered asking Jerome to take her to the market, but the idea of traipsing around a store sounded like pure torture when her legs, feet, and back screamed for her to go to bed.

Jerome scratched his clean-shaven jaw. "Would you—um—like to eat with me?"

She studied his uncomfortable expression, and for a moment she considered declining his invitation. When her stomach gurgled again, only louder this time, she tried to ignore her flaming cheeks and gave him a thin smile. "Danki, Jerome. That would be *wunderbaar.*"

He nodded before making a sweeping gesture toward the back door. She followed him down a flagstone line path to the small house that looked like a daadihaus, where he wrenched the door open and then gestured for her to walk in first.

She entered the simple kitchen and glanced around, finding a table with four chairs, light-colored cabinets, and sink with faucet, just like her grandmother's. Darkness crept in through the window above the sink, and Jerome switched on a few battery-operated lanterns before flipping a couple of knobs on the stove and then retrieving a casserole dish from the refrigerator.

"Mei schweschder insists on cooking for me," he muttered, setting the dish onto the counter.

"Jeannie, right?"

He turned toward her, and his mouth was still set in a frown. "Ya."

She smiled. "I remember playing with you and Jeannie. Our mamms were friends."

He gave her a quick nod and then turned his attention toward the cabinet.

"I can set the table if you need to do something else."

Relief traveled across his face before he disappeared from the kitchen. Renee set the casserole in the oven and then busied herself with pulling out dishes, utensils, and glasses. She glanced around the room looking for something to tidy up, but she found nothing. The counters and floor were clean. Crossing to the window, she peered out, taking in the rolling patchwork fields as the sun began to set.

Jerome finally reappeared a few minutes later wearing a blue shirt that complemented his clear eyes. His face was still set in a frown. Was he always so sullen? Or did he not approve of her being on his farm or in his home?

The questions swirled through her mind as he crossed the kitchen, opened the oven door, and then closed it.

"I think it needs a few more minutes," he said.

More silence suffused the air between them, and she racked her brain for something to say. The delicious smell from the chicken, cheese, and broccoli casserole overtook the kitchen, and Renee hugged her arms to her middle, hoping to prevent another embarrassing, loud growl from escaping.

"How's Jeannie?" she asked.

At the same time, he said, "Have you called your mamm?"

"What?" she asked with a chuckle, but his expression remained grim.

He pointed toward the doorway. "You can use the phone in the shanty to call your mamm. Let her know that you got here safely."

"Oh." She leaned on the back of a kitchen chair. "We don't have a phone."

His eyes studied her for a moment. "Not even a community phone?"

She shook her head. "I'm going to write her a letter."

He shrugged and then checked the casserole. "Looks done," he mumbled, before grabbing a potholder and pulling the bubbling casserole from the oven and setting it on a hot pad on the table.

Soon they were sitting across from each other. After a silent prayer, they each scooped casserole onto their plates and began eating.

Renee peeked across the table at Jerome and found him staring at his plate. Once again she longed for the tense silence between them to dissipate. "How's Jeannie doing?"

"Fine." He sipped from his glass of water.

"Is she married?"

"Nee." Then his blue eyes met hers. "Are you?"

She scoffed. "Nee."

He returned his focus to his plate.

"How long have you worked here?" she asked.

"Couple years," he muttered without meeting her gaze.

"Do you like it?"

He gave her a half shrug without looking over at her.

"Your folks own a store, right?" she asked.

"Ya. Graber Fabrics."

"Did you ever work there?"

"Ya." He paused for a moment. "I prefer farming."

Renee pressed her lips together while questions about Jerome occupied her mind. Once again she longed to know if he was simply a grouch or just a loner. Or did he long for her to leave and go back to Ohio? What if he'd hoped to inherit the farm himself or even perhaps purchase it?

The question gripped her mind, and the pieces came together. Jerome might resent her for taking over the farm when he had been the person doing all of the chores for the past couple of years. Perhaps when she met with the lawyer on Monday, she should suggest the lawyer help her sell Mammi's place and then return to Ohio. If she sold the farm, she could secure her future since most likely one of Ike's children would inherit his property. If Ike passed away before her mother, Renee could use the money to take care of her mother. And if Renee never married, she could possibly purchase a home of her own.

But she couldn't sell the farm before she found out what happened to push her father out of the community. She was still convinced God had led her here to discover the truth about her family's past.

Jerome took another drink of water, and his eyes met hers.

"How long has this haus been here?" The question leapt from her lips without any forethought.

Jerome's brow wrinkled.

She set her fork beside her plate. "I don't remember this daadi-haus being here when I was little." Pointing toward the door, she added, "Only mammi's haus and the barn were here on the land. Did mei mammi build this haus for you?"

"It's been here for as long as I've worked here. Martha said her previous farmhand lived here before I did."

"Oh." She almost smiled. Jerome had spoken to her using two complete sentences, and his expression was almost…friendly. Almost. Once again she wondered if he resented her, and a plan to win him over took shape. She adjusted herself on her chair. "What chores can I do for you while I'm here?"

"Chores?"

She waved her fork in the air. "You know. I could take care of the chickens, clean for you, maybe cook. Do you need any clothes mended?"

He studied her with a blank expression.

"Or maybe—" She stopped speaking when a yawn gripped her, and she covered her mouth with her hand. "I'm sorry. It was a long trip. What I meant to say was that I could I wash your clothes too." Then she yawned again.

Jerome's eyes crinkled at the edges. "Why don't you get some rest before we worry about assigning you some chores?"

"Okay."

They finished their meals and then Renee gathered up their plates. "Supper was appeditlich. Danki for sharing it with me."

"No problem. *Gern gschehne.*" His *you're welcome* was almost inaudible. Reaching over, his hands brushed hers, and he took the dishes from her. "I'll clean up. You rest."

"Oh." She slid her hands down her apron. "Danki."

He nodded and carried the dishes to the sink.

She stood still while he turned on the faucet and added dish detergent to the water. She had to pump water into the sink with a hand pump at home. The faucet seemed so much easier—and from the steam rising it looked like he had warm water too. She watched him work for a moment.

He swiveled to face her, but then a strange look flickered over his face. He dashed out of the kitchen and returned a few moments later with a flashlight and two lanterns. "Do you want me to show you around Martha's haus?"

She shook her head. "I think I can find everything."

"Linens are in the dresser in the bedroom. You should have everything you need."

"Except food," she reminded him. "Could I use your horse and buggy to go to the grocery store tomorrow?"

"We'll go together." He handed her a key ring with two keys on it, along with a flashlight and a battery-operated lantern. "There are more lanterns in the utility room. You'll have enough to keep one in each room."

She studied the lantern and then looked up at him. "Why don't you use kerosene?"

His light eyebrows drew together. "You don't use battery-operated lanterns?"

She shook her head.

"These are safer. There should be spare batteries in the utility room too, but if you need extra, just ask."

"I will," she said. "Danki." Jerome seemed so kind and caring. But then she took in his frown, and she wondered if she'd ever get a chance to see him smile. Hear him laugh.

What was wrong with her? Must be the exhaustion talking.

"If you need anything, let me know."

"I will. *Gut nacht*, Jerome," she said before heading out into the cool evening air. She trudged toward the house, her steps bogged down by the weight of her exhaustion while the lantern guided her way along the rocky path.

When she reached the house, she found her way to her grandmother's bedroom and located linens. She made the bed while contemplating how different it was to be back in her grandmother's home with a faucet, battery-operated lanterns, and an indoor bathroom with a flush toilet and a tub with a shower.

After bathing and pulling on her nightgown, Renee climbed into the comfortable bed and snuggled under the sheets.

Chapter Four

Bird-in-Hand, Pennsylvania
Saturday, April 12

Movement out of the corner of Jerome's peripheral vision drew his attention to the barn door, where Renee stood. She was clad in another dark-colored dress, and her expression was unsure while she fiddled with the hem of her apron. It was early in the morning, and the air was cool and smelled of wet wood.

He lifted his straw hat and swiped the back of his hand over his brow while he plodded over to her.

"Gude mariye." Her voice was perky, and her soulful brown eyes sparkled in the low light. She looked well rested. If only he could find the secret to a good night's sleep.

He nodded.

"I was wondering if I could make you breakfast." She bit her lower lip. "That's if I can use your groceries and then buy you some to replace them."

"I'm almost done out here. Wait a few minutes, and we'll cook together."

Her posture relaxed. Did she truly believe he'd let her starve?

"Gut. Danki." She scanned the barn, and a wistful expression moved across her face. "I remember playing out here with mei *daadi*. He always let me help him feed the animals, and I remember he told the best stories." She smiled. "There were always barn cats, and one time I found one with a new litter of kittens. Daadi and I sat together and while I played with the kittens, he talked about the farm where he'd grown up."

Jerome folded his arms over his middle.

Her brow furrowed, and she pointed toward the cows. "What kind of contraption do you use to milk the cows?"

"They're milkers that run on diesel." He studied her. "What do you use in your community?"

She held up her hands. "These."

He shook his head. All her questions made him wonder if her father had moved his family to a more conservative community when they went to Ohio.

Interesting.

He suddenly recalled a conversation he'd had with Martha shortly before she passed away. On that day he'd noticed that Martha had been unusually quiet, and when he'd found her wiping her eyes while sitting at her kitchen table, he sat with her and asked her if she was okay. She'd given him a sad smile and said, "If it wasn't for my mistakes, mei sohn wouldn't have felt the need to take his family away and join a Swartzentruber community."

Jerome hadn't felt it was his place to ask more questions, but he couldn't escape his curiosity. Instead of questioning her, he had made her tea and sat with her, hoping his presence would offer some comfort.

"Do you sell the milk?" Renee's question yanked him back to the present.

"Ya. The milk truck comes on Mondays."

Renee nodded while glancing around the barn. "Would you like me to feed the chickens and collect the eggs?"

"Sure." He pointed toward the tack room. "The chicken feed and a couple of baskets are in there."

She hurried off, and he finished milking the cows and feeding the horses.

Jerome walked outside and met Renee as she ambled toward him carrying two baskets. He held his hand out to take them from her.

"I got it," she said as they walked together toward his house.

While they moved down the dirt path, he could feel her eyes studying him, but he kept moving forward.

"Jerome," Renee began, "Are you okay?" Her voice held an undercurrent of curiosity and concern.

He stopped moving and faced her. "Yeah. Why?"

"You're...limping." She pointed to his left leg.

"Old injury," he muttered before continuing his journey toward the house. He set his jaw and hoped she wouldn't ask for details. But even if she did, he wouldn't answer. He never discussed the accident—no matter what.

Once inside, she placed the basket on the counter. "Would you like me to make us eggs?" she asked.

"Sure." He gathered up a pan and butter before pulling out bread and bacon. When he turned toward Renee again, he found her staring at the stove. "Something wrong?"

"Um." She pointed toward the stove. "How do I start it?"

He lifted an eyebrow. "You've never used a stove?"

"Not like this. We have a wood-burning stove."

Jerome was silent for a moment, once again wondering about her father's decision to move his family. He clicked the dials on the propane-powered stove, and then she set to work making eggs and bacon while he started the percolator for coffee.

Soon they sat down with their meal of eggs, bacon, and toast.

"Could I take your horse and buggy to the grocery store?" she asked. "I don't want to inconvenience you if you have something else that you need to be doing."

He buttered a piece of toast. "I can still take you." He tried to ignore the worry that always nipped at him when he took Jeannie or another woman out in his buggy. Having a passenger with him always brought back visions of the night that changed everything, but he shoved the anxiety deep inside himself.

They ate in silence, and he was relieved she didn't ask more questions about his injury or his life. He finished his bacon and took a sip of coffee.

When he peered across the table, he spotted her staring at her plate, looking as if she were working through something in her mind. He almost asked her what was wrong, but he didn't want to risk getting close to her. The sooner she made a decision about his job on the farm, the better off he'd be.

Finally, her deep brown eyes met his. "How was my mammi paying you?"

Jerome rubbed his clean-shaven chin. "Room and board and a small salary."

"I see." She wrapped her hands around her coffee mug. "I'm not able to pay you a salary, but I can buy groceries and cook for you while I figure out what to do with the farm."

"It's not a problem. I met with the lawyer last week, and Martha left me a few months of salary.'"

"Oh. Gut."

He nodded slowly. "Are you going to sell it?" He tried to ignore how his gut tied itself into a knot at the thought of losing his job. He needed to start asking around to see if there was another farm that needed a hand.

"Mei mamm wants me to let it go."

He sipped more coffee. "Let it go?" he asked.

Renee pressed her lips into a thin line. "Donate it to the Amish community."

"Is that what you want to do?"

She blew out a deep sigh. "I don't know yet. I might also consider selling it."

He took a bite of bacon and wondered what would happen if she donated it to the community. Would the bishop let him work and live there? They could share in the profits from the milk. That could be a good solution for him and the community.

And if she sold the farm, Jerome was in no position to buy it, but he could see if the new owners needed a farmhand.

But no matter what, Jerome needed to start checking around the community to see what jobs were available. He didn't want to work in his parents' fabric store, but he would consider working on another farm. He'd start checking the bulletin boards in the local stores and talk to members of his church. Another job had to be out there, but he would miss working on this farm.

Renee added a bag of pasta to the grocery cart and then walked toward the deli, where she examined the display of meats. She tried to calculate how to make her money last until August while she was in Bird-in-Hand.

Jerome stayed a few steps behind her, leaning on the cart while she chose her groceries. He'd been quiet during the ride to the store in his buggy, only giving one-word responses to her questions about the farm and the community, and he'd continued his reticence once inside. She wondered if he was always quiet or if his standoffish behavior was due to her presence.

Renee looked at the meat, comparing prices. When she heard someone call Jerome's name, she spun around just as a middle-aged Amish woman approached him.

"Jerome! Wie geht's?" the woman asked. "How are your folks doing?" Her prayer covering was heart-shaped in the back, which was different from Renee's cone-shaped covering, and her dress was maroon, a color she rarely saw in her community.

He continued to lean on the cart and frowned while he muttered responses to the woman's questions. His fingers were wrapped tightly around the handle of the shopping cart as if he were holding on to it for dear life.

Renee chose a package of pork chops, along with a couple of packages of ground beef and chicken. She set them in the cart just as the other woman walked away.

While she and Jerome wove through the remainder of the store, a few more Amish folks greeted Jerome, but he only responded with a curt nod. Renee had a sneaking suspicion that his grim mood wasn't directed at her. Instead, this was his constant disposition, and she wondered what had happened to make him close himself off.

When they reached the cashier, Jerome helped load their groceries onto the conveyor. A young Englisher woman with a nose ring and blue-dyed hair rang up their items and bagged them, and Renee pulled out her wallet from her plain black purse. As she handed money to the clerk, she felt a tap on her shoulder.

Jerome said, holding out a handful of bills, "Take this."

"Nee," she told him. "I said I would pay for—"

"Please, Renee. Just take it." His sky-blue eyes seemed to plead with her.

"Okay," she conceded. She added the bills he gave her to the ones she'd retrieved from her wallet, and the cashier handed them change, which she split with Jerome before they headed out to the parking lot.

After loading their groceries into the back of his buggy, they were on their way to the farm. Renee kept her gaze fixed on the passing traffic, and the patchwork of farms in the distance looked familiar somehow.

She turned toward Jerome beside her, and his eyes were trained on the road ahead.

"How long have you worked for mei mammi?" she asked. "You said about two years, right?"

He adjusted his body in his seat while keeping his eyes focused on the windshield. "Ya."

"Did you always work as a farmhand?"

Somehow the permanent frown that graced his chiseled jaw seemed deeper. "Nee," he grumbled.

More questions taunted Renee. Jerome seemed like such a complicated man. What kind of work did he do before moving to the farm? And what inspired him to work for her mammi? Was he a loner or did he have a girlfriend? And what kind of injury caused his limp?

But it was none of her business. She didn't mean to be so nosy, but Jerome was so…intriguing.

When they reached the farm, Jerome halted the horse. "I'll check the mail."

"I'll get it," she offered.

"It's fine." He limped over to the mailbox.

Renee peered out the window, and she found the man across the street staring at her with a menacing expression. Her stomach plunged as a sick feeling rolled over her.

Jerome got back into the buggy and set a pile of envelopes on the seat between them. "Was iss letz?" he asked.

"That Englisher," she said, lifting her chin toward the neighbor. "He was staring at me yesterday when I first got here. And he's staring at us now. He seems so angry."

"That's Murray Robertson." Jerome guided the horse up the dirt driveway toward the barn.

"Is he…okay?" she asked.

Jerome shrugged. "He's a loner. Martha told me that he's always kept to himself ever since he moved here. He's a little peculiar, but he seems fine. Every once in a while he talks to me, but he's not very social."

An eerie feeling moved through her.

After they carried the groceries into her grandmother's kitchen, Jerome began stowing the meat in the propane-powered freezer.

"I can take care of it," she said. "You can tend to the horse."

He nodded and started for the door.

"Jerome," she called to him. "Do you have church tomorrow or next week?"

"Tomorrow."

"Do I need to bring anything?" she asked.

"The women normally bring a dessert."

"Oh." She glanced at the groceries. "I could try to throw together a cake." Then she studied the oven. "I'll have to figure out the oven."

"I think the Lord would understand if you don't bring something to service this week."

A ghost of a smile played on his lips, and she was fascinated. She stilled for a moment trying to imagine what he'd look like if he actually grinned. He was...handsome, with his strong jaw and bright blue eyes, and if he smiled, he'd be even more attractive.

She waited for his lips to turn upward, but the frown reappeared.

His eyebrows lifted, and she realized she'd been staring at him. *Ach, nee!*

Heat filled her cheeks. She needed to say something in order to end this awkward moment.

"C-could I...?" she stammered.

"Have a ride to church?" he finished her question, and she nodded. "Of course. Your mammi gave up her horse and buggy years ago, and I drove her where she needed to go, or she got rides from others in the community."

"Danki," she said, and an uncomfortable silence hung in the air between them. She returned to the counter and began unpacking a grocery bag. "I'll have supper ready at five, and I'll do my best not to burn it."

"Burnt supper is better than no supper at all," he muttered on his way toward the door.

As she watched him go, she wondered if she'd ever get to know Jerome and what had happened to him. Had God sent her here to help soften his heart?

She almost laughed out loud at that ridiculous notion. Why would God want her to work in Jerome's life when Mamm had made it clear she needed to take care of Mammi's farm and return home to her own Amish community?

Banishing those ridiculous thoughts, Renee focused on stowing the groceries. She put the pasta and soups in the pantry, and when she turned toward the counter, her eyes focused on a china cabinet at the far end of the kitchen.

As she spotted a teapot decorated with colorful flowers, another memory unlocked in her mind. She recalled sitting in the kitchen with her grandmother and sharing a cup of tea.

She gasped. That was the same memory she had recalled when she felt God leading her back to Pennsylvania.

Tears welled in her eyes as she opened the china cabinet door and picked up the porcelain teapot. She sniffed and traced her fingertip over the flowers.

"I'm sorry I never saw you again after we left, Mammi, but danki for leaving me the farm. I'm going to find out the truth about why mei dat left you and the community behind, and if I need to, I'll make things right," she whispered, before setting the teapot back in the cabinet and focusing on what to make for supper.

Chapter Five

Bird-in-Hand, Pennsylvania
Sunday, April 13

Jerome guided his horse down the driveway toward the road the following morning. The mid-April air was cool, and the sky was blue and dotted with fluffy, white clouds. The clip-clop of the horse's hooves and the whirr of the wheels filled the silence while they made their journey to the Zook family's farm for church service. He tried to ignore the anxiety that always rose inside him when he had a passenger in his buggy. He would do everything to keep his passenger safe.

Out of the corner of his eye, he spotted Renee beside him clasping and unclasping her hands before she swiped them over the skirt of her black dress. During the past few days, she'd only worn a black or a gray dress, which seemed unusual since the young, unmarried women in his district wore brightly colored frocks to church. It was confirmation that she lived in a much more conservative community in Ohio.

She met his gaze, and her lips tipped up in a nervous smile. "Will your parents and Jeannie be at church?"

He nodded.

"Do you and Jeannie have more siblings?" she asked.

His brow wrinkled. "What do you mean?"

"I haven't seen you in twenty years," she began. "I didn't know if your mamm and dat had more kinner after I left."

"Oh. Nee." He shook his head. "It's still just Jeannie and me."

He turned his attention back to the road, but he could feel her watching him. Shifting in his seat, he tried to think of something to say, but after the accident, he'd lost his social skills. He used to love being with his friends—playing volleyball, going camping, swimming at their favorite lake, or just even spending the evening laughing. He'd almost considered himself the life of the party.

But now Jerome was more comfortable observing people rather than participating in conversations, which was why the thought of attending youth group with his sibling sounded like pure torture.

"Aside from some stepsiblings, I'm still an only child," Renee suddenly said. "My stepfather has six grown children and more than two dozen grandchildren. My best friend back home is Anna, and she lives on the farm next door to mine. She's the second oldest of seven, and her mamm is expecting another one." She chuckled to herself. "Anna has the best stories about her siblings. Since she's the eldest girl, she's always babysitting them. One time she took them to the park, and the four youngest decided to go swimming in a mud hole. She brought them home caked in dirt. Anna said she had to use a bucket to rinse them off outside. Can you imagine?"

He peeked over at her while she laughed, and he enjoyed the sweet sound. Her voice was soothing, reminding him of a warm, comfortable blanket. He felt the tense bundles of nerves in his back relax while she smiled at him.

Somehow she looked even prettier now with the sunlight from the windshield highlighting her ivory skin, deep brown eyes, petite nose, pink lips, and the dark brown hair peeking out from under her prayer covering.

Whoa.

He needed to dismiss those thoughts. He had no business admiring Renee or even considering pursuing another relationship.

Jerome deserved to be alone. He was no good to anyone else, and he was going to be a bachelor for the rest of his life.

"I'm going to write a letter to Anna," Renee continued. "She's like mei schweschder since I don't have any siblings. I also need to write to mei mamm. I was going to write letters last night, but I was too tired and I knew I had to get up early for church."

Jerome settled in the seat and enjoyed the sound of her voice for the remainder of the ride while she detailed more stories about her friend Anna and her family, Renee's stepfather's farm in Ohio, and how pretty the flowers were there.

When they arrived at the Zooks' farm, Jerome's mare followed the line of horses and buggies toward the barn. He halted the horse and then turned toward Renee.

She swallowed, and her eyes flittered around the farm before meeting his. "We're here."

He nodded.

"Gut." She gripped the door handle and then stopped.

He felt the urge to encourage her but couldn't find the words. Three years ago, he would've known what to say to calm her nerves, but the accident had stolen so much from him—including how to speak to people without feeling like a *dummkopp.*

Jerome hopped out of the buggy and began unhitching the horse while Renee came to stand beside him. Her hands shook while she fiddled with her apron.

"Jerome! Jerome!" his twin sister hollered while she sprinted toward him, her light blue dress and white apron flowing around her legs. "I was looking around for you and I—" She stopped moving as her eyes focused on Renee, and her already bright smile shone even brighter.

"Renee?" she asked, her voice coming out in a squeak. When Renee nodded, Jeannie flung her arms around Renee and pulled her in for a tight hug. "I was wondering when you'd come! How are you?" Then she stepped away and giggled. "I should've introduced myself. I'm Jeannie, Jerome's twin. We used to play together. Do you remember me?"

Relief flickered over Renee's attractive face. "Of course I remember you. You and Jerome were my favorite friends."

"Why didn't you tell me Renee was back?" Jeannie pinned Jerome with an annoyed expression.

"I haven't had a chance," he said.

"Well, you're here now." Jeannie looped her arm with Renee's. "Come meet everyone."

"Okay." Renee smiled at Jerome. "See you after the service."

He nodded while his sister and Renee walked away.

"When did you arrive?" Jeannie asked while they walked side-by-side, arms linked, toward the house.

Renee scanned the farm, taking in a line of buggies parked in the large, green field. "Friday."

"Jerome should've called me," Jeannie said. "I would've come over to see you. I need to introduce you to all of my friends."

She steered Renee over to a group of young women who looked to be around her age, and Renee was struck by their light-colored dresses. They wore cheerful shades of pink, blue, yellow, and green, colors she'd never seen worn in her community. She glanced down at her black dress and felt out of place.

"Everyone," Jeannie began, "this is Renee. She moved away twenty years ago, and she's back now. Her mammi was Martha Mast." Jerome's sister's smile was as bright as the midday sun. "Renee, this is Lucy, Maribeth, and Sarah."

Renee nodded hello.

"Where are you from?" Lucy asked. With blond hair and green eyes, she reminded Renee of Anna.

Crossing her arms, Renee moved her hands over her long sleeves. "Ohio."

Maribeth had copper-colored hair. Her gray eyes seemed to study Renee. "Did you move back here?"

"No," Renee began. "Mei mammi left me her farm, and I'm here to settle the legal matters. I'm meeting with the lawyer tomorrow."

"Do you have a boyfriend?" Sarah's hair was light brown, and her dark eyes sparkled with intrigue.

"Nee," Renee said.

"Gut." Jeannie laughed. "Then you fit in perfectly with us."

They all laughed, including Renee, and she felt as if the awkwardness had been broken. She looked out toward the barn, where

Jerome leaned on a fence and spoke to a young man with brown hair who looked to be about their age. He nodded with a sullen expression while the man spoke. When his blue eyes met hers, he lifted his chin in a greeting, and she felt a strange flutter in her chest.

"Jerome is so handsome," Maribeth said with a dreamy sigh.

Renee's eyes snapped to Maribeth. Did Maribeth like Jerome? And if so, was he off-limits? She hoped her face didn't reflect her worry.

"That's true, but he never shows interest in any of the young women," Lucy said. "Not since…well, you know."

Renee divided a look between the two young women. What had happened to Jerome to cause him to not show any interest in the young women in his community? She couldn't imagine why a young Amish man wouldn't want to date, but at the same time, she certainly didn't want to overstep, especially if one of Jeannie's friends liked him. Not that he was interested in Renee.

Just then the congregation began filing into the barn for the service.

"You're going to sit with me during the service, right?" Jeannie asked.

Renee chuckled. "Where else would I sit?"

Jeannie looped her arm around Renee's shoulder and grinned.

Renee followed the line of unmarried women over to their section and then took a seat on the backless bench. The scent of animals and moist earth floated over her while she scanned the congregation seated in the different sections. A murmur of conversations provided backdrop while the married women sat together across from the married men. Renee looked over toward the unmarried men's section and found Jerome sitting beside the man she'd seen talking to him earlier. She recalled Maribeth and Lucy's comments about him, and once again, she wondered if Maribeth had hoped to mend his heart. If so, then Renee would have to respect that—especially since she wouldn't be in Bird-in-Hand very long.

Glancing around the unmarried section where she sat, Renee felt self-conscious. She hugged her arms over her middle as if to shield her dress. She was also the only woman in the congregation wearing a cone-shaped prayer covering. She yearned to not stick out so much.

"How does it feel to be back here?" Jeannie asked.

Renee's eyes bounced around the barn again. "Strange, but also familiar."

She turned toward her friend. Jeannie's striking blue eyes and golden-colored hair mirrored her brother's. She was lovely, and with her ever-present smile, she seemed as sweet as she was attractive.

"I remember attending church with my parents when I lived here," Renee added.

"And all of the fun we had on the swing set and in the sandbox at our haus while our mamms talked for hours and hours." Jeannie touched Renee's arm. "I was telling my folks and Jerome that I hoped you'd come back. Gott answered my prayers."

Renee's heart expanded as she smiled at her friend. Just then the service began, and Renee joined in as the congregation slowly sang the opening hymn. As she expected, this district's services were much like her own. A young man sitting across the barn served as the song leader. He began the first syllable of each line and then the rest of the congregation joined in to finish the verse.

While the ministers met in another room for thirty minutes to choose who would preach that day, the congregation continued to sing. During the last verse of the second hymn, Renee's gaze moved to the back of the barn as the ministers returned. They placed their hats on two hay bales, indicating that the service was about to begin.

The chosen minister began the first sermon, and Renee tried her best to concentrate on his holy words. But her thoughts turned to her parents and Anna at home. They would also be attending church now. She hoped they were having a good day, and her heart squeezed. She missed them, but she was also anxious to learn about her family's past. Renee had done some searching around her grandmother's house last night, but she hadn't found anything. She planned to also search the barn and to talk to a few of the women in the congregation after the services. Surely someone in her grandmother's church district knew something. She hoped God would lead her to the answers she longed to find.

When her thoughts wandered to Jerome, her eyes moved toward the young men across the aisle. Jerome sat with his head bowed, focusing on his hands in his lap. She yearned to know what weighed on his heart. Would she get a chance to know him well enough to find out why he always appeared so sad?

She redirected her thoughts to the sermon, taking in the message and concentrating on God. When the first sermon ended, Renee knelt in silent prayer beside Jeannie. She closed her eyes and thanked God for her new friends, and she asked God to lead her to the answers she sought. She also prayed for Jerome, asking God to send healing and comfort to him if that was what he needed.

After the prayers, the deacon read from the Scriptures, and then the hour-long main sermon began. Renee willed herself to concentrate as the deacon preached from the book of Acts.

Relief flooded Renee when the fifteen-minute kneeling prayer ended. The congregation stood for the benediction and sang the closing hymn. While she sang, her eyes moved again to Jerome. She wondered if he could feel her watching him, but he didn't look her way.

When the service ended, Jeannie touched Renee's hand. "Let's help serve lunch."

They slipped past men converting benches into tables for the noon meal on their way out the barn door. Jeannie hurried down a rock path and into the Zook family's kitchen, where women fluttered around the space, preparing the meal. The appetizing scents of coffee, bread, and lunchmeat wafted over her.

Jeannie tugged Renee's sleeve and towed her over to a middle-aged woman busy pouring pretzels into bowls. The woman wore a maroon-colored dress and black apron, and her sky-blue eyes reminded Renee of Jeannie's and Jerome's.

"Mamm," Jeannie exclaimed. "Renee's here!"

The woman grinned and pulled Renee in for a hug. "Renee! Did your mamm come with you?"

"Nee," Renee said. "She's home in Ohio."

"How is she?"

"She's gut," Renee said.

"I've missed Lovina so much. I often longed for her address, so I could write her a letter." Jeannie's mother chuckled. "I'm Delilah.

I'm sure you don't remember my name. You must come for supper sometime."

"I'd like that. I'd love to talk to you about my parents and why they left."

Delilah nodded. "Let's plan a time to get together."

Renee's heart lifted. "Could you introduce me to *mei mammi's* friends here at church?"

"I'd be happy to after we serve the meal."

"Danki."

Women moved past them, balancing trays full of food.

"We should help," Jeannie said before picking up two coffee carafes. "Let's go fill *kaffi* cups," she said.

Jerome sat at the table across from his best friend, Tim. They'd been buddies since before they started first grade together, and Jerome was thankful that their friendship had remained constant, despite the ups and downs he'd faced after the accident. Just like Jerome, Tim was still a bachelor, and they were two of the few unmarried men left from their original youth group.

Jerome dropped a few pretzels onto his plate. He'd tried to concentrate on the minister's holy words during the service, but he'd spent the time sneaking looks over at Renee and his sister. He was relieved that Renee had seemed comfortable, and he was certain that his sister had helped her overcome her anxiety. Jeannie had a way with people, and he was grateful for his sister's gift.

"Kaffi?"

Jerome looked over his shoulder to where Renee held up a coffee carafe. Her lips were turned up in a smile, and her brown eyes sparkled. "Ya. Danki." He handed her his cup, and their fingers brushed. Her skin was warm and soft beneath his touch.

She reached across the table to fill Tim's cup as well before moving down the line.

"Who's that?" Tim asked.

"Renee Mast," Jerome said. "Martha's granddaughter."

Tim's dark eyebrows lifted. "She inherited the farm?"

"Ya. She's here from Ohio. She's meeting with the lawyer tomorrow to discuss Martha's will."

"Huh." Tim's dark eyes followed Renee while she continued down the table, filling cups. "She's schee."

That's true. She's the prettiest woman I've ever seen.

But he kept that thought to himself and simply shrugged. It didn't matter what he thought of Renee. She'd never be interested in him, and he certainly wasn't interested in ruining another young woman's life.

"Is she keeping the farm?" Tim asked.

"Not sure, but I don't think so."

"What are you going to do?"

"I don't know."

Tim studied him, and Jerome felt itchy under his scrutiny. "You're acting like you don't care, Jerome, but it's your livelihood."

Jerome chose a piece of bread and piled roast beef on it. "I definitely care, and I'm going to start asking around to see if there are any farming jobs available. But until she puts it up for sale, I'll keep running the farm."

"Well, I hope it works out for you."

"Ya," Jerome said with a sigh. "Me too."

Chapter Six

"J erome!" Jeannie called. "I have news."

He turned toward his sister and Renee, and they traipsed toward him. He'd just finished hitching up his horse, and he was waiting for Renee to join him at his buggy so that they could head back to the farm. He planned on spending the rest of his Sunday resting before he had to care for the animals again.

"I'm moving in with Renee!" Jeannie announced.

"What?" Jerome studied his twin.

"I said I'm moving in," she repeated. "I talked to Mamm about it and since you and Renee are both single and living on the farm alone, I'm going to be your chaperone. Isn't that great?" Her grin was wide.

Jerome shrugged. "Sure."

"We're going to have so much fun, Renee," Jeannie told her, and she sounded as if she might burst with excitement. "We can cook, clean, and sew together. It'll be wunderbaar."

Renee smiled. "I can't wait."

"I'll pack tomorrow morning, and then I'll come over," Jeannie said.

"I'm meeting with the lawyer in the morning," Renee told her. "But I'll see you when I get back to the farm."

"Perfect." Jeannie tapped Jerome's arm. "Call that new driver I told you about for her. She has great rates on rides."

Jerome nodded. "I will."

After telling Jeannie goodbye, Jerome and Renee climbed into his buggy and started their journey home.

When they were well underway, he turned to Renee beside him. Her attention was focused out the window while she kept her arms folded over her middle. He had expected her to be chatty on the trip home, after she'd spent their ride to the Zooks' farm sharing stories about her life in Ohio.

For some reason, he couldn't stand the silence, which was unusual for him. Normally, he loved silence since it didn't require him to participate. But at the moment, he craved her voice, which made no sense at all. He racked his brain for something to say that might start a conversation with her while he also focused on the road, watching for any hazards.

"Was the service different from what you're used to?" he asked.

She faced him, and her eyes were round. Had she expected him to be quiet just as he'd expected her to be talkative?

"Ya. It was shorter, and we eat a different meal."

"Was this meal better or worse?" he asked.

She smiled, and her pretty face lit up. "Much better."

He snorted, and she laughed.

"Could I borrow your horse and buggy tomorrow to go to the lawyer's office?" she asked.

He gave her a sideways glance. "Where's the lawyer's office?"

She shared the address, and he shook his head. "Renee, that's more than twenty miles from the farm."

"That means I'll have to leave early."

His brow furrowed while he studied her. Was she making a joke? "You don't want to take a horse and buggy that far. We'll call the driver, just like Jeannie suggested."

"But it's not an emergency," she said, her dark brows drawn together.

"Ya, I know."

"That means we must take the buggy. We can't pay for a ride."

Jerome stared out the windshield while he once again recalled his conversation with Martha about Emmanuel joining the Swartzentruber Amish. He glanced over at Renee once again. "Does your bishop only allow rides in cars for emergencies?" he asked.

She nodded.

"Martha once mentioned that your dat had moved you and your mamm to a Swartzentruber community."

"She did?" Her eyes lit up when he nodded. "What else did she tell you?"

"She didn't say much about it. She only mentioned it to me once, and she was sad." He explained how he had found Martha crying in the kitchen, and he'd made tea and sat with her. "I got the impression that she blamed herself."

Renee gasped, and tears appeared in her eyes.

Ach nee. He made her cry. "I'm sorry. I didn't mean to upset you."

"It's okay." She sniffed and wiped her eyes. "One of the reasons I came here was to find out why mei dat made us leave."

"You don't know?"

She shook her head. "Do you?"

"Nee, I have no idea. Martha talked about when Emmanuel was little, and she shared stories about how she loved to cook with you and how Abner always told you stories and loved to hear you laugh, but she never discussed why you left, except for that one time."

"Oh." Renee folded her arms over her waist and stared out the window. She said nothing more.

Great. He'd managed to ruin the conversation. He struggled to think of something else to say. His thoughts wandered back to her comment about not taking a car tomorrow morning. "Our bishop allows us to ride in a car when necessary, but if you're more comfortable taking the horse and buggy, then we'll need to leave very early in the morning."

She sat up straighter in her seat. "I can take myself."

"Is that right, Renee?" he asked, and she nodded. "I suppose you know how to get there?"

She blushed, and the pink tinging her cheeks made her even prettier. Not that he was interested.

"I guess that means I'll arrange for a ride, ya?" he asked.

She swallowed. "But isn't it too late to arrange for a ride?" she asked. "Are you permitted to make phone calls on Sundays?"

"I'll call first thing in the morning," he said. "Drivers are used to Amish calling early."

"Danki," she said.

He nodded. "Gern gschehne."

Monday, April 14

"The driver will be here shortly," Jerome told Renee the following morning. "Her name is Autumn Martin. Also, Jeannie left a message on the voicemail, and she's packing up her things to move in. She'll be here this afternoon."

Renee looked over from the counter, where she scoured their breakfast dishes. "Okay." She set the dishes on the drainboard.

He spotted two envelopes sitting on the end of the counter. "You wrote your family last night?"

"Ya." She stood the utensils on the drainboard. "I wrote to mei mamm and Anna. I'll put them in the mailbox on my way out." She hung the dishtowels on a hook near the counter. "I'll take care of my chores when I get home. I need to find my letter from the lawyer with the address." She worried her lower lip, and she was adorable.

But he dismissed the thought. "Want me to ride with you?" he asked.

"Oh, nee." She waved off the suggestion. "What about the milk truck?"

"He comes in the afternoons. We'll be back before then," Jerome said. "I need to go to the farm supply store."

"You do?" she asked, and he nodded. Then her expression relaxed. "Ya, that sounds gut."

"See you in a little bit." He started for the door.

A half hour later, Jerome and Renee sat on the back seat of a white van.

"I'm Autumn." The driver angled her body from the front seat.

"I'm Jerome, and this is Renee," Jerome told her.

"Great to meet ya both," Autumn said. "Thanks for giving me a call this morning. So, you're headed to a lawyer's office in Lancaster?" She programmed the address into the GPS in her smartphone, which rested in a phone mount on her dashboard.

Renee folded her hands on her lap and moved her fingers over her purse strap.

Autumn started the engine and backed down the driveway. "I hope everything's okay." Her hazel eyes watched Renee in the mirror.

"Ya. I think it will be." Renee continued to touch her purse strap, and she gave Autumn a nervous smile.

Jerome was tempted to touch Renee's arm to offer her some encouragement, but that would be forward. He didn't want to cross a line.

"You don't dress like the other Amish women around here. Where are you from, Renee?" Autumn asked.

Jerome pursed his lips. He couldn't stand when Englishers boldly questioned members of his community. Most likely Autumn didn't mean any harm, but it was rude.

"Ohio," Renee said.

"Really?" Autumn glanced at her in the rearview mirror again. "What brings you here?"

Renee folded her hands in her lap. "I inherited my grandmother's farm."

"Oh no. I'm so sorry for your loss." Autumn seemed to study Renee in the mirror, and Jerome considered telling her to watch the road instead. "And that's why you're going to the lawyer's office," she continued, filling in the blanks. "Makes sense." Then she shook her head. "I'm sorry for all my questions. I just moved here, and I'm so curious about your community."

Renee nodded while playing with her purse strap. An anxious smile flickered over her mouth.

Irritation nipped at Jerome. Why couldn't those nosy Englishers let the members of his community be? Wasn't it obvious Renee was stressed enough without her invasive questions? He needed to change the subject.

"Autumn," Jerome began, "after you drop Renee off, would you mind taking me to the farm supply store?" He held up his list. "I need to get a few things. Then we can head back for Renee."

"Sure thing," Autumn exclaimed. "I'm familiar with the business complex where the lawyer's office is, and there's a farm supply store close by."

"Gut," he said.

Beside him, he spotted Renee settling back and saw her shoulders relax.

He glanced over at her, and she gave him a hesitant smile.

When they arrived at the lawyer's office, Renee gathered up her purse and tote bag before giving Jerome a worried look.

"It will be fine," he told her softly in Pennsylvania Dutch.

She nodded, her expression relaxing slightly. "Danki." Then she hurried across the parking lot and into the brick building.

While they drove out of the parking lot, Jerome silently asked God to calm Renee's nerves during her meeting with the lawyer.

Renee's head spun as she walked out of the lawyer's office nearly ninety minutes later. She was relieved when she spotted the white van waiting for her in a nearby parking spot. She hugged her sweater to her middle and got into the back seat next to Jerome, who watched her with a concerned expression.

After buckling her safety belt, she turned toward him.

"How'd it go?" he asked.

She kneaded her temples. "It was…a lot." She settled back in the seat while the driver steered into an intersection. "Mei mammi left me everything—the farm, her possessions, and her bank accounts."

"That's what you expected, right?" Jerome's question was gentle. "Isn't that what the letter said?"

Renee looked up and found Autumn watching her in the mirror. "Ya, but it's so much," she responded in Pennsylvania Dutch. "I already told you that mei mamm wants me to surrender or sell the farm, but I feel…torn."

"What do *you* want, Renee?" he asked in English.

She took a shuddering breath. "I want to find out why my dad made us leave Bird-in-Hand," she said in English. "Why did he take us out to Ohio when our family is here?" She pointed to the floor. "Mei dat wouldn't ever bring us here to visit, and he forbade mei mamm from writing to anyone in the community. Mei dat would never tell us what happened or why he completely cut his parents out of his life. And even though mei dat has been gone for eight years, mei mamm still won't answer my questions. She didn't even want me to come here after I received the letter from the lawyer. I had to beg her, and my stepfather was the one who convinced her to let me come.

"I've searched the house a few times, and I haven't found any clues. I also asked around at church, and no one knows anything. Your mamm said she wants to get together to talk, and I'm hoping she knows something. Even the lawyer told me that mei mammi didn't tell him anything except that mei dat made the choice to leave. The only clue I have so far is that you said mei mammi blamed herself for what happened." She shook her head. "Mei mamm will only give me until August to make a decision about what to do with the farm, but she made it clear that I can't keep it or stay here."

Renee leaned her head back, closed her eyes, and rubbed her temples where a headache began to throb. "I have a lot to think about. I can't make any decisions yet."

"Take your time, Renee." Jerome's deep voice was soft. "If you're confused, then don't make any hasty decisions. Take all the time that your mamm has given you and think it through."

She opened her eyes and found his handsome face full of concern, which sent warmth swirling through her. Jerome was a good and thoughtful man. Why was he so sad? It seemed he had so much love to give. Why was he still single?

Shaking off the thought, Renee sat up straight. "There's enough money that I'll be able to keep paying you. And I'll reimburse you for the supplies. Let's stop at the bank on the way back to the farm."

After visiting the bank, the van parked in the farm's driveway, and Renee pulled out her wallet and retrieved a few bills. She leaned forward and paid Autumn. "Danki for the ride."

"You're welcome." Autumn's smile was wide. "If you need anything, let me know. You can call me anytime, and I'll be here to pick you up. No ride is too long or too short."

Renee exited the van and collected the mail while Jerome unloaded his supplies. She sifted through the piles of letters, finding postcards from Realtors offering to help sell the land. She assumed that they had read about her grandmother's death in the obituary section of the newspaper, which inspired their offers to sell the property.

The questions that had hounded her for years bubbled up as she headed for the back porch. She turned toward Jerome, who carried a bag of feed into the barn.

"Jerome," she called, and he faced her. "Are you sure mei mammi didn't say anything about mei dat that might help me understand why they left?"

He set the bag of feed down, and his frown seemed to deepen. "I'm sorry, but nee." He pointed to a box of supplies near the driveway. "I'm going to put away the feed. The milk truck should be here soon."

She nodded, and he limped into the barn.

Renee opened the back door and entered her grandmother's den just as Jeannie sprinted toward her from the hallway.

"You're home." Jeannie pulled her in for a hug. "I was just unpacking." She grimaced. "I hope it's okay that I chose the first bedroom. It looked like you're staying in the larger room."

"Jeannie!" Renee exclaimed. "Ya, the first bedroom is perfect."

"Wunderbaar!" Jerome's twin nearly danced toward the hallway. "I'll finish unpacking and then we can discuss what to make for supper. I'm so excited to be here. We're going to have such a gut time!"

Relief twined through Renee. She was grateful to have her two friends staying on the farm with her while she worked to solve her family's mystery. Sinking onto the sofa, she scanned the small family room. She was going to continue her research, looking for clues in her grandmother's house.

Renee's eyes focused on her grandmother's bookshelf. She was determined to find the truth. Stooping, Renee pored over the shelf.

Chapter Seven

Thursday, April 17

"It's lunchtime," Jeannie sang as she entered the barn Thursday afternoon. "Aren't you hungry?"

Jerome looked over from brushing his mare and studied his twin. She held two grocery bags in her arms.

The past few days had flown by while he, Jeannie, and Renee had fallen into a routine. While he managed the animals, his sister cleaned his little house and took care of his laundry when she wasn't working at his folks' fabric store, and Renee managed chores at her grandmother's. Both Jeannie and Renee cooked, and the three of them ate their meals together. Renee was starting to feel like part of his family—which was strange. But he had to admit he appreciated company. Being alone had gotten old after Martha passed away.

Jerome pointed toward her bags. "Did you go to the market this morning?"

"Ya." She made a face. "I told you at breakfast that I was going to go to the market. You obviously weren't listening."

"Do I *ever* listen to you?" he teased.

She harrumphed, and he bit back a laugh. He had always enjoyed giving his twin a hard time—jokingly, of course.

He peered out through the barn door and spotted the white van backing out of the driveway. "Did Autumn Martin take you to the store?"

Jeannie nodded. "She's so nice and affordable."

"And nosy," he mumbled. His lips turned down as he recalled how uncomfortable she'd made Renee when they went to the lawyer's office.

"That's true. She asked all about you and the farm." Jeannie shrugged. "You know how Englishers are. They're always fascinated with our lives, even though we're plain and practical." She took a step toward the barn door and beckoned him to follow. "Come in for lunch."

Jerome set the brush down and started toward Martha's house beside his sister. He took a grocery bag from her to lighten her load.

Jeannie elbowed his side. "Renee is schee, ya?" She grinned and waggled her blond eyebrows.

"Don't start." He groaned. He was tired of Jeannie bugging him about dating. He was done with it and happy to spend his life as a farmhand. In fact, he'd noticed a couple of ads for farmhands on the bulletin board at the farm supply store, and he planned to call and ask about them later this week.

Jeannie's grin flattened. "Jerome, what happened to Amanda wasn't your fault."

Jerome froze, and his body vibrated at the sound of that name. "Jeannie, I refuse to have this conversation with you," he growled.

"So, *drop it*." His twin flinched at his sharp tone, and guilt walloped him. "Please," he added.

"Fine, fine," she sang, her smile returning. "I picked up roast beef, ham, and turkey lunchmeat, and Renee baked bread earlier." They entered the house. "I'm back," she called. "Let's eat." Jeannie started assembling the ingredients.

Renee appeared in the doorway and smiled at Jerome before setting the table. Soon they were sitting together eating sandwiches and chips.

"Saturday is the craft show and mud sale," Jeannie said. "Do you have those in Ohio?"

"I've never been to one, but I've heard of them," Renee said.

"It's a Lancaster County tradition. They happen in the spring when it's often muddy from the rain, which is why it's called a mud sale," Jeannie explained. "It's like an annual auction, and it benefits the fire department. We auction off everything from antiques to lumber to farm equipment. Thousands of people attend looking for bargains."

"That sounds like fun."

"I've made a few quilts for it, and I'm going to have a booth. You have to come with me, Renee. You can meet more people in the community."

Renee nodded and took a bite of her roast beef sandwich.

Eyeing Jerome, Jeannie said, "You need to come too."

"Nee." He shook his head. "You two can go. I'll handle my chores. There's always plenty to do around here, and I don't need anything from the mud sale."

Jeannie rolled her eyes. "You need to stop being such a grouch, *bruder.*"

He turned toward Renee and found her watching him with interest. Then he shook his head. "We'll see."

Jeannie leaned toward Renee and said, "That means 'ya,' in Jerome's language."

Renee giggled, captivating him.

Jeannie spent the remainder of lunch discussing the mud sale and sharing her excitement over it, along with details about the quilts and crafts she planned to sell.

After they finished eating, Jerome gathered up their plates.

Renee's eyes lit up. "Your mamm had mentioned getting together for supper sometime, and I'd love to talk to her about my folks. Do you think we could plan something?"

"Absolutely," Jeannie said.

"I'll call her and see if we can visit Sunday since it's an off Sunday with no church service," Jerome suggested while stacking the dishes on the counter.

"Ya. Danki," Renee agreed.

"And you're coming Saturday too, Jerome," Jeannie told him. "I already asked Autumn to pick us up early for the mud sale. We have a lot of goods to bring with us to sell, along with supplies, so we'll need her van to help us get it there. You can help us set up. You can carry a table or two."

Jerome sighed on his way out to the barn. His twin never gave up. No wonder their parents called her stubborn.

Saturday, April 19

The aromas of popcorn, ice cream, coffee, and fried foods filled Renee's senses while she worked in the booth Saturday morning.

She and Jeannie had gotten up early to make breakfast and take care of the chickens before Autumn Martin picked them up and took them to the Bird-in-Hand Spring Festival, which included a mud sale and craft show.

Booths selling everything from food to collectables to clothes to homemade items took over the large open field. Beyond it was a fair, featuring rides and games. A large stage was ready for live acts, and an auction, including everything from livestock to furniture to tools and farm equipment, was set to start later in the day.

Renee was disappointed that Jerome insisted he had to stay at the farm to take care of his chores, but she hoped that he would join them later in the day. She enjoyed the way he'd begun to talk to her more, and she even felt him opening up to her a little bit. She hoped that their friendship had become important to him. Renee sighed. She was kidding herself, thinking that her friendship with Jerome had become something special. Besides, if Maribeth liked him, she didn't want to hurt her feelings or stand in the way of Maribeth and Jerome. Besides, Renee needed to keep her focus on finding out why her father had moved them from Ohio and cut off his parents.

When they arrived at the festival, Jeannie introduced Renee to the other young Amish women who were working in the booth before she assisted in setting up the items for sale. She couldn't help noticing that the women wore beautiful shades of maroon, green, and blue dresses, while she was clad in another black dress today.

She longed to wear a color other than black or gray. The idea of making a dress like Jeannie's occurred to her, but she shooed it away. There were more important things to worry about, such as how to help in the craft booth.

Jeannie was busy talking to a customer about a set of potholders she'd made, and Renee moved her hand over a colorful quilt sewn in a log cabin pattern.

"Do you like to sew?"

Renee turned to Jeannie's friend Mary. "I can mend clothes, but I've never sewn a quilt."

Mary gave her a knowing look. "Jeannie is a very good quiltmaker." She pointed toward a queen-sized rose and pink pinwheel quilt.

"I could teach you how to quilt, Renee," Jeannie said as she joined them. "We can make a quilt together if you'd like."

Renee's heart swelled with appreciation for her friend. "I'd love that." She gestured to Jeannie's dress. "I'd like to make a brightly colored dress for church too." She said the words, but then doubt crept into her mind. What would her mamm and her bishop at home say if they found out she was wearing bright-color clothes?

"Ooh! Ya!" Jeannie clapped. "We should do some sewing together next week, ya?"

Mary nodded toward the front of the booth. "We have customers."

For the next few hours Renee helped fairgoers purchase pot holders, blankets, quilts, pillows, and wall hangings. She enjoyed conversing with folks as well as laughing with Jeannie and her new friends.

Later that afternoon Renee was handing a customer her change. After thanking the woman, she turned to find Jerome standing nearby, holding two plates with a tasty-looking snack on each.

"Jerome," she said, her heart thumping against her ribcage. "What a surprise. I didn't think you were going to come today."

He held up a plate. "Can you take a break?"

Renee turned to Jeannie, who beamed at her.

"Go, Renee." Jeannie gave her a gentle push. "Have fun."

Renee hurried out to where Jerome stood. A knot of people milled around the booths, and conversations floated over them. She followed him to a quiet corner away from the sea of people.

"Have you ever had a funnel cake?" he asked as he handed her a plate with the sugary treat.

She shook her head and then took a bite. The flavor made her taste buds dance with delight. "This is amazing. Danki, Jerome."

"Gern gschehne." His lips twitched and curled upward. Then, suddenly, he finally graced her with a real smile for the first time since she'd met him. For a moment she was mesmerized. He was even more handsome this way, and the smile was more magnificent than she'd ever imagined. In fact, she couldn't take her eyes off him. She longed for him to smile for her all the time, every day! She wanted to bask in this light—*always.*

Jerome tilted his head, and his brow furrowed.

She realized she was staring, and she chuckled as heat invaded her cheeks.

"You okay?" he asked.

Renee cleared her throat. "Ya. I wasn't expecting to see you here."

"Ya, well." He shrugged. "I finished my chores and then decided to use Jeannie's scooter and check out the mud sale."

She took another bite.

"Would you like to walk around for a few minutes and see the other vendors?"

"I'd love to."

They wove through the crowd, taking in the different booths and pointing out unique items for sale. After their funnel cakes were gone, they returned to the craft booth.

"I'd better get back to work," Renee told him.

He nodded. "Danki for taking a break with me."

"It was fun," she said. "Are you going back to the farm now?"

He shook his head. "I'm going to check out the auction and see if there are any gut deals on farm equipment or tools. I'll meet you and Jeannie when it's time to head home, and we'll ride together. I'm sure the scooter will fit in the back of Autumn's van."

"Gut."

They stared at each other for a moment, and when he smiled again, her heart did a funny little dance.

"See you later," she said.

When she turned toward the booth, she found Jeannie grinning while she watched them. An imperceptible look passed between the twins before Jerome disappeared into the crowd.

"Did you have fun with mei bruder?" Jeannie asked as Renee sidled up to her.

Renee tried to ignore how her face heated. Why was she always blushing when she was around Jerome? "Ya, I did."

"Gut," Jeannie said before turning toward a customer. "Can I help you?"

Renee smiled. She was starting to feel at home in Bird-in-Hand and part of the community, and she really, really liked it.

Later that evening, Autumn Martin parked her van in the driveway at the farm. Jerome got out of the vehicle and unloaded the scooter before helping Renee and Jeannie unload their supplies from the mud sale. Then he pulled out his wallet while Renee and Jeannie started toward the house. The sky above was dark and sprinkled with bright stars. A chorus of frogs sang nearby while a dog barked somewhere in the distance.

"Danki," he said then handed Autumn a few bills.

"Give me a call when you need another ride," she said before backing out of the driveway.

"My feet hurt," Renee announced as they moved up the path. "But the day was fun."

Jeannie spun around, holding a flashlight in the air and balancing tote bags on each of her shoulders. "Ya! I sold all of my quilts, pot holders, and pillows! Now I have to make more, and I love creating them. Renee, you can help me make inventory for the next sale, and we can split the profits next September."

Renee's pretty face clouded with a frown. "I won't be here in September."

"You won't?" Jeannie's smile flattened. "Why not?"

"Mei mamm wants me home by August, but I'd love to help you work on quilts for the next mud sale."

Renee's sad expression mirrored the feeling rolling through Jerome. He was going to miss her, which made no sense at all. He hardly knew her.

Pushing away the thought, he pulled his small flashlight from his pocket, flipped it on, and stood by the path leading to his little house. "Gut nacht," he called.

"Danki for coming with us today," Renee called to him. "I had a great time."

He had too. In fact, he couldn't shake the feeling an invisible magnet was yanking him to her, and it was unsettling. He hadn't felt that since…

No, no, no!

He couldn't even think her name. He refused to remember how it felt to want to plan a future with a special woman. Never again!

"We're going to Mamm's tomorrow, right?" Jeannie's question broke through his mental tirade.

"Ya." He nodded. "She's excited to spend time with us."

Jeannie did a little dance. "Ya." Then she looped her arm around Renee's shoulder. "We're going to have so much fun spending the day with my folks." His twin spun to face him. "Gut nacht, Jerome."

He lifted his hand in a wave and then started toward his house. He unlocked the door and opened it. When he heard a scream, he spun toward Martha's house.

"Jerome! Jerome!" his sister screamed. "Come quick!"

He sprinted up the path toward the house, as fast as his injured leg would allow. His heart felt as if it might beat out of his ribcage while panic welled up inside of him.

When he reached the porch, he found Renee holding a piece of paper. Tears sparkled in her wide, brown eyes. "Jerome," she said, her voice sounding strange. "L-look at this." Her hand shook as she gave him the paper.

He read in large, bold, red handwritten letters, *GO HOME! YOU DON'T BELONG HERE! IF YOU DON'T LEAVE, YOU'LL REGRET IT!*

"Who could've sent that?" Jeannie asked, her voice trembling.

"I don't know." Jerome shook his head and studied the piece of paper. Then he scanned the farm. Could the person who sent this still be around—possibly hiding in the barn and waiting to harm Renee and his sister? His lungs felt tight, and his pulse hurtled. "Where did you find this?"

Renee pointed to the door. "It was hanging right there."

Jerome thought back to earlier in the day when he was working on the farm. He hadn't noticed any strange cars or spotted anyone hanging around. And he couldn't recall seeing the note before he left to go to the festival. The letter must have been hung on the door after he'd left.

And that meant whoever left it knew they were gone. Had the person sat out in the street in a car, waiting for them to leave? Was someone spying on them?

Unease spread through his veins. He would have to ask Murray if he'd seen someone watching the farm.

He studied his sister's and Renee's worried expressions. "I'll check out the haus for you. Stay on the porch and yell if you see anyone."

Jerome pushed open the door, picked up a lantern from the table in the den, and moved around the house, checking every room and closet.

After confirming the house was empty, he returned to the porch, where the women stood close together, their eyes still full of anxiety.

"The haus is clear," he said. "I can sleep in the den tonight if you'd like."

Jeannie shook her head. "We'll be fine," she said, and Renee nodded. "We'll make sure the doors and windows are locked."

"Okay." He studied the note again and more worry wound through him. "We should call the police."

Renee shook her head. "Nee. We never involve Englishers in our problems."

"I disagree," Jerome said, holding up the letter. "This is a threat, Renee. We don't know how serious this person could be."

"But it might also be a prank," Renee countered. "I think we should be vigilant but not call the police."

Jerome and Jeannie shared a troubled expression.

"I'll agree to that now, but if this happens again, then I'll insist we call the police," Jerome said.

"Okay," Renee said.

"Do you want me to stay here tonight?" he asked again.

"Nee, but danki," Renee said. "I'll make us warm milk to help us sleep."

Jeannie touched his bicep. "If we need you, we'll come and get you."

"Okay," he said, but he knew he wouldn't be able to sleep tonight. Instead, he'd lie awake and worry about his sister and Renee and the threatening letter they'd received.

Gott, protect them!

Chapter Eight

"G ude mariye!" Delilah sang as Renee, Jeannie, and Jerome entered her home the following morning. "We're so glad you're going to visit with us today."

"Danki." Renee handed her a plate of cookies she'd picked up at the fair. "Jeannie and I didn't have time to bake since we were helping out at the craft booth all day yesterday, but we picked up a box of chocolate chip *kichlin*."

Delilah took the box of cookies from her. "Great choice. They're my favorite." She waved Renee over to where a tall, middle-aged man with light brown hair stood. "Do you remember Harvey?"

"Hi." Renee shook Harvey's hand, and his kind smile reminded her of Jerome's.

"I remember when you were barely up to my knee."

Renee chuckled.

"Let's put some kaffi on and visit." Jeannie scooted through the den and into the kitchen. "Come on in, Renee. Make yourself at home."

Renee helped Jeannie retrieve mugs, creamer, and sugar. She set five mugs on the table assuming the men would join them, but when she turned toward the doorway, she was surprised Jerome lingered there, speaking softly to his father, who stood in the den.

She studied Jerome's stoic profile, and the dark circles beneath his eyes. He'd been reticent at breakfast and during their buggy ride to his parents' house this morning. She'd longed to try to pull him into their conversation, and although Jeannie had done enough chatting to fill the empty space between them, it did little to settle her worry about him and also about the threatening note they'd received. She hoped it had been a prank, but she couldn't stop the feeling that it wasn't.

"Jerome," she said, and his dull blue eyes snapped to hers. "Aren't you going to join us for kichlin and kaffi?"

He shook his head. "I'm going out to the barn with mei dat."

"Okay." She gave him a stiff smile.

The men's heavy footsteps echoed on their way out of the house. Renee peeked out the kitchen window as they made their way toward the barn.

Soon the welcome scent of coffee rose from the pot, and Renee sat at the table with Jeannie and her mother.

"These kichlin are appeditlich," Delilah announced. "How was the mud sale yesterday?"

Jeannie's face brightened. "It was fantastic. We sold everything we brought. The booth was empty when we left." She tapped Renee's arm. "I think Renee had fun too."

"I did. I hadn't been to a mud sale like that before."

Delilah looked surprised. "You haven't? Don't you have sales like it in Ohio?"

"We do, but I couldn't ever go." Renee shook her head. "My community doesn't participate in events like that." She moved her fingers over her warm mug. "Do you know why mei dat insisted that we move away?"

"Nee, I don't." Delilah's smile flattened. "I was heartbroken. Your mamm was my best friend from school, and she'd become like family to me."

"I've spoken to mei mammi's friends at church, but no one knows anything. They've only told me that Mammi was heartbroken when mei dat left, and she blamed herself. Do you know anyone else I could talk to?"

Delilah moved her finger over the table. "Have you spoken to Naomi?"

Renee let the name filter through her mind, but it wasn't familiar. "Who's she?"

"She's your mamm's schweschder, and she doesn't live far from here."

Renee's thoughts spun. "Mei mamm has a schweschder?"

"Ya." Delilah's brow puckered. "You don't remember her?"

"Nee. She never talks about her. I thought she was an only child like me."

Delilah hesitated. "She's your mamm's older schweschder. She might be able to give you some answers about what happened with your dat. I can give you her address if you'd like."

"Ya, please." Renee's pulse sped up as more questions overwhelmed her. Why would Mamm stop speaking to her sister? And could her aunt hold the answers to all the mysteries that burdened her heart? "Where does she live?"

Delilah pulled out an Amish community directory and flipped through it. After a few moments, she placed her finger on the page.

"Naomi lives in White Horse, about ten miles from here." She wrote on a notepad and then held the piece of paper out to Renee. "She's out of town visiting her dochder who recently had a boppli. I ran into her in a grocery store a couple of weeks ago, and she told me that she planned to go out to western Pennsylvania to visit with her when the boppli was born. You can talk to her when she gets back. She might know more."

"Danki." Renee's hand shook as she studied the paper. Naomi and Dennis Beiler, her aunt and uncle. She'd had no idea they even existed! Why had her mother never spoken about her sister? Why had her parents broken all contact with them when they left Pennsylvania?

"I only received two letters from your mamm after you moved, but they didn't have a return address." Her blue eyes brightened. "I think I still have the letters. Would you like them?"

Hope swelled within Renee. "Ya. Please."

"I'll go get them." Delilah disappeared down a hallway.

Jeannie chose a cookie from the box and took a bite. "I remember playing in the backyard with you and Jerome while our mamms drank tea and talked. And I remember how mei mamm cried when you moved away." Her eyes sparkled. "I'm so glad you're back, and I think mei bruder is too." She winked, and Renee's heart bumped.

"I found the letters." Delilah reappeared holding two envelopes. She set them on the table.

Renee's hands vibrated as she picked up the top envelope. She immediately recognized her mother's beautiful, slanted handwriting. She started to open the envelope, but her eyes stung. What if she read something that made her cry in front of Jeannie and Delilah? She'd look like a dummkopp for sure!

"You don't have to read them now," Delilah said. "Take them with you."

"Danki." Renee slipped the letters into her apron pocket. She couldn't wait to dive into them later when she was alone in her room. "Would you like our address so that you could write to mei mamm?"

Delilah's eyes widened. "I would love that. I miss her so much."

Jeannie jumped up from the table and retrieved a notepad and a pen. "Here you go."

Renee wrote down the address and handed the notepad to Delilah. "I'm sure she would love to hear from you, and Ike won't mind when she writes you back."

"Danki, Renee. I'll write her a letter and mail it tomorrow." Delilah sipped her coffee. "So, your mamm never told you why your dat decided to move?"

"Nee." Renee blew out a deep sigh. "We were forbidden from discussing it, and after mei dat passed away, mei mamm kept her promise to him to never discuss it." She tilted her head. "No one seems to know what happened. Were there ever any rumors about why we left?"

Delilah shook her head. "I don't remember ever hearing any, except that your dat was very angry about something, and that was why he moved."

Renee nodded slowly while disappointment moved through her. She didn't feel like she was getting any closer to the truth, but she wasn't going to give up either.

Sympathy traveled across Delilah's face. "I'm sorry you lost your dat. What happened?"

"Cancer. He passed away eight years ago. Mei mamm met Ike, who also lost his spouse to cancer, and they married seven years ago.

Ike is a kind and soft-spoken man. He's been gut to us. He convinced mei mamm to let me come here, but I have to be home by August. I'm hoping to find out the truth about why mei dat made us leave before I go back to Ohio."

Jeannie rubbed Renee's shoulder. "I'm sorry that you lost your dat, but I'm grateful that Gott sent Ike to you and your mamm."

Renee smiled at her. "Danki."

"I had always hoped that Lovina would call me, but she never did," Delilah said. "After I received those letters with no return address, I never heard from her again. The only thing she told me was that your dat insisted that they had to go, and there was no discussion."

Renee set her elbow on the table, and her chin on her palm. "That sounds like mei dat. No discussion. No explanation. He made the rules, and we followed them—no questions asked." She cupped her hand to her mouth to shield a yawn. Her restless night of tossing and turning was catching up to her.

"You didn't get much sleep either, huh?" Jeannie asked, and Renee shook her head. "We need to tell mei mamm about what happened last night."

Delilah divided a look between them. "What happened?"

"We found a threatening note on our door," Jeannie began, before explaining to her mother how they found it and what it said.

Shock moved over Delilah's face. "Who do you think left it?"

"We don't know." Jeannie's expression was grim.

"Did you call the police?" Delilah asked, and when Jeannie shook her head, she added, "Why not?"

Renee set her hands on the table. "In my community, we don't involve Englishers in our problems. I told Jerome and Jeannie that

I'd rather we figure this out ourselves. It could just be a prank." Her thoughts moved to Murray—the odd man who lived across the street from her grandmother's farm. Could he have been the person who left the note?

She mentally shook the thought away. Surely he wouldn't want to threaten them. After all, Jerome insisted he was harmless.

"Or it could be serious." Delilah looked unconvinced. "Don't take this lightly. If you feel threatened, you need to call the police. You should tell the bishop about this."

Jeannie nodded. "If it happens again, we'll call the police." She eyed Renee. "Agreed?"

Renee nodded. "Nothing happened last night, so hopefully it was just a prank and an isolated incident." She sipped her coffee and smiled at Delilah. "I'd love to see your fabric store."

Jeannie's expression brightened. "Let's finish our snack and then I'll give you a tour of the store."

After their cups were empty, they walked out into the warm April morning, and Renee spotted the family's small pasture and barn. She followed Jeannie and Delilah down a path leading to a one-story cinderblock building with large windows and a sign reading Graber Fabrics. A few parking spaces and a hitching post sat out front. Renee vaguely remembered visiting as a child.

Delilah unlocked the door, and they walked inside the large store. Displays of patterns sat toward the front by the counters, and nearby were aisles with signs for material, buttons, zippers, thread, needles, and other supplies.

"This place is amazing," Renee said while peeking down the aisles. "How long have you owned it?"

Delilah tapped her chin. "We opened it shortly after we were married, so almost thirty years now."

"Some of this is familiar." Renee meandered down an aisle featuring brightly colored material, and the yearning she'd felt for a week now resurfaced. She turned to Jeannie. "I'd love to make a brightly colored dress for church. Would that be okay?"

"Are you kidding? That would be fantastic," Jeannie insisted, and when Renee nodded, Jeannie clapped. "Let's pick out a color for you." She consulted her mother. "What do you think of green?"

Delilah nodded. "Green would be lovely." She moved farther down the aisle and beckoned Renee. "Let's find a shade you like."

Renee's heart skipped a beat as she followed her friends toward the bolts of material.

Jerome grimaced while his father studied the letter that Jeannie and Renee had found hanging on the door last night.

He was relieved that Jeannie had already arranged for her and Renee to spend the day visiting their folks since he planned to get his father alone to ask his opinion about the situation, after enduring a restless night pondering the letter and what it could mean.

He'd spent more than an hour staring out his window facing Martha's house, watching for any sign of a prowler and ready to jump into action if he had to protect his sister and Renee. As if he could do much to protect them. Any person who was in decent physical shape could outrun him thanks to his leg injury, but he was determined to do what was needed in order to protect those who meant the most to him. And Renee was quickly becoming important to him, which also concerned him. But he shoved that thought away and focused on the threat.

"What do you think, Dat?" he asked.

"Hmm." Dat rubbed his graying, light brown beard. "I'm not sure what to think. It's definitely concerning."

"But..." he said, prodding his father to continue.

"But it also could be some Englisher kinner playing a prank. You remember a few years ago when the group of kinner kept opening pasture gates and letting the cows out, right?"

Jerome nodded. "Ya, I do."

"Maybe this is also some kind of practical joke."

"Remember the Englisher kinner that were setting fire to barns? They killed several horses."

Dat's frown illustrated that he understood Jerome's point. "You're right, sohn. It could be a real threat."

"Exactly." Jerome sank down onto an overturned bucket while the worry that shadowed him all night long rose inside him.

"I can tell when you're concentrating on something. So go ahead and tell me what's on your mind, sohn."

"I'm really concerned about Renee and Jeannie." Saying the words out loud sent a wave of relief through him. "I couldn't sleep last night." Nighttime restlessness wasn't unusual for Jerome, but this new concern was different than his past burden of guilt. "I kept watching out my window, waiting for someone to try to hurt them." His frown deepened. "Renee doesn't want me to call the police, but I almost did." He scrubbed his hands over his face. "What would you do if you were in my situation?"

Dat patted his shoulder. "I would be cautious. Don't spend your nights staring out your window since you need to get your sleep to stay aware. But don't take the threat lightly. And if you receive another letter or something worse, call the police, even if Renee doesn't want you to. It's your job to protect them."

"I know." Jerome blew out a deep puff of air. He intended to do everything in his might to keep them safe. He just hoped he could.

Jerome's worries followed him around while he spent the remainder of the day with his family and Renee. He tried his best to participate in the lively discussion during lunch, but he couldn't stop wondering who had taped that letter to the back door of Martha's home. And what was their point in trying to scare Renee? What did they hope to accomplish if she returned home? What was their goal?

Later he hitched up his horse and buggy while Jeannie hugged their mother and said goodbye.

"This was so fun, Mamm," Jeannie announced.

Renee shook Mamm's hand. "Danki for having us and for giving me the material and the letters." She held up a bag, and he spotted green fabric sticking out of it. "I'm going to write mei mamm. I'll be sure to tell her that you miss her, and that she should write you."

"I'll write her too." Mamm pulled Renee in for a hug. "We'll see you soon."

Jerome waved goodbye to his folks before they piled into his buggy.

Renee looked over at him while he guided the horse toward the road. "Are you okay, Jerome?" she asked.

He nodded. "Ya. Why?"

"You've been so quiet." She leaned toward him. "If you ever want to talk, I'm here to listen, okay?" Her sweet expression made his pulse skip a beat.

"Danki," he managed to whisper. He knew deep in his heart that Renee was sincere, and for the first time in years he started to feel his heart coming back to life.

Renee jumped onto her bed and pulled the letters out of her apron. She'd been grateful when Jeannie suggested that they rest for the remainder of Sunday afternoon until it was time to eat supper. She'd hoped for some time alone to read the letters her mother had sent to Delilah.

Her chest clutched as she examined the postmark on the envelopes. Both were from twenty years ago. One was marked May, and the other was marked June. She opened the May letter first.

> *Dear Delilah,*
>
> *By the time you receive this letter, you'll know that Emmanuel has moved us to Ohio. I'm sorry for not telling you the exact date that we were leaving. He insisted that we keep it a secret. While I want to tell you why we left, Emmanuel has insisted we keep the reason to ourselves. You know that you've always been like a sister to me, but I must honor my husband's wishes. I'm sure you understand.*
>
> *Emmanuel said we needed a new start in a community that's more focused on God. I tried to convince him to stay in*

Bird-in-Hand, but he wouldn't listen. He insists that mistakes from the past can't be forgiven, and when I try to remind him that the Lord tells us to forgive, he instructs me to remember my place—he's the head of the family, and I'm not.

Life out here is different than what we're used to, but Emmanuel assures me it's for the best. I'm thankful that Renee is small enough that she'll adapt easily. I'm praying that I will too.

Please give my love to Jerome and Jeannie. Also, tell Harvey that we said hello.

Emmanuel doesn't want me to share our address, so I'll write to you again when I can.

Sincerely,

Lovina

Tears streamed down Renee's face while she read the letter over and over again, and her eyes kept focusing on one sentence:

He insists that mistakes from the past can't be forgiven...

She studied the sentence until she had it committed to memory.

"What mistake from the past could you not forgive, Dat?" she whispered to the empty room. "What happened to make you so angry that you had to leave your family and your home?"

Wiping her eyes, Renee's glance slid around her grandmother's room. Was the answer hidden somewhere in this house? She'd been searching since the day after she'd arrived. Each day she retraced her steps. If the answer was here, would she ever find it?

Her questions echoed through her mind as she opened the second letter and read it.

> *Dear Delilah,*
>
> *It's been more than a month since we moved out to Ohio, and I miss you every day. I miss our weekly talks while we'd drink tea and watch our children play. I could always be open and honest with you. The women here are different—more reserved. Right now, I feel like an outcast, but I suppose it will take some time before I feel like a part of the community.*
>
> *Emmanuel has insisted that I cut all ties with the people in our past and that includes you and my sister. I'm heartbroken since you're my dearest friend, but I must do as he says. I'm sorry to tell you that this will be my last letter to you.*
>
> *We're doing okay here. I'm adjusting to a plainer lifestyle. My chores take longer, but it gives me a chance to do more praying and reflect more on the Scriptures.*
>
> *I hope you, Harvey, and the twins are doing well. I miss you dearly. Please take good care of yourself and your family and don't forget me.*
>
> *Sincerely,*
>
> *Lovina*

The second letter sent more tears flooding Renee's eyes. She could feel her mother's loneliness and sadness in her words. More than ever, she yearned to know the source of her father's decision to take her mother away from her home. She couldn't wait for her aunt to return so she could not only reconnect with her but also ask her what she might know.

Closing her eyes, she whispered a prayer:

"Gott, please lead me to the answers I seek and help me understand why we left this community."

Chapter Nine

Monday, April 21

The sounds of a car on the driveway reached her ears, just as Renee hung her dress on a line extending from the back porch to the barn. She swept her hand over her brow and walked down the porch steps toward the fancy, black sedan.

Renee approached the car, and a woman got out. She was tall and slim and had short, copper-colored hair. She wore a navy-blue suit and high heels, along with a copious amount of makeup. She looked to be in her late thirties or early forties.

"Good morning," the Englisher exclaimed. "I heard Martha Mast passed away last month. Are you related to her?"

Renee smoothed a hand over her black apron and dress. "She was my grandmother."

"I am so sorry for your loss, honey." The woman's dark eyes studied her. "Are you the heir?"

"Ya."

The woman's smile reminded Renee of a photo of a tiger she'd seen in a children's book years ago. "Are you going to keep the farm?"

"I'm not sure what I'm going to do yet," Renee admitted.

"Well, it's always good to keep your options open." The woman shoved a business card and a postcard into Renee's hand. "I'm Belinda Walker, and I'm a Realtor. I mailed you a few postcards, but since I haven't heard from you, I thought I'd stop by to visit and introduce myself. I'm well known around here. I'm the top seller at my firm. In fact, I've had the best sales record for the past three years, and I can get you a fabulous price for this piece of land. I'm talking a good solid seven figures, honey."

"Seven figures?" Renee whispered with awe.

"That's right. That's a million dollars in case you didn't know, sweetheart." The woman's condescending tone sent a jolt of irritation through Renee.

Jerome exited the barn and limped over to join them, his face set in a glower. "What's going on here?"

"Hi, there!" The woman waved at him, but he continued to scowl. "I'm Belinda Walker, and I'm a Realtor. I was just telling your wife..." She paused and pointed between them. "You're married, right?"

"No," Jerome said.

Heat traveled up Renee's neck to her cheeks. She was blushing in front of Jerome—*again*!

"Oh. Okay." Belinda shrugged. "Anyway, I was telling..." Pausing, she looked at Renee. "What's your name again, honey?"

"Renee Mast."

The woman snapped her fingers. "Right. Renee," she repeated. "I was telling her to let me know when you're ready to sell, and I'll talk to some of the developers around here. I know they'd love to scoop up this land and put in a new neighborhood, condos, or even a nice hotel. Folks love to buy authentic Amish farmland."

Renee and Jerome shared a look of disbelief.

"Well, I'm sure this might all be confusing for you," Belinda continued, "but I'm here to help. I respect your customs and your culture, and if you want to sell, please call me first." She pointed to Renee's hand. "You have my card, so don't be shy. Okay?"

Renee nodded.

"Fantastic." Belinda rubbed her hands together, showing off bright red, well-manicured nails. "Well, I'll leave you to your chores. I'll be in touch." She waved her hands and then returned to her fancy car and drove off.

Renee spun toward Jerome, who glared after the car. "Was iss letz?"

"She was awfully pushy and arrogant," he said.

Renee frowned. "Ya, that's true." She consulted the business card. "I recognize her name. She's sent a couple of postcards since I arrived here."

"Seems like she really wants your business."

Something in Jerome's tone caught her attention, and her eyes snapped to his.

"I wonder if she's the one who left the note in order to scare you into selling," he said.

Renee gasped. "Do you think so?"

"Some people will do anything to get what they want," Jerome said before limping toward the barn.

Her stomach twisted while his words whirled through her mind.

Wednesday, April 23

Renee fixed the hem on one of her black aprons Wednesday afternoon. The window in her grandmother's sewing room was open and a warm breeze mixed with the scent of fresh grass and honeysuckle drifted in. She finished mending the apron and then examined the Kelly-green material Delilah and Jeannie had given her on Sunday.

Her fingers itched to sew a dress to wear on Sunday, but something deep inside held her back. What would her mother say about her wearing such a bright color?

But her mother had loved this community. The letters she wrote to Delilah after she'd moved to Ohio were laced with sadness. Perhaps her mother would understand why Renee wanted to blend in and feel like she was part of this district again.

At the same time, her mother hadn't wanted her to return to Pennsylvania. Would she be disappointed in Renee's longing to blend in?

"But it's only a dress," she whispered. "Surely Mamm would understand."

Renee found the pattern that Jeannie had loaned her, picked up the material, and began measuring out pieces for the dress. The floor creaked, and she turned toward the doorway just as Jerome stuck his head in.

His sky-blue eyes were bright, and his expression was warm. "I got the mail." He held up a handful of envelopes. "Do you want me to leave it in the kitchen?"

"Ya. Danki."

His gaze moved over the sewing table. "What are you doing?"

"Your mamm and Jeannie gave me this material. I was thinking about making a dress for church on Sunday."

He was silent, and she held on to the edge of the table, awaiting his reaction. Finally, his gaze met hers. "That color will look schee on you."

Air whooshed out of her, and her face felt hot.

"I'll leave the mail on the counter," he said before turning and walking toward the kitchen.

Curiosity propelled her from the sewing chair and down the hallway to the kitchen. "Did I get any interesting letters?"

"It looks like your friend Anna wrote to you." He handed her an envelope.

Anna! "Danki."

"And there are more postcards from Realtors." He pressed his mouth into a flat line. "That Belinda Walker woman wrote to you." He held out the postcard, and when she took it, their hands brushed, sending a tingle of warmth up her arm.

She read the postcard.

Renee: Are you ready to sell your farm? Give me a call!

She studied the woman's fancy handwriting. "Do you really think she's the one who left the threatening letter?" she asked.

Jerome shook his head. "It's hard to tell, since the letters are printed and not written in script." He dragged his fingers over his angular jaw. "Mei dat thinks it was kinner playing a prank. I hope he's right."

"Ya, me too."

He touched the brim of his straw hat. "I'll be in the barn."

"Do you need help with chores since Jeannie is working at the fabric store?" she offered.

"Nee." He pointed toward the hallway. "You should work on that dress for Sunday." And when his lips quirked, her heartbeat tripped over itself.

While Jerome ambled outside, Renee decided that the dress could wait a little longer. Instead of sewing, she brewed tea in her grandmother's beautiful teapot. She smiled and ran her fingers over the white porcelain decorated with colorful flowers. Happy memories of time spent in the kitchen drinking tea with her grandmother occupied her mind.

Then she settled at the kitchen table with her cup of tea and opened Anna's letter.

> *Dear Renee,*
>
> *It was so good to hear from you! I'm glad you're doing well at your grandmother's farm. Jerome and Jeannie sound so nice. I'm happy that you're reconnecting with old friends.*
>
> *I have news! You'll never guess… Noah proposed! I'm so excited. He asked my father for permission a couple of weeks ago, and my dat said yes, of course. Well, he finally asked me to marry him the other night. I wish you were here to celebrate with me, Renee.*
>
> *We want to get married in October. I'd love for you to help me with plans. We can make the dresses together, and we can also talk about the menu for the reception.*

I hope that your visit is going well, and you're able to find the answers to the questions you've had for so many years. You mentioned checking with some of your grandmother's old friends. Have they helped you at all? Were you able to talk to Jerome's mother, Delilah? I hope she was able to help you figure out why your father made you leave.

The basket shop has been busy. Your mamm and I have made and sold quite a few baskets. We have fun when we work together.

I know you have plenty to do there, but I miss you so much, Renee.

Write soon!

Sincerely,

Anna

Renee sipped her tea and smiled. She was so happy for her friend, and she believed God would bless Anna and Noah with a fruitful marriage full of happiness and children. But she felt conflicted when Anna asked her to help with her wedding plans. She longed to be a part of her best friend's wedding preparation, but she also needed to figure out why her father had chosen to leave this community. She'd been talking to members of the church district and searching the house, but she wasn't any closer to finding the truth. She was going to run out of time sooner rather than later. Renee was determined to take care of her grandmother's affairs and find answers to her questions before she went back to Ohio, and she needed to do that quickly.

She chose a piece of stationery and began to write.

Dear Anna,

It's so good to hear from you too! Congratulations on your engagement! I'm so happy for you and Noah. Your wedding is going to be amazing. I can't wait to help you plan it.

Things are going fine here. Jerome is still running the farm, and his twin sister, Jeannie, moved in with me to help as well. I've met with the lawyer, but I haven't made any plans for the farm yet. I've received letters from Realtors who want to help me sell it, and one has been very aggressive.

Renee paused and nibbled on the end of her pen. She considered telling Anna about the threatening letter she received, but she didn't want to worry her or risk Anna telling her mother. If Mamm found out, then surely she and Ike would insist Renee return to Ohio. She couldn't take a chance on being told to go home before she found out her family's secrets.

Movement drew her attention to the kitchen window, where she glimpsed Jerome and Jeannie talking by the barn. Her lungs squeezed when she considered going back to Ohio and leaving the Graber twins. It had barely been two weeks since she'd arrived in Pennsylvania, and she was already becoming attached to her friends. But she couldn't share that with Anna and accidentally hurt her feelings. She missed Anna, and she would miss the Graber twins when she returned to Ohio too.

Renee poised her pen and continued writing.

I'm still searching for the answers to my questions. I'll keep you posted on what I find out. Thank you for working in the basket shop. I'm so glad you're enjoying it.

Please give my love to my parents. And write soon. Keep me posted on your wedding plans.

Sincerely,

Renee

She folded the letter and sealed it in an envelope before addressing it and sticking a stamp on the upper right corner.

Renee poured herself more tea from her grandmother's beloved teapot before studying the Realtors' postcards. She found postcards from different companies, along with another one from Belinda Walker. It seemed strange that she would send one nearly every day. Was she that desperate to get her hands on Mammi's farm?

She considered how Belinda had insisted that the farm was worth a million dollars. She tried to imagine having that much money but couldn't fathom such wealth. It seemed like a fantasy—a story in a book.

What could she even do with it? Give some to her parents, save some for her future, and do something for others? Perhaps she could open a medical clinic to help to serve the members of her community?

She let that thought settle over her. But would that be what her grandmother would want her to do with the farm? She couldn't be certain what Mammi would want, but she had a feeling Mammi wanted Renee to make that choice for herself. Still, it seemed crazy to imagine having that much money when her community was so very plain.

Renee drank more tea and studied Belinda's photo. The woman looked artificial from her long, red nails to her copper-colored hair to her fancy black suit. Her career seemed to be very important to her.

Could Belinda have a darker side? And if so, how far would an Englisher go to make a big profit on a real estate sale?

Renee didn't know, but a chill traveled through her as she recalled the threatening letter that had been left on her grand-mother's door.

Chapter Ten

Sunday, April 27

Jerome hitched his horse by the barn and looked toward Martha's house. He had woken up early to take care of the animals and have a quick breakfast before getting ready for church. He expected his sister and Renee to come out soon. They needed to leave in the next five minutes if they were going to make it to the Dienner family's farm in time for the service.

Martha's back door opened, and when Renee stepped out onto the porch, Jerome did a double take. She was effortlessly beautiful in her new green dress, coupled with a white apron and a Lancaster County heart-shaped prayer *kapp* that Jeannie had given her. His mouth dried as she descended the stairs and padded down the path toward him. She looked like she belonged in his community.

But she didn't belong here. And she would be gone by August.

As she approached him, an unsure expression overtook her pretty face. She brushed a hand over her apron and then touched her prayer covering. Was she worried that he wouldn't like how she looked? If so, then she couldn't be more wrong.

"G-gude mariye," she stammered.

He started to reach for her hand and then dropped his arm to his side. "You look schee."

"Danki," she said softly as her face flushed. He was certain she had no idea just how attractive she was.

A memory of his late fiancée, Amanda, flashed through his mind, and his happy mood evaporated. The scene of the accident rolled through his memory, and every muscle in his spine tensed. It was all his fault—*all his fault*, and he had no business even admiring another woman after what he'd done. He deserved to be alone and to live with a limp that served as a constant source of guilt and regret for his unforgivable actions.

Renee was better off without him. If he let her into his battered heart, he would bring her nothing but disappointment and pain. She needed to return to Ohio and forget him. That's what God would want.

His lips turned down, and he moved away from her while focusing his attention on his horse.

Renee rushed over to him. "Is everything all right?"

"We need to get going. Is Jeannie ready?" he asked.

"I'll check on her." Renee hurried into the house and reappeared a few moments later with Jeannie behind her, holding a portable container.

After Jeannie ran back into the house one last time, she finally climbed into the back of the buggy, and Renee took the passenger seat. Jerome tried to shake off his suddenly murky mood by concentrating on guiding the horse toward the Dienner family's farm. He couldn't stop thinking about the past, and he tried in vain to shake off the familiar worry that threaded through him when he traveled with passengers in his buggy.

The sound of his mare's hooves and road noise filled the air. Out of the corner of his eye, he spotted Renee moving her fingertip over the hem of her apron. Anxiety rolled off her in waves. He tried to think of something to say, but he fell mute. At that moment, he longed for his bubbly twin to start a conversation. If Jeannie started chatting, then the ride would fly by instead of feeling like a long and painful journey.

A few more minutes ticked by, and Jerome yearned for someone to break the silence and help him turn off his memories of Amanda.

"Jerome," Jeannie began from the rear of the buggy, and he felt the tense muscles in his back relax slightly. "We were discussing that threatening letter at breakfast, and we realized it's been eight days since it was left on the back door."

Renee turned toward him. "Right. We've decided that we think your dat was right, and it was just a prank."

"Exactly," Jeannie said. "If the person was really trying to scare us, wouldn't they do something else?"

Jerome brushed a hand over his clean-shaven chin.

"What do you think, Jerome?" Renee asked.

He glanced over at her, and her soulful brown eyes seemed eager for his opinion or possibly for his agreement. "I hope you're right."

Jeannie and Renee discussed their theories about the threatening letter during the remainder of the ride.

When they reached the Dienners' farm, he guided his horse toward the barn, and they got out.

"See you after service," Jeannie said before heading toward the house holding the portable dish.

Renee stood beside him for a moment. "Are you okay, Jerome?" Concern colored her face.

"Ya." He tried to smile, but it felt more like a grimace.

"Are you worried that the letter wasn't a prank?"

He studied her anxious expression and for a moment he considered telling her the truth, sharing everything that had happened with Amanda and the accident, but his mouth clamped shut. This was the wrong place and time to even consider such a thing. After all, they were headed into the church service.

"I'm just tired," he said, his voice croaking.

She studied him, and when her forehead furrowed, he was certain she could see right through his fib. A few moments ticked by, and he waited for her to question him and demand the truth.

"Renee!" Jeannie's voice crashed through his thoughts. "Are you coming?"

Spinning toward his twin's voice, Renee waved. "Ya!" Then she pivoted to face Jerome. "I'll see you later," she said before trotting off to meet his sister.

Jerome finished taking care of his horse and then trudged through the lush green grass to where Tim stood with a few of their friends by the barn.

"Cuttin' it close, huh? I was wondering if you were going to be late today," Tim quipped with a grin.

Leaning against the fence, Jerome said, "I had to wait for mei schweschder to get ready."

"Jeannie's staying at the farm?" Tim asked.

"Ya, in Martha's haus. She and mei mamm decided it would be a gut idea for Jeannie to be our chaperone since Renee and I are both single."

Tim's gaze darted to something behind Jerome. "Renee looks... different. She's dressing like a member of the community." His best friend lifted a dark eyebrow. "Is she staying?"

"Nee." Jerome crossed his arms over his middle.

"How would you feel if she stayed?"

Jerome glowered. "She's not staying."

"But what if she did?" Tim's expression challenged him.

Jerome pushed off the fence and then pointed toward the barn, where the congregation had started filing in for the service. "It's time to go."

He was relieved he'd escaped Tim's question. Thinking about Renee staying in the community was preposterous, and he couldn't allow himself to imagine getting close to her. If he did, it would only end with him nursing another broken heart.

Renee took a bite of her sandwich while Maribeth shared a story about working at her parents' bakery. She glanced around the barn and pulled in the scent of animals mixed with coffee and peanut butter spread. A buzz of conversations hung in the air while the women had their turn to eat lunch.

She enjoyed the church service, especially when the minister discussed the book of John. Although a small part of her ached for her parents and Anna, Renee felt like a member of this community, not only because she was dressed like the other young, unmarried women in the congregation with her bright green dress, but also because Jeannie's friends had seemed happy to see her and were including her in their conversation.

She'd tried her best not to stare at Jerome during the service and instead concentrate on the minister's holy words, but her eyes had defied her a few times and found him staring into his lap. Worry for him lingered in the back of her mind. His posture had been stiff, and his smile that she'd enjoyed so much hadn't reappeared during their ride to church. And when he had glanced her way during the service, his lips remained fixed in a flat line, which sent more concern coursing through her.

Although he'd insisted he was only tired, she couldn't shake the feeling that he wasn't telling her the whole truth. She yearned to know what was troubling him. When she could get Jeannie alone, she would ask her if she knew why Jerome seemed so down.

"The Englishers actually asked us if we baked over a fire pit in our backyards," Maribeth continued her story with a laugh. "I showed the women our propane-powered ovens in the back of the bakery, and they seemed very impressed that we could operate them."

Sarah snorted. "I'm always surprised by the questions they come up with. One woman asked how my family managed to live without electricity. I told her that it's not as difficult as you think. Candles, flashlights, lanterns, and propane lamps work just as well as overhead lighting."

Renee chuckled and popped a pretzel into her mouth.

"Green is your color, Renee," Lucy announced. "It's nice seeing you wearing it."

Renee sat up a little taller, surprised by the compliment. "Danki."

"I agree." Jeannie lifted her cup of coffee. "You look lovely."

Renee felt Sarah studying her, but she kept her eyes focused on a small pile of pretzels on her plate.

"Are you dating Jerome?" Sarah finally asked.

Renee gasped. She would never date a man without her stepfather's permission. "Nee." Her cheeks warmed as her gaze darted to Maribeth, expecting to see her disapproval, but Maribeth's expression seemed curious instead of angry. Did that mean she wasn't interested in Jerome? Had Renee misread Maribeth the first time she'd met her?

"Ach." Sarah frowned. "That's a shame. I'd hoped maybe you could bring him out of his shell and his sadness." She shook her head and clucked her tongue. "Jerome needs to start dating again."

Jeannie heaved a deep sigh, and her ever-present smile wobbled. "Ya, I remind him often that he needs to start dating again, but he doesn't want to listen to his twin."

"I'm sure he still misses Amanda." Maribeth's voice was soft.

"Ya. We all do," Lucy chimed in. "And what happened was so *bedauerlich*."

"It was tragic, but it was Gott's will and not our place to question it," Maribeth added.

Renee's thoughts spun as she glanced around the table. Who was Amanda, and what had happened to her? The sad expression on her new friends' faces also indicated that this wasn't the place to ask.

Her mother had taught her to mind her business and not pry, but she cared about Jerome. She longed to help him through this painful season of his life—if he'd allow her to.

Renee did her best to focus on her friends' conversations while they finished lunch and then helped the other women clean up. Questions about Jerome and Amanda continued to nip at her while she and Jeannie walked toward the waiting line of buggies.

When she and Jeannie were out of earshot from the rest of the women, Renee stopped moving and touched Jeannie's arm. "Wait," she said. "Who was Amanda?"

Jeannie swallowed before scanning the area. "She was engaged to Jerome."

"Oh." Renee tried to mask her surprise. Jerome was engaged? This news shocked her. "What happened to her?" she asked slowly.

Jeannie's eyes glittered. "She...died." Her words sounded thick.

Renee gasped, and her eyes stung as the pieces came together in her mind. Jerome's sadness, his reticence, and his constant frown all made sense now. Her heart felt heavy for him. The man had been through so much. He said his limp was caused by an old injury. But could his limp have something to do with how Amanda died?

Gott, please heal Jerome's broken spirit and help me be a balm to his soul.

Jeannie placed her hand on Renee's shoulder. "We can't walk over to him looking sad. He'd be upset if he knew I was talking about Amanda." She sniffed. "Let's talk about something happy, okay? So we can laugh."

Renee turned to where Jerome was talking to Tim by his buggy. Jerome's expression was set in stone while Tim spoke. She suddenly felt as if she knew him better and understood his heart, and at the same time, she felt compelled to help him. If only she could convince him to open up to her and tell her what happened. Maybe she could convince him that God would want him to find joy again. Perhaps she could show him how to be happy.

But that wasn't her place. She wasn't planning to stay in Bird-in-Hand.

Yet she felt herself being drawn to Jerome. Did God want her to help him?

That question settled over her heart, along with a small nagging feeling that she couldn't quite identify, while she and Jeannie plodded through the grass toward the buggy.

Jeannie never stopped talking while Jerome guided his mare toward Martha's farm. She went on and on about Maribeth's family's bakery, Sarah's cousins who were coming to visit next month, and about the afternoon youth group gathering at the Fisher family's farm, which she insisted Jerome and Renee needed to attend.

Beside him, however, Renee remained quiet. With her hands folded on her lap, she peered out the side window as if avoiding his gaze. Her demeanor was puzzling, especially after she'd nearly insisted he open up to her earlier. What had changed?

When his twin paused between stories, Jerome leaned toward Renee. "You okay, Renee?"

"Huh?" She jumped with a start. She faced him, and her expression was sad. "Ya. I'm just...tired."

So, she was his own words now. Interesting. But perhaps she was homesick after receiving a letter from her best friend.

"Now, you two *are* going to join me for youth group today, right?" Jeannie prodded from the back of the buggy. "We're going to play volleyball over at the Fisher family's farm. It's going to be so wunderbaar!"

Jerome shook his head. Youth group led to dating pressure, and he would never, ever date again. It was best that he stay home and rest on the Lord's day.

"Nee, danki," Renee said. "I'm going to rest this afternoon."

For a brief moment, Jerome wondered if she could read his thoughts. Not that he believed in such a thing.

Jeannie frowned. "You *have* to come, Renee. It's a bright and sunny day, and a youth group from over in Paradise is going to join us. You'll love it. I promise!"

"Maybe," Renee said, and Jeannie cheered.

Jerome guided the horse to the barn, and when he got out of the buggy, he turned toward Martha's house and found the back door wide open. His gut knotted as a sense of foreboding trickled through him.

"Jeannie," he called, "did you close the door when you left for church?"

"What? Why?" Jeannie's nose wrinkled. When she turned toward the house, her blue eyes widened. "I think I closed it." She gulped. "Was someone in the haus while we were at church?" she asked.

Renee shook her head. "I'm sure we closed the door," she said. "I walked out behind Jeannie, and the hem of my new dress got caught in the door as I closed it. I had to open it and then close it solidly behind myself." She started toward the house. "So, why is the door open?" She stopped, and a dark expression flickered over her face. "We've had someone leave us a threatening note. Maybe it was a prank, but maybe it wasn't. What if the real estate agent came over here and decided to snoop around, knowing we'd be at church?"

Jeannie studied Renee. "You think someone came here and broke into the haus?"

"Ya." Renee's dark eyes bounced around the farm. "What if the person who did this is still here, hiding in the barn?"

Jerome shook his head. They all needed to calm down. Why would someone want to break into the house, hide out, and then hurt them? That thought was preposterous.

He had been pondering the threatening letter all week, and he'd checked with Murray to see if their neighbor had witnessed anyone leaving the note that day. Murray didn't say much, but he insisted he hadn't seen anything. Jeannie and Renee were definitely overreacting.

"Hold on." He held up a hand. "I don't think anyone is hiding in the barn or anywhere else, and I don't think anyone is planning to hurt us."

Renee pointed to the house. "Then why is the door open?" she asked. "I remember closing it, Jerome."

"I'll check out the haus. You can come inside with me." Jerome ascended the porch steps and entered the house. He panned the family room, looking for signs of a robbery, forced entry, or vandalism, but the room looked as it always had, with a sofa and armchairs in the center of the room, along with end tables, a coffee table, propane lamps, and a bookshelf. Nothing seemed to be amiss.

He continued, room by room, with his sister and Renee in tow, and nothing was disturbed. After checking the last room, he returned to the hallway. "Is anything missing?" he asked.

Jeannie shook her head. "My room seems fine."

"I don't know." Renee's brows drew together. "I'll take another look around." She fluttered toward the kitchen while he remained in the hallway with his twin.

Jeannie tapped his arm and looked contrite. "What if it's my fault? What if I left the door unlocked or open?"

Jerome tried to remember if Jeannie had locked the door before they left for church, but he'd been too focused on how pretty Renee was in her new dress to recall any other details from that morning. He should have paid more attention, and he couldn't stand for his twin to take the blame. "It's not your fault."

"But what if it is?" Jeannie's eyes widened. "I ran back into the haus for the second *kuche*. You and Renee weren't paying attention. What if I left the door open and someone came in?"

"I don't think—"

"Ach, nee!" Renee cried.

Jerome took off toward the kitchen, where Renee stood in front of the china cabinet with tears glistening in her eyes. "What happened?"

"Mei mammi's teapot is missing." She pointed to the cabinet. "It's always on that shelf there." She rested her hand on her forehead. "I'm trying to remember the last time I used it." She closed her eyes and then opened them. "It was Wednesday when I wrote a letter to Anna. I had brewed myself a cup of tea."

She pointed to Jeannie. "You were at work at your parents' store." Her lower lip trembled, and his heart squeezed. "But why would someone steal mei mammi's teapot? Maybe I didn't put it back where it belongs." Her voice was raspy. "I could've misplaced it." She swept the backs of her hands over her eyes.

"Let's look for it," he said.

For the next several minutes, Jerome, Jeannie, and Renee searched the cabinets and pantry for the teapot but weren't able to find it.

Renee stood in the middle of the kitchen and made a sweeping gesture. "Why would someone break in and take a teapot?" she asked. "It doesn't make sense. It's narrisch."

"Ya," Jeannie said. "I agree. It is crazy."

Jerome rubbed a hand over his jaw. He agreed that it didn't make sense, but his stomach pitched with unease. Something wasn't right, and he didn't like it one bit.

"What's on your mind, Jerome?" Renee stood so close to him that the flowery scent of her shampoo or possibly her lotion drifted over him, and his pulse blipped.

"Make sure your windows and doors are locked tonight," he said. "From now on we're going to be extra cautious."

Renee nodded. "Okay."

Jeannie looped her arm around Renee's shoulders. "Come to youth group with me. It'll take your mind off this."

Renee hesitated and glanced over at Jerome. Was she looking for his permission? "Should I?"

"Ya." He nodded. "That's a gut idea. I'll look after things here."

She bit her lower lip. "Will you be okay alone?"

The tenderness in her expression sent warmth blooming in his chest. "I'll be fine," he said.

Renee gave his sister a tremulous smile. "Ya, I'll go."

"Yay! Let's get ready." Jeannie steered Renee toward the bedrooms.

Jerome remained in the doorway while an eerie feeling gripped him. He couldn't shake the sense that someone had been in Martha's house, and he was determined to find out who it was and why.

And he would do everything in his power to protect Renee and Jeannie.

Chapter Eleven

Wednesday, April 30

Renee pushed a mop around the kitchen Wednesday afternoon. While she worked, her gaze kept flicking over to the china cabinet. After finishing her chores, she'd spent the past two days searching for anything that might explain why her father had left the community. She'd continued looking in the house and had also searched the barn, all while keeping an eye out for the teapot. She couldn't figure out where she'd put it, and despite Jerome's insistence that no strangers had been inside the house, she couldn't shake the feeling that someone had taken it.

She had enjoyed her time with Jeannie and her friends on Sunday while they'd played volleyball and then sang hymns until late in the night. Laughing and talking with her new friends had been good for her soul.

When she and Jeannie arrived home Sunday night, Renee was not really surprised that Jerome had waited up to make sure they got home safely. He insisted on walking through the house one more time, checking all the window locks as well as the front door, before he said good night, reminded them to bolt the door behind him, and retreated to his house.

Renee had hoped her hunch was right and the missing teapot would turn up, but Jerome's warning still sent a jolt of worry through her. She'd also continued wondering about Jerome's past and the story behind his fiancée's death. She'd almost asked him about it when Jeannie was at work on Monday and again earlier in the day, but she was afraid to bring up the painful subject and risk alienating him.

After she finished mopping the kitchen, Renee headed out the front door, descended the porch steps, and followed the path to the driveway and out to the mailbox. The sky above was covered with gray, foreboding clouds, and the air smelled like rain.

She opened the metal mailbox and pulled out a stack of letters and postcards. Rifling through them, she stopped when she came to an envelope addressed to her in familiar, beautiful, slanted handwriting. When she realized the letter was from her mother, her heart skipped a beat. She couldn't wait to read it.

But first Renee perused the postcards, which were all from local Realtors. When she came across one from Belinda Walker, her stomach clenched. A handwritten note on the back said, *Renee— Just wanted to check in and see if you've considered selling the farm. Give me a call if you'd like to discuss it. Sincerely, Belinda.*

The woman wouldn't give up! And Renee couldn't help wondering if Belinda might be the person who had left the threatening note and also broken into the house.

The hair on the back of her neck suddenly stood up, and a chill trickled down her spine. She was certain someone was watching her.

Renee slowly turned toward the street. Her eyes hunted around until they landed on the neighbor's house. Something glinted from behind a front window, and when it came into focus, she found Murray Robertson watching her through binoculars.

Feeling violated, she hugged the mail to her chest and scurried up the driveway, through the front door of the house, and locked the deadbolt before rushing to the den and dropping onto the sofa. She slid her hands over her face and tried to calm her raging pulse.

Murray Robertson was an odd bird. Was he strange enough to leave a threatening note on her door or to break into her home and steal her grandmother's teapot? But why would he be compelled to do that? Was he an Englisher who didn't approve of the Amish, and he wanted Renee to sell the farm to a non-Amish person?

She would tell Jerome and Jeannie about Murray Robertson when they arrived back at the farm. Jeannie was at work at her family's fabric store, and Jerome had gotten a ride to run for supplies.

Renee shoved away her worry and picked up the letter from her mother. After opening the envelope, she began to read.

Dear Renee,

I hope this letter finds you well. I was so grateful to hear from you. Ike and I were discussing you last night and wondering how your visit is going.

Anna has been a great help in the basket store. We sold six baskets last week, and we're working on creating some more. I miss having you at the basket stand with me.

Noah and Anna announced their engagement at church last week. Anna said she was going to write to you and tell you. She's anxious for you to get home so you can help her with her plans. Maybe you can come home sooner than August so you can help her?

Also, her engagement got me thinking about your future. I know you've dated a bit, but you need to seriously consider finding a husband. You should get back here so you can get more involved with youth group. Once this business with your grandmother's farm is settled, you can focus on your future and God's plan for you.

How did the meeting go with the lawyer? Have you asked the lawyer to start on the paperwork to hand the land over to the Amish community or are you going to put the land up for sale? If you're still unsure about how to handle the farm, you should speak to the bishop. He can help you figure out the best way to handle the farm.

We miss you. You should wrap up the legal issues with that farm and get back home. Write soon and let me know what progress you've made with Martha's estate.

Love,

Mamm

Renee's lungs constricted while she studied her mother's letter. She could feel her mother pressuring her to give up the farm and return home at once.

The room suddenly felt too small, and she was certain she couldn't breathe. Dropping the letter onto the sofa, she stood and dashed out to the back porch, where Murray couldn't see her with the binoculars, and sucked in air. A cool mist of rain kissed her cheeks. She couldn't allow her mother to force her to leave before she found out the truth about her past. Surely God would understand why she had to disobey her mother and stay until she had the answers to all of her questions.

She looked up at the sky and whispered a prayer, "Gott, forgive me for not leaving before I'm ready. I don't mean to be a disobedient dochder, but I need to find the answers I'm craving before I go home."

When she walked back inside, Renee was overcome with the urge to look for clues and for the teapot again. She returned to the kitchen and after confirming the floor was dry, she began searching the china cabinet for what felt like the dozenth time. She pushed the dishes and cups around, looking for…something. She didn't know what, but she was determined to find some sort of clue about the past.

She pulled open the top drawer and lifted serving platters, peeking under each one. In the center section of the cabinet, she found larger portable containers, and when she jostled them around, she came up empty.

After investigating drawers containing serving utensils, she pulled a chair over and sank down next to the bottom drawers. Disappointment weighed heavily on her as she yanked open a large drawer and found it was full of tablecloths. She lifted them out, one by one, and ran her hands over the soft fabric. Renee had almost given up hope when she glimpsed something stuck at the back of the drawer.

She grabbed it, and her pulse galloped when she realized it was a large envelope with *Renee* written across it in script. She opened it to find a sealed and postmarked envelope addressed to her father at their Ohio address. The return address was for her grandmother. *Return to Sender* was written in block letters across the top, and the postmark was from ten years ago.

This was it! This had to be a clue that would help her understand the past! And it seemed that Mammi had left it for her to find!

Her heart beat like a drum, and her hands shuddered as she turned the envelope over in them.

Renee began to open it.

"Do you need to stop anywhere else?" Autumn Martin asked Jerome as she merged the van onto Old Philadelphia Pike.

A sign for Tim's family's hardware store came into view. "Could we make a stop at Kings' Hardware?"

"Sure thing."

After taking care of the animals and eating breakfast with Jeannie and Renee, Jerome spent the morning running errands, going to the farm supply and grocery stores. Since he needed to buy supplies to fix the barn door, he'd called for a ride. He'd had such a long list of materials that it made sense to get a ride instead of trying to fit it all into his buggy. Aside from that, he also had become more comfortable traveling by car since the accident.

He'd been contemplating the possible break-in and the threatening letter during the past few days, and he couldn't seem to shake off his worry. His sleepless nights had become routine even before the door to Martha's home had been left open, and he'd sat by a window for hours watching the farm, waiting for a delinquent to trespass and harass them.

Jerome had considered stopping by his parents' store to discuss his worries with his father, but he assumed Jeannie would fill them in. Instead, he longed to talk to his best friend and get his thoughts on the stressful situation.

Autumn parked in front of the store, and Jerome wrenched the door open. "I won't be long," he said.

"Take your time." She flipped on the radio, and pop music sang through the speakers.

Jerome strode into the shop, the bell above the door announcing his entrance. He glanced at a colorful display of birdhouses and bags of birdseed and then chose a cart before slipping through the aisles, where he grabbed a box of nails, hinges, a pile of wood, a few paint brushes, and a half-gallon of paint.

He took his place in line behind an older Amish man who had a basket full of painting supplies.

"Jerome. Wie geht's?"

He whirled around just as Tim walked up to him. "Hi. Do you have a minute to talk?"

"Ya." Tim waved him over to the second register next to where his younger brother, Levi, rang up a customer.

Jerome waved to Levi and then paid Tim for his supplies.

Tim gave him his change and receipt. "What did you want to talk about?"

"Can you walk outside?" Jerome asked.

Tim told his brother he'd be right back and then he walked out to the van with Jerome.

"You look troubled," Tim commented.

"Ya, I am." Jerome set the box of nails on the back seat of the van and then moved to the front end to stand beside his best friend. "Things have gotten a bit tense at the farm."

He leaned on the hood of the van and shared how they had received the threatening note taped to the back door of Martha's house over a week ago and then came home after church on Sunday to find the back door open and Renee's grandmother's teapot missing.

"Mei dat insists that the threatening note was some Englisher kinner playing a prank, but I can't escape this terrible feeling that something bad is going to happen," Jerome confessed. "I think it's more than just a prank. We've gotten postcards from a few Realtors wanting to help Renee sell the farm, and one seemed very pushy. She's stopped by and keeps sending postcards. I wonder if someone is trying to scare Renee into selling the land because they want to make a big profit."

Jerome rested his hands on his hips. "All I know for sure is that I haven't slept since last week. I'm up nearly all night watching out the window, determined to protect mei schweschder and Renee." He licked his lips and stood up straight. "Do you think I'm overreacting or I'm narrisch? Or that I'm imagining the threat in my mind?"

Tim pursed his lips and shook his head. "Jerome, I've known you for eighteen years, and I've never known you to overreact." He paused for a moment. "Has Renee decided what she's going to do with the farm yet?"

"Nee. She needs some time to work through a family situation." He felt it was his duty to protect Renee's privacy and the questions she wanted answered about her father's past. "I've been checking into a few jobs since I'm not in any position to buy the land myself."

"To be honest with you, I would take the threat seriously, and I wouldn't trust anyone who seemed to be out to gain something from the farm. I think you're *schmaert* to protect your schweschder and Renee, but you need your sleep, Jerome." His best friend gave him a knowing look. "You're not going to be in any shape to help Renee or Jeannie when they need you if you're running on an hour's sleep."

"Tim!"

They both looked toward the store, where Levi stood waving at him.

"Dat needs you to finish up the inventory," Levi said before slipping back inside.

"I gotta go," Tim told Jerome before patting his shoulder. "Keep me posted on everything, and if you need my help, let me know."

"Danki," Jerome told him before loading up his supplies in the trunk and returning to the back seat of the van. He fastened his safety belt and realized that the radio had been turned off. The only sound in the car came from the soft rumble of the engine.

Autumn angled her body so that she faced Jerome. "Everything all right?"

"Yeah. Danki." He managed to plaster a smile on his lips. "Could you take me back to the farm now?"

She grinned and slipped on her sunglasses. "Absolutely."

A loud knock sounded on the back door.

"Renee?" Jerome called. "I have groceries."

She folded the letter and stuffed it into the pocket of her apron, sniffed, and wiped her eyes before unlocking the door and pulling it open.

"Danki," she said as he carried bags to the counter.

"Was iss letz?" he asked, concern clouding his handsome face.

She waved off his question. "Nothing. I'll put away the groceries." She pulled out a package of lunch meat and headed toward the refrigerator.

"Hold on." A warm hand covered hers, sending goosebumps chasing each other up her arm. "Renee, sit with me."

She placed the package in the refrigerator and then allowed Jerome to gently guide her to the table, where they sat together. "How'd your errands go?"

"Nice try, but you're not going to change the subject." A smile tugged at the corners of his mouth. "Please, Renee. Talk to me." Worry flashed across his features. "You can trust me. I promise."

The sincerity in his expression made her feel lightheaded for a moment. She managed to get her wits about her, then pulled the letter out of her pocket and pushed it toward him. "I found this."

Jerome unfolded the letter, and his eyes scanned it for a moment before his brow wrinkled. "This is personal." He moved the letter back over to Renee. "I can't read this."

"Ya, you can," she insisted. "Because I *do* trust you. I trust you completely, Jerome. Please read it."

He shook his head. "I don't feel right about it."

"I'm giving you permission, Jerome."

He hesitated and then began reading it. While his eyes moved over the letter, Renee could almost recite the words verbatim since she'd read it over and over again after finding it. Her heart clenched as the words echoed in her mind.

Dear Emmanuel,

It's been ten years since you took your family away from me. I miss you every single day, and daily I beg God to bring you back to me.

I want to know my granddaughter—my only grandchild unless the Lord has blessed you and Lovina with more children. I built a small home on my land, and I'd like you to come home and take over the farm, which is rightfully yours. Then we can be together again as a family.

Let's start over, Emmanuel. Please forgive me as God has forgiven our sins. I miss and love you, son. Please bring my family back to me and allow me to live out my last days with you all at my side. This is your home, and you should be here.

Always,

Mamm

When Jerome finally looked up, his intelligent, sky-blue eyes glistened with tears.

Renee blotted her eyes with a napkin and sniffed.

"Where did you find this?" he asked softly, his voice sounding raspy.

She pointed to the china cabinet. "It was in the bottom drawer under a pile of tablecloths. It was unopened. Mei dat had written 'return to sender' on it." She swallowed against the lump expanding in her throat. "What do you think it means?"

"I don't know, but it confirms what Martha told me. She said that she'd done something that hurt your dat, and that's why he took you and your mamm away from home," he said. "Martha loved to cook for me, and we used to eat all of our meals together. She used to share memories of when Emmanuel was little, and she'd talk about you and how much she loved your visits." He paused. "I know she missed her family and never got over losing you."

"I missed her too." Renee dipped her chin toward the wooden tabletop and drew invisible circles with her fingertip. "And I missed mei daadi. I remember his booming laugh, which was so infectious. He would carry me on his shoulders while we'd walk around the farm and he'd tell me stories about when he was little and he worked on his dat's farm. Somehow mei dat got word when Daadi passed about eleven years ago." She settled back in the chair. "It was sad to hear that he was gone. I feel like I missed out on so much with my grandparents."

"Your daadi was loved in the community. The church district was devastated when we lost our bishop."

She sighed. "I've been here two and a half weeks, and I still don't know anything about why my parents left. I've spoken to mei mammi's friends at church, and I've asked some of the women who knew mei mamm. I've also searched the haus, the barn, and the little outbuildings, but I can't find anything in this house that will tell me anything. No clues at all. I can't wait until my aunt gets back in town so I can talk to her. Maybe she'll be able to tell me something that helps me understand why mei dat made us leave."

She frowned. "I received a letter from mei mamm, and she wants me to wrap up the legal issues here and come home. I feel guilty for wanting to stay until I get my questions answered, but I also feel like I'm owed answers."

Covering her face with her hands, she groaned. "I sound like a petulant and entitled child, but I can't rest until I know what happened."

"Renee, look at me." Jerome's voice was soft and smooth, reminding her of velvet.

She set her hands on the table. When he covered her hands with his, the feel of his skin sent a thrill dancing up her arms.

"I promise you that I will help you figure this out," he said, and the affection in his eyes warmed her from the inside out. "We'll do it together."

"Danki. Let's make a plan." She smiled, and relief fell across his face. "I guess I need to stop blubbering, put the groceries away, and figure out what to make for supper for you, Jeannie, and me."

They worked together to stow the groceries, and when she pulled out her grandmother's cookbook, she suddenly recalled what she'd wanted to tell Jerome.

"When I went to collect the mail earlier, I saw Murray Robertson staring at me with binoculars." A chill traveled up her spine at the memory. "Do you think he could be harassing us because he wants us to sell the land?"

"Nee." Jerome shook his head. "I don't think he would do anything like that."

"Then why would he watch me with binoculars?"

"He once told Martha that he likes to watch wildlife. A couple of weeks ago, I was getting the mail, and he called over to me and told me that he saw a bobcat out this way. He said to make sure that the chickens were secure, which they always are. Maybe he was looking to see if it came back?"

Renee frowned. "If that's true, then why was he watching *me*?" She pointed to her chest.

"I don't know."

She eyed Jerome. "But what do you *really* know about him?" she asked. "You told me that he was a loner and always kept to himself, but did he ever bother mei mammi?"

Jerome shook his head. "Nee. He never bothered her. In fact, he was kind to her. I always worried about Martha going for the mail, but she insisted she liked walking down the driveway. She called it her walk, and she loved to see if any of her neighbors had planted flowers. One day she fell by the mailbox. I was in the barn, and I had no idea she was hurt." He frowned and brushed a hand over his mouth. "Murray saw her, and he ran over. He got her up and helped her to the house, where I bandaged up the cuts on her leg."

"That was so kind of him." Renee's heart squeezed.

Jerome grimaced. "Ya. I felt terrible that I never heard her call for help, and I told her that if she insisted on going for the mail, then she needed to use her cane. I was grateful Murray had heard her."

"I guess that means he doesn't have something against Amish people."

"I don't think so." He tilted his head. "Why would you assume that?"

She shrugged. "I don't know. I was wondering if he wanted me to sell the farm so that an Englisher could buy the place." She tapped her finger against the counter. "If he was kind to mei mammi and he doesn't mind Amish people, then why would he spy on me with binoculars?"

Jerome's eyes widened for a fraction of a moment before his handsome face twisted with a glower. "I don't know, but I'll definitely keep an eye out now."

Chapter Twelve

Friday, May 2

Renee collected the eggs from the chicken coop and set them into her large basket Friday afternoon. The sky was azure blue, and the afternoon sun was warm on her cheeks. Birds sang in the nearby trees, and bees buzzed past her. She hummed to herself on her way back toward the house. When a familiar dark-colored sedan motored up the driveway, she quickened her steps on her way to meet the car.

Belinda Walker got out of the vehicle, gave Renee a big wave, and retrieved a large basket from the back seat. "Renee," she said. "So good to see you." She lifted her chin toward the sky. "Such a beautiful day, isn't it? I'm so glad it's finally May. I can't wait for the summertime. Do you like the summer?"

Renee shrugged. "I suppose so."

"I wanted to stop by and see how you're doing. Have you received my postcards?"

"Ya." Renee studied the woman's face and tried to imagine her leaving the threatening letter and breaking into the house to take her precious teapot. She couldn't determine whether or not Belinda was capable of that, but she also couldn't shake the possibility either.

Belinda closed the distance between them and held out the basket. "This is for you."

Renee blinked at the open hamper filled with oranges, apples, pears, and bananas. A large pink bow adorned the handle, along with a notecard attached with a smaller ribbon. What an unusual gift to receive from a stranger. "What's this for?"

"It's for you." Belinda held it out. "Take it. I insist."

"Uh… Thank you." Renee balanced the container of eggs in one hand and took the fruit basket in the other.

"Now don't forget that if you want to sell, you just give me a call. I'm ready when you are."

Renee paused for a moment, and all the questions and doubts she'd had about the real estate agent whirled through her mind. Was Belinda giving her a gift so Renee wouldn't suspect her?

She needed to know the truth. *Now's my chance to confront her. I have to be brave, firm, and direct.*

Mustering all her courage from deep inside herself, Renee leveled her gaze on the Realtor. "Have you been harassing us?" she asked.

Belinda's eyes widened. "I beg your pardon?"

"Someone left a threatening letter taped to my back door, then broke into my house while we were at church and stole my grandmother's teapot. Did you do those things in order to try to convince me to sell the farm and go back home to Ohio?"

Belinda looked offended. "Honey, I'm sorry that happened to you, but I can assure you, I didn't have anything to do with it. I don't have to harass or threaten people in order to get business. I know how to take no for an answer." She pointed to the basket. "Enjoy the fruit, and if you decide to sell, call me any time." Spinning on her high heels, she strutted to her car and drove away.

Renee toted the two large baskets into the house and set them on the kitchen table. She removed the envelope from the fruit basket, opened it, and read the note.

> Renee,
> Enjoy these treats. Call me if you need any help selling your farm.
> Sincerely,
> Belinda Walker

After retrieving the threatening letter from the drawer next to the sink, she set both the letter and the note on the table and compared the handwriting. She had tried to compare the postcards to the threatening letter, but the postcards were written in script while the letter was printed. Since the card with the baskets was printed, it could offer a clue. Her mind spun with the possibility that Belinda could've been the one who left the letter and also broke in.

The back door opened and clicked shut before Jerome wandered into the kitchen.

"Where'd that come from?" he asked as he set his straw hat on the counter.

"Belinda was here again."

"I thought I heard a car." He came to stand beside her, and she tried to ignore how his nearness sent her senses spinning.

Renee held up both documents. "Do you think she could've written the letter?"

Jerome's eyes narrowed as he perused them. "The writing might be similar, but you don't know who wrote the cards. The person who sold her the baskets could've written the note for her."

"Good point." Her shoulders slumped.

He shook his head. "We may never know."

"I asked her if she did."

His blond eyebrows careened toward his hairline. "You did?"

"Uh-huh."

"What'd she say?"

"She looked shocked, and she said that she doesn't need to threaten or harass people in order to get their business." Renee sighed. "I don't know what to think. She seemed genuine, but she could be a very convincing liar too."

To her surprise, he laughed, and she enjoyed the deep, rich sound. In fact, she wanted to hear it more often.

"I'm impressed, Renee."

"You are?"

"Ya, I am. Gut for you for being outspoken and asking her outright if she did it. If it was Belinda, maybe she'll realize that we're not country bumpkins just because we're Amish, and she can't pull one over on us." He grinned. "I'm proud of you. Gut job."

Her heart felt buoyant. "Danki."

"I came in to tell you that there's a voicemail message for you." He pointed toward the door. "Jeannie called from the store. She was excited to tell you that she and Mamm want to invite you for a sisters' day tomorrow. She's stopping at the store to get some supplies so you can bake kichlin or a kuche tonight."

Renee scrunched her nose. "A sisters' day?"

A grin flickered about his lips, and she thought she might melt into a puddle. "A sisters' day is when a group of women get together to work on a project. Most likely you'll be sewing. Jeannie mentioned something about needing to get a few more quilts done for an auction."

"That sounds great." She indicated the counter. "I'd better get started on supper."

"I need to take care of a few more chores."

As she watched him walk toward the door, Renee smiled. She felt as if Jerome was starting to open to her, and she hoped someday soon, he'd trust her enough to tell her about his past and what happened to him and Amanda.

Saturday, May 3

"We're making such gut progress on those quilts," Jeannie announced the following afternoon. "I'm so glad you could all come and help. Mamm and I want to support the auction next month, and we fell behind on our schedule. We're raising money for the new fire station, and I want to be able to donate a few of my quilts to help the community."

Renee added a few stitches to the colorful queen-size lone star pattern quilt. She had enjoyed not only helping Jeannie and her friends, but she cherished the fellowship, along with learning how to quilt.

"Lucy," Maribeth began from her side of the table, "are you going to ride home from youth group with Jeremiah Blank again tomorrow?" She grinned while studying her friend.

When Lucy's cheeks turned bright red, her friends began talking at once, and Renee couldn't stop her own smile.

"You do like him, huh?" Sarah asked.

Jeannie paused her stitching work. "I always thought you'd make a cute couple."

"Has he asked your dat's permission to date you yet?" Maribeth asked.

"Whoa now. One question at a time." Lucy held her hand up. "Ya, I do like Jeremiah." She beamed. "And I think he might like me too."

"Well, obviously, if he gave you a ride home…" Sarah muttered.

"And I think he asked mei dat for permission."

"When?" Jeannie demanded.

"Mei schweschder said she saw him stop by the farm Thursday afternoon. She said he talked to our dat and then left," Lucy said, her voice picking up speed. "So, I think he's going to ask me tomorrow at youth group." She made a little squealing sound, and Jeannie, Maribeth, and Sarah all clapped their hands.

Sarah leaned over and pulled Lucy into a side hug. "I'm so excited for you."

"How about you, Sarah?" Maribeth asked. "I saw you talking to one of the men who had visited from Paradise last week. Did you like him?"

Sarah smiled while she worked on stitching. "His name is David, and he seemed nice. He works in construction."

The women turned to discussing other dating prospects, and Renee continued sewing and lost herself in thoughts of home. She had hoped to receive another letter from Anna this week with an update about her engagement and wedding plans. She missed her best friend, and she missed her parents. Her throat ached.

Perhaps Mamm was right, and she needed to settle the legal matters and get back home. Maybe she should call the Realtor, put the farm on the market, and leave. Her eyes stung.

"What about you, Renee?"

Renee lifted her chin and found all eyes in the room focused on her. "I'm sorry," she said. "I didn't hear the question."

"Did you meet anyone last week at youth group who you found interesting?" Maribeth's gray eyes sparkled.

"Oh." Renee glanced around the table at the curious stares. The only man she'd met who had caught her eye was Jerome, but she wouldn't be in Bird-in-Hand long enough to see if their friendship might lead to anything. And then there was the issue of her parents insisting she return home by harvesttime...

"Nee." She shook her head. "I didn't notice the young men. Instead, I was concentrating on my new friends—all of you."

They all responded with wide smiles before moving on to the subject of community news and discussing people Renee didn't know.

Later that afternoon, Renee gathered up the empty container from the apple pie she and Jeannie had baked last night using apples from the fruit basket Belinda Walker had given her. She started toward the door just as Delilah walked into the kitchen.

"I had fun today," she told Jeannie's mother. "Danki for inviting me."

"Of course we would invite you. We appreciate your help. Many hands make light work." Delilah nodded toward Renee's container. "And that pie was appeditlich." Her eyes brightened. "I was going to call you to tell you Harvey ran into Naomi's husband, Dennis. He said that Naomi will be home sometime this weekend. That means you can visit her Monday. Do you still have her address and phone number?"

Renee could hardly hold back her excitement. "Ya, I do."

"Great. Reach out to her. She might be able to help you find out what happened." Delilah smiled. "We don't have church tomorrow. You and Jerome need to come visit with us."

"I'll come too," Jeannie announced before hugging her mother. "We'll see you tomorrow." She pointed to the door. "Our ride's here." She took Renee's arm and steered her in that direction. "Bye, Mamm!"

"See you tomorrow, Delilah." Renee rubbed her hands together. She couldn't wait to visit her long-lost aunt.

The sound of tires crunching on the driveway pulled Jerome's attention from the board he was fixing on his small porch to the white van parking near his house. His thoughts had lingered on Renee while he'd taken care of his chores, and he hoped she'd enjoyed her day at his mother's house. For some reason, it was important to him.

As he made his way to the van, he realized that he'd missed her, and he tried to shut those feelings down.

Jeannie popped out of the van. "Hey, bruder! How was your day?"

"Gut. Yours?"

"Great! We finished one quilt and made a dent in the other." She dashed toward Martha's house. "I'll preheat the oven and put in the roast chicken I made last night."

He snickered. Sometimes she reminded him of a hummingbird, fluttering off to do something important. Then he turned his attention toward Renee. She had her wallet out, and she was paying the driver, Autumn Martin. "How was your day, Renee?"

"Great." Her pretty face lit with a smile. "Your mamm told me that mei *aenti* is coming home this weekend. I want to visit her Monday." She handed Autumn a couple of bills. "She's over in White Horse."

"White Horse isn't far at all," Autumn chimed. "I can take you if you'd like."

"Let's plan to go see her on Monday," Jerome agreed.

Renee's eyes widened. "You'll go with me?"

"Oh." Embarrassment crawled up his neck. "I'm sorry. I didn't mean to invite myself."

A layer of relief moved over her face. "I'd love for you to come with me. Danki. Also, your mamm wants us to visit tomorrow. Jeannie said she's going to stay home from youth group and go too."

"That sounds gut." He jammed his thumb toward his house. "I need to finish fixing my porch, but I'll see you at supper." He was grateful Renee wanted to include him in her search for the truth about her family. He hoped he could offer her some strength.

But he also needed to remind himself that she'd be gone soon, and he would miss her.

Chapter Thirteen

Sunday, May 4

"You actually asked the Realtor if she was harassing you?" Dat sounded surprised as he gazed across the table at Renee the following afternoon.

Jerome sat at the kitchen table with his parents, Jeannie, and Renee. A spring breeze meandered in from the open windows, and the scent of flowers wafted into the kitchen. His eyes cut to Renee, and she was lovely in a new pink dress. He'd grown accustomed to seeing her in a Lancaster County prayer kapp instead of the cone-shaped covering she'd worn when she first arrived in Bird-in-Hand. The brighter color and the prayer covering suited her. She fit in with his community, and as she gave his father a shy smile, he couldn't help but think that she fit in with his family too.

"I did." Renee shrugged. "The words jumped from my lips."

Dat actually grinned. "I'm impressed."

"That's what I told her," Jerome said. When he met her gaze, her lips formed a smile that seemed to be only meant for him, and his chest swelled. He swallowed a forkful of his mother's meatloaf, and when his eyes moved to his mother, she gave him a knowing smile.

Uh oh. He didn't want to give Mamm the wrong idea about his feelings for Renee. Sure, he cared for her, but he couldn't plan on being any more than her friend.

"How are things at the farm, Jerome?" Dat asked.

"Gut." Jerome wiped his mouth with a napkin. "I finally finished fixing the fence, and I repaired my little porch yesterday. I'm going to start painting the fence this week. Has the store been busy?"

Mamm nodded. "Oh ya. We're having a big sale, and we ran a few ads in the local newspapers. The ads have been a great success."

"I agree with that," his sister added. "Business is steady from when we open until we close."

Jerome glanced around the table while his parents discussed their store, and happiness fizzled through him.

It was the first time he'd felt joy since...

He dismissed the thought. He couldn't allow himself to believe that he deserved happiness. It was an illusion that would evaporate as soon as Renee sold the farm and returned to Ohio. Then Jerome would lose his job, his home, and his friendship with sweet Renee.

After lunch, Jerome and his father moved to the porch, where they sat on rocking chairs and looked out toward his father's barn and small pasture.

Jerome forked a piece of Renee's moist chocolate cake into his mouth and then sipped his coffee. The sun shone in a cloudless, bright blue sky, and the colorful flowers in his mother's garden swayed in the breeze. A couple of chipmunks chased each other up a tree while birds ate at nearby feeders.

Setting his mug on the small table beside him, Jerome blew out a happy sigh and felt his entire body relax for the first time since...

Well, he had no idea how long it had been since he'd felt completely at ease.

"It's gut to see you smile again, sohn."

Jerome lifted an eyebrow as he turned toward his father.

"It's apparent you and Renee have a special friendship, and that makes your mamm and me very happy."

Jerome's smile flattened. "Dat, we're only friends. Nothing more than that."

"Your mamm and I started off as friends."

"Renee is going back to Ohio," Jerome explained. "Her parents told her that she has to be home by August. She's figuring out what she's going to do with Martha's farm. I've been checking into other jobs. I have a lead on a farm that's going to need a hand out in Gordonville soon. Their farmhand is going to move out of state. Right now, I'm focusing on getting my life in order and moving on from Martha's farm since Renee has made it clear that she doesn't want to stay."

"What if you told her that you want her to stay?"

Jerome stilled. That thought hadn't occurred to him, but it was a bad plan. It would never work out. "No, Dat. I'm not ready for that. I can't allow myself to..." The words trailed off. He couldn't even say it aloud.

"Why?" Dat leaned toward him. "What if Gott's will is for you to move on?"

"How can I move on after what happened?" His voice sounded gravelly. "It was *my* fault." He pointed to himself.

Empathy covered his father's face. "Jerome, it was Gott's will."

Jerome shook his head. It was so much more than that. He had no business being on the road that night. And if he'd done what he'd been told to do, Amanda would still be alive.

Dat patted Jerome's shoulder. "You need to allow Gott to open your heart again. You can't stay alone forever."

Jerome nodded, but deep in his heart he couldn't allow himself to believe that he deserved a loving wife and family after what he'd done.

Delilah pulled Renee in for a hug later that evening. "Your kuche was appeditlich," she said. Then she lowered her voice to a whisper. "Danki for making my sohn happy again." She released Renee, and happy tears glistened in her eyes.

Renee stared at the middle-aged woman. "What do you mean?"

"Harvey and I see a difference in him, and we know it's because of you." Delilah wiped her eyes. "You're a blessing to us, Renee. We thank Gott you came back to Bird-in-Hand."

"Oh." Renee nodded, still unsure of what to say while her heart raced. Jerome had become important to her, and if his parents noticed a difference in him, did that mean that she and Jerome could be more than friends? Had God brought them together for a reason? But she was planning to return to Ohio. How could she and Jerome have a future when her parents made it clear she needed to return home?

"You ready?" Jerome appeared in the doorway, and his smile faded as he turned to his mother. "You okay, Mamm?"

Delilah waved off the question. "Ya, ya. Have a gut week." After he said goodbye to her, he headed back out the door, and she winked at Renee.

During the ride back to her grandmother's farm, Renee sat in the passenger seat and tried to process Delilah's words. She glanced over at Jerome and took in the pleasant expression on his handsome profile, and her heart swelled. Could Jerome care about Renee the same way she cared about him? Her stomach flip-flopped at the thought, and she tried to bite back the smile threatening to overtake her lips.

Jeannie sat in the back of the buggy, prattling on about her plans for the week, including how she hoped to finish rearranging a few of the displays in her parents' store, as well as tidying Jerome's little house.

Jerome halted the horse at a red light and gave Renee a sideways glance. "Did you have a gut visit today?"

"Ya. Your family is great."

Jeannie leaned over. "And we all love you, Renee."

When Jerome smiled, Renee's heart leapt with joy.

While they continued their journey back to her grandmother's farm, her thoughts turned to the mystery about her father's past, and her plan to visit her aunt.

"Do you think mei aenti will be happy to see me tomorrow?" Renee asked.

"Of course she will," Jerome said.

"I agree," Jeannie chimed in. "She's going to hug you as soon as she sees you, Renee."

"What if mei mamm hurt her feelings before they left?" Renee asked.

"Even if she did, *you* didn't," Jeannie said. "I imagine I would want to see mei *bruderskinner* no matter what happened between Jerome and me."

"I completely agree," Jerome said. "But I can't imagine that you and I would ever stop talking."

"Of course not. We're *zwillingbopplin*!" Jeannie exclaimed.

Renee chuckled and felt herself relax.

When they reached the farm, Jerome tied his horse to the fence. "Let me check the haus before you go inside."

They walked up the back steps, and Jerome unlocked the door. "Wait here," he said.

Renee and Jeannie sat on the glider and looked out toward the field.

"Are you sorry you skipped the youth group gathering today?" Renee asked her friend.

Jeannie shook her head. "Why would you ask that?"

"I know Sarah and Maribeth were excited to see if Jeremiah asked Lucy to be his girlfriend," Renee said.

"I'm sure I'll find out the news tomorrow." Jeannie pushed the glider into motion with the toe of her shoe. "Lucy will probably stop by the store and tell me."

Renee nodded.

"Are you active with your youth group in Ohio?"

Renee shrugged. "Ya, but I haven't had a boyfriend. My best friend Anna recently got engaged, and she wants me to help plan the wedding."

"That's so exciting," Jeannie said.

"Ya, it is."

"You must miss her."

"I do, but I'm enjoying my time here."

"We are too." Jeannie looked toward the door and then at Renee. "I'm really glad you're here."

"All clear," Jerome said as he limped out to the porch. "You can go in now."

Jeannie popped up from the glider. "I'm going to relax and read a book I found on Martha's shelf." She waved to her twin. "See you later," she sang as she disappeared into the house.

"I wanted to make sure nothing looked disturbed in the haus," Jerome said.

Renee stood. "Danki."

Jerome hesitated for a moment, and his expression became intense. He lifted his hand and brushed it across her cheek. The featherlike touch of his warm fingers on her skin was a sweet caress, something she'd never felt before.

Her lungs hitched as she studied his radiant blue eyes.

"Call out to me if you need me, Renee," he whispered.

While he limped down the steps and started on the path toward his horse and buggy to stow them in the barn, she yearned to ask him if he could ever allow his heart to love again, but her voice didn't want to work.

Monday, May 5

Renee's thoughts spun as she glanced out the window from the backseat of Autumn's van Monday morning. She smoothed her hands down her black apron and the cranberry-colored dress she'd sewn last week. She hoped her aunt didn't consider her dress to be too worldly or fancy. Perhaps she should've worn her gray dress instead, not wanting to offend her aunt the first time they met.

A warm hand covered hers, and her worries immediately ceased.

"You have nothing to worry about." Jerome's deep, smooth voice was soft in her ear. "Your aenti is going to be thrilled to see you, and you're going to have a gut day with her." His caring gaze was just what her soul needed.

Autumn parked her van in the driveway at a two-story, white clapboard house, with a wraparound porch featuring two rocking chairs and a glider. A cheerful garden full of colorful flowers adorned the front, and a large, red barn sat beyond the home.

Vague memories rolled through Renee's mind. Had she been to this home in the past? She was almost certain she'd sat on that porch and played with a doll at one time.

"Are you ready, Renee?" Jerome asked beside her.

She nodded and lifted the container of cookies she'd baked for her aunt early that morning. Then she pushed open the door.

"I hope you get the answers you need," Autumn said from the front seat.

"Danki," Renee said, and they agreed on a time when she would pick them up.

Palms sweating, Renee started toward the front door of the home with Jerome at her side. She knocked on the door before taking in Jerome's reassuring smile.

The door flew open, revealing a woman who appeared to be in her late fifties, with familiar dark eyes and graying dark hair. Her brows knitted. "May I help you?"

"Naomi?" Renee asked.

"Ya?"

Renee's hands trembled. "Gude mariye. I'm your niece, Renee Mast."

Naomi's eyes sparkled as recognition flickered over her face. "Renee?" she asked.

"Ya." Renee nodded.

"Oh!" Naomi pulled her in for a tight hug. "I haven't seen you in so long!" She cupped her hand to Renee's face. "You look just like your mamm," she said, clucking her tongue. "It's so gut to see you." Her dark eyes searched Renee's. "What are you doing here?"

"I'm in town taking care of mei mammi's affairs. She passed away and left the farm to me." She glanced at Jerome and then Naomi. "This is mei friend, Jerome. His mamm, Delilah Graber, gave me your address."

"Delilah Graber," Naomi repeated, and Renee and Jerome nodded. "Your folks own Graber Fabrics."

"That's right," Jerome said.

"Come on in. Let's visit for a while." Naomi led them through a den to a spacious kitchen with large windows looking out toward the pasture.

Renee helped her aunt serve a cheesecake, the cookies she'd brought, and cups of coffee. Then they sat together.

"Delilah told me that you were out of town helping your dochder with her first boppli. Where does she live?"

"Frannie is out in New Wilmington. She had a girl," Naomi said. "I'm hoping to visit her again soon."

"Do you have other kinner?" Renee asked.

"Ya, Judy lives a few miles away. She's married and expecting her first in the fall." Naomi smiled, and her smile reminded Renee of her mother's. She lifted an oatmeal raisin cookie from the container. "Are you married?"

Renee stirred milk and sugar into her coffee. "Nee."

Naomi swallowed a bite of the cookie. "Your mammi, Martha, passed away?"

"Ya."

"I'm sorry to hear that." Naomi paused. "She left you everything?" she asked, and Renee nodded. She hesitated as if unsure for a moment. "Is your dat still alive?" she asked gently.

Renee shook her head. "He passed away eight years ago."

"I'm sorry to hear that." Naomi hesitated again. "How's your mamm?"

"She's gut. She remarried seven years ago. She and my stepdad both lost spouses to cancer and bonded over that. Ike is a gut man." Renee moved her fingers over her warm mug of coffee. "He calms her. He's very patient and soft spoken."

Understanding flickered over Naomi's face. Perhaps she recalled Renee's father's quick temper and stubbornness. "Did your mamm come with you?"

"Nee." Renee explained how her mother didn't want her to come to Bird-in-Hand, but her stepfather helped convince her mother to allow her to visit until August. "I want to take care of mei mammi's affairs." She stopped speaking and glanced at Jerome, who gave her an encouraging expression. "I also want to know the truth about why mei dat moved us out to Ohio and left everyone from our family behind. Mei dat would never discuss it, and even though he's gone, mei mamm still believes it's not her place to tell me. He made her promise not to, but she said I can find out on my own."

Naomi nodded.

Renee folded her hands on the table. "Aenti Naomi, do you know why mei dat took us to Ohio and joined a more conservative Amish community? And cut off all ties with everyone here?" Her mouth dried while her aunt seemed to ponder the question.

Please tell me the truth. Please!

Her aunt opened her mouth and then closed it, and her face seemed to cloud with uncertainty.

Renee's stomach sank. Her aunt wasn't going to open up to her after waiting all this time to meet her. "Aenti Naomi, if you know what happened, would you please tell me?"

Naomi licked her lips and folded her hands. "Renee, this hasn't been fair to you, and I'll tell you what I can."

Renee's shoulders loosened with relief. *Finally!*

"I know in my heart that there is more to the story than what my sister told me. But I don't know what that is, and I don't think anyone alive except your mother knows the whole truth." Sadness overtook her aunt's countenance. "Your mom and I had a falling out and Lovina stopped speaking to me."

"What happened?" Renee asked.

Naomi grimaced. "Our husbands had an argument, and, well, even though Dennis wanted to make things right..."

"Mei dat wouldn't forgive him," Renee whispered.

"Ya," Naomi said. "Dennis and I tried everything to fix it, but Emmanuel shut us out. Then one day Lovina called to say she couldn't speak to me ever again. I was devastated. She's my only schweschder. We'd lost our parents years earlier, and then I lost her too." She sniffed and dabbed her eyes with a napkin.

Renee worked to hold back her own tears as a pit swelled in her belly.

Jerome touched her arm, and his sad smile gave her the courage to keep digging.

"What did they argue about?" Renee asked.

Naomi shook her head. "Money. Your dat was going to start a new business, and he asked Dennis for a loan. When Dennis told him no because he'd had a bad year with his shed business, Emmanuel was furious. Their heated discussion turned into a huge argument, and Emmanuel left in a fit of rage."

Renee couldn't speak as a wave of embarrassment, anger, and disappointment curdled in her belly.

"Ach, mei *liewe*." Naomi scooted around the table and looped her arm over Renee's shoulder. "I didn't mean to upset you."

"You didn't," Renee whispered. "I'm just so upset with mei dat. Why did he have to cut off our family for something so petty and minor?"

Jerome handed her a napkin, and she blotted her wet eyes.

Renee felt a stab of anguish in the center of her chest. "Was that the last time you heard from Mamm?"

"Nee." Naomi chose a cookie from the box, and her eyes focused on the cookie as if the memory were projected there. "Lovina called me out of the blue three years later. She left me a message and she said something like, 'I want you to know that Emmanuel and I are taking Renee to Ohio. He had a falling out with his mamm, and I have to go. Give my love to Dennis and the girls.'"

Naomi's lip quavered. "I called her and left her a few messages, begging her to come and see me before she left. I prayed and prayed for Gott to bring her back into my life, but she never replied. I even prayed for her to write me, but that was the last message I received." Her eyes moved to Renee. "But now that you're here in my haus, it feels like my prayers were finally answered twenty years later."

"Do you know why mei dat made us move?"

"All she told me was that your mammi betrayed your dat, and he couldn't find it in his heart to forgive her, no matter how much your mammi begged or how much your mamm tried to convince him."

Renee stared at her aunt as the words from the returned letter she'd found echoed in her mind.

Let's start over, Emmanuel. Please forgive me as God has forgiven our sins. I miss and love you, son.

Jerome touched her arm. "I can tell something's bothering you. What's on your mind, Renee?" he asked softly.

Renee cleared her throat. "I don't understand what mei mammi could have done that would cause mei dat to shun her and completely cut her and the rest of the community out of his life. What would cause a child to turn their back on their mamm like that?" She looked at her aunt. "Do you have any idea what could have happened?"

"I don't, but your dat had a quick temper. It might have been something that he blew out of proportion."

"That's true." Renee ate a cookie while pondering her aunt's words. "But uprooting our family was a major decision. That's why I think it couldn't have been something minor. Can you think of anyone else who might know what happened?"

"Nee, I'll let you know if I remember anything or think of someone else who might know."

When Autumn arrived, Renee's aunt walked her and Jerome out to the van.

"I'm glad you came to see me," Naomi told Renee before pulling her in for a hug.

"Me too." Renee held on to her aunt for a moment before pulling away. "I promise I'll come see you again before I go home."

"Let's plan an afternoon together. I'll call Judy, and she can come over too."

"I'd love to meet my cousin." Renee touched her aunt's hand. "I'm going to tell mei mamm that we talked, and I'll try to convince her to write to you."

Tears filled Naomi's eyes. "That would mean so much to me. I've missed mei schweschder."

"I'm sure she misses you too," Renee said. "I'll write her and encourage her to write to you."

"Danki. Let's get together again soon."

Renee climbed into the van with a heavy heart. She also had the overwhelming feeling that God was calling her to stay in Bird-in-Hand and reconnect with her family. Perhaps He wanted her to mend the bonds that her father had broken.

But it would be up to her mother to reestablish her own connection.

Chapter Fourteen

With her gaze trained on the side window, Renee softly sniffed and wiped her eyes with a tissue. Jerome could feel tension and anxiety radiating off her.

The entire day had been an emotional roller coaster, while she became acquainted with her aunt and learned more about the rift her father had caused within their family. Jerome could only imagine the inner turmoil she was wading through. Seeing her suffer hurt his heart.

The muscles in his back knotted. The silence between them was eating him alive. There had to be something he could say to soothe her anxiety.

He gently touched her arm, and she startled before facing him.

"I'm sorry." He held his hands up. "I didn't mean to scare you."

"It's okay." Her bottomless brown eyes were so sad. She offered him a watery smile. "I was just deep in thought."

"Wanna talk about it?"

She licked her lips, and her eyes moved to her apron.

"You don't have to. I don't mean to pry."

She inched closer to him, and his shoulders loosened. "I'm so… overwhelmed." She rested her head on the back of her seat. "I had no idea I had cousins since mei dat was an only child. I still don't know why he made us leave our community and family, except that his mamm betrayed him."

Her chin wobbled. "How does a mamm betray a child? And aren't we supposed to obey and honor our parents? Why couldn't Dat get past it? Mei mammi died alone because—" She stopped speaking, and her eyes focused on his. "You took care of her, didn't you?"

He shrugged. "I did the best I could."

"Danki." Tears streamed down her face, and sadness trickled through him. "She wanted me in her life, but because of mei dat, I missed out on knowing her, knowing mei aenti, and knowing my cousins."

He linked his fingers with hers, and he cherished the feeling of her soft, warm skin. "You know Naomi now. You can write her letters and visit her." *And visit me.*

She swallowed. "But I feel Gott calling me home."

His eyes widened as he tried to read her hesitant expression. "What exactly do you mean by that?" he asked her slowly.

"I'm starting to feel like a part of this community, and I'm wondering if Gott is calling me to stay here. But how can I stay when mei mamm told me I have to go back to Ohio? How can I disobey my mamm like that?" She covered her face with her hands. "I'm so confused."

Jerome noticed movement out of the corner of his eye, and when he looked toward the front of the van, he spotted Autumn watching them in the mirror. She was listening to their conversation, invading their privacy. He couldn't imagine why she'd care about their business, but her nosiness had made him uncomfortable in the past.

Leaning closer to Renee, he responded to her in Pennsylvania Dutch and hoped Autumn couldn't understand it. "Pray about it and see how Gott leads you. Your mamm said you had to be home by August, and you still have time. It's only May."

His pulse leapt at the idea that Renee might stay, but he also understood that she couldn't imagine disobeying her mother, no matter what her father had done in the past.

She responded by threading her fingers with his and giving his hand a gentle squeeze. He thought his heart might explode.

She held his hand for the remainder of the ride, and when they arrived home, he paid Autumn.

"Thank you for the ride," he said.

Autumn pocketed the money. "I'm here for you any time you need me." Her eyes darted to Renee and settled on her for a few moments before she backed out of the driveway.

"Jeannie will be home from work soon. I'll start supper," Renee said.

"Okay." Jerome missed her hand holding his and slipped his hands into his pockets. "I'll take care of the animals."

He ambled toward the barn, and for a moment he wondered what might have happened if Renee had grown up in his community. They would've gone to school together and possibly attended the same youth group. Would they have dated? Possibly fallen in love? Maybe gotten married?

But she'd grown up in Ohio and now she was considering staying in Bird-in-Hand. Could that mean that God was giving them a second chance?

As he entered the barn an idea hit him—what if he offered to go back to Ohio with her? Could he join her community, ask her stepfather for permission to date her, and possibly plan a future with her?

Jerome laughed out loud at his ridiculous thought. Love and marriage weren't within his grasp. After all the mistakes he'd made, he wasn't fit to be a husband or a father. Instead of dreaming of a future with sweet Renee, he had to accept that she was leaving.

And he knew to the depths of his soul that he had to prepare for another heartbreak. Only this time, he'd have a chance to say good-bye. He had no idea how he'd ever form the words to tell her how much she meant to him or how much he'd miss her.

Wednesday, May 7

Renee sat up with a jolt. She scanned her pitch-black bedroom while her breath came in short bursts and sweat clung to her body. The green numbers of her battery-powered digital clock read: 12:47.

She rested her back on her headboard and pondered what had awakened her. Possibly a bad dream? But she normally recalled her dreams. She tried to concentrate on what she could have dreamt, but nothing came to her mind's eye. No, it was something else.

Renee thought she heard something, and she froze.

Footsteps sounded. Maybe Jeannie had gotten up to use the restroom. But she didn't see Jeannie's flashlight glowing in the hallway.

More footsteps—only heavier this time. No, they weren't inside the house. They were outside, moving along the flagstone path leading to the front porch, which was beyond her bedroom.

"Jerome?" she whispered. But why would he be on her porch after midnight?

The footsteps ceased and a few beats of silence passed before a hissing noise sounded. What could that be? Maybe an aerosol can? But why would someone have an aerosol can on her porch? And what would they be doing with it on her porch in the middle of the night?

It couldn't be for a good reason. Renee's pulse thrummed as a chill moved through her.

A crash sounded—like glassing shattering.

What was that?

With tremors rolling through her, Renee grabbed her lantern and her robe.

"Jerome?" she called out. "Jeannie?"

Was she asleep and imagining this? But the sounds outside were as real as the feel of the cool handle of the lantern in her hands.

She tiptoed out to the hallway and placed her hand on the lantern switch. Had someone broken into the house? She hadn't heard the front or back door open or close. But what if the uninvited guest broke in through a window?

Dread pooled in her stomach, and she lifted her hand from the switch. If she turned on the lantern, she'd give away her location. Instead, she'd remain in the pitch-black house until she was certain the trespasser had left.

If only Jerome's house was closer...

Hopefully Jerome heard the crash and the footsteps, and he's calling for help!

Shoes moved along the rock pathway again, and Renee remained still, flattening herself against the wall. Fear gripped her, and she tried not to breathe.

Was a person breaking into the house? And if someone did, would they hurt her or Jeannie? A scream built up in her chest, but she swallowed it.

Please, Gott. Please protect Jeannie and me!

A car door slammed, and an engine revved before a vehicle peeled out of the driveway.

Flipping on the lantern, Renee padded down the hallway to the back door. She peeked out the window, but the porch was clear. She flipped the dead bolt on the door and pushed it open, but she didn't see anything amiss.

What had caused the crash?

Renee dashed down the hallway to the front of the house and peered out the window before approaching the door.

When she opened the door and scanned the concrete porch, tears blurred her vision before she fell to her knees, and her whole body shook as sobs erupted.

Jerome sat up with a gasp and looked around his dark bedroom, confused. But when he heard a car door slam and an engine rev, he was suddenly wide awake.

Why was a car in the driveway in the middle of the night?

Renee and Jeannie! Were they safe?

Adrenaline pumped through his veins as he leapt out of bed, flipped on his lantern, threw on a plain white T-shirt over his trousers, and rushed out of his house. He hoped to catch a glimpse of the vehicle, but the driveway was empty.

Worry clawed at him as he hurried toward Renee's house. Finding the back porch empty, he rounded the house and raced up the front porch steps.

"Jerome?" Renee called, her voice sounding thin. "Jerome? Is that you?"

"Ya." He hurried toward her, and when he spotted her on her knees, crying, icy fingers of dread gripped him. "Renee!" He rushed over to her.

A sob tore from her, and her head dropped into her hands while she knelt on the porch floor.

Rushing over, he dropped onto his knees, ignoring the pain spiraling up his bad leg. He tried to pull her against him. But she remained cemented in place with her head in her hands.

"Renee. Talk to me," he begged while his gut constricted.

She leaned her shoulder against his side.

"Renee," he pleaded again, his words coming at a fast clip while his head spun. "What happened? Are you okay? Do you need help? Should I call an ambulance?"

Then his eyes moved around the porch, and suddenly, the puzzle pieces came together in his mind. He glanced down the length of the porch and read the words scrawled in bright red paint: *GET OUT! GO BACK TO OHIO!*

He gasped and shifted his eyes to a pile of broken pieces of porcelain.

Oh no.

"The teapot," she said, her voice coming out in a whimper. "I knew I hadn't lost it, and I was right."

"Come here," he said, pulling her into his arms.

She froze for a moment and then wrapped her arms around his neck while her tears continued to fall.

"Renee," he whispered against her dark brown hair. It was the first time he'd seen her hair uncovered, and it was glorious—more beautiful than he'd ever imagined. Her thick locks cascaded in waves down her back to her small waist. "You're safe now. I promise nothing will happen to you. We're in this together." He rubbed her back and breathed in her flowery scent. His fingers raked through her hair, and he silently marveled at how soft it was.

After several moments, her sobs dissipated, and she rested her cheek on his shoulder. Holding her close felt right. It was as if she belonged in his arms, and for a moment, he yearned to believe that he deserved a woman in his life as kind and caring and beautiful as Renee.

"I knew someone had taken the teapot. I couldn't convince myself that I'd lost it because I'd never lose something so precious." Her voice shook. "And now the person who stole it from me returned it—in pieces. I'm devastated, Jerome. Just devastated." She took a deep, shuddering breath.

"I-I'm sorry for being so—so emotional. Seeing the teapot unlocked something deep inside me. It's grief. I'm grieving mei mammi and also grieving for the lost years I could have had with relatives I never knew existed because mei dat held on to this petty rift. Mei dat stole my family and my home from me because he couldn't find it in his heart to forgive his family. And now my home has been vandalized, and someone trespassed on my property— again! And I'm afraid, and I'm confused. What have I done to upset someone enough to do this to mei mammi's farm? It's—it's too much for me. I feel broken—just like that teapot." Her voice broke, and she wept softly.

"It's okay," he whispered, his own voice sounding raw. "Let it out. I'm here for you, and I won't let you go. And I'll protect you and Jeannie, no matter what." He held her close while anger, sadness, and fury warred inside him.

After several moments, she sniffed before sitting up and turning toward the front door. "Where's Jeannie?" Worry flickered over her face. "Do you think she's okay?"

"Mei schweschder could sleep through a tornado. She would snore even if the haus fell down around her." He pushed a lock of Renee's hair behind her ear. "We need to figure out who did this." His eyes narrowed. "What did you see and hear?"

She lowered herself onto the porch beside him. "I woke up to the sound of someone on the path outside my window. I thought I was dreaming, and then I thought maybe it was Jeannie going to the bathroom or you coming to the haus. But when I didn't see Jeannie's flashlight or hear your voice, I realized it had to be a trespasser."

She explained how she heard what sounded like an aerosol can, a crash, more footsteps, and then a car door slam before the vehicle sped off. "I hid in the hallway." She grimaced and sniffed. "I should have looked out the window, but I was afraid."

"It's okay, Renee." He touched her cheek. "You did the right thing. I'm glad you're safe." He moved his fingers through a lock of her hair, and his heartbeat kicked. She was stunningly beautiful, and for a moment, he couldn't stop staring at her.

A strange expression traveled over her face, and then she gasped. "Ach, nee!" She hugged her arms to her middle. "My hair's not covered. This is so inappropriate." She jumped to her feet. "I should get a scarf," she said, disappearing into the house.

Jerome pushed himself up from the porch floor, and more discomfort traveled from his knee down to his ankle. He shook off the pain before examining the threatening message written in red paint, and the smashed teapot.

Who would want to scare Renee? Who held so much animosity toward her that they would deliberately destroy something she loved and leave such a hateful message on her porch? What were they trying to accomplish with this horrible act of vandalism and intrusion?

The front door opened with a squeak, and Renee appeared with a blue scarf covering her gorgeous hair. "I peeked in on Jeannie, and you're right. She's snoring."

"Let's let her sleep. We can fill her in on everything in the morning."

"Okay." Her face clouded with a glower. "Do you think he did this?" She pointed in the direction of Murray Robertson's house across the street.

Jerome considered the question. Murray had seemed like a harmless guy, but how could he know for sure? "I don't know, but I don't think it's safe for us to be out here." Taking her hand in his, he pulled her into the house, locked the door, and towed her down the hallway to the den, where he sat on the sofa. "We should call the police."

She shook her head. "Nee."

Frustration rippled through him. "Renee, this was a direct threat, along with a theft and vandalism, which are also crimes. Next time this person might actually try to break in while you're home, and I can't let anyone hurt you or mei schweschder."

Her lower lip started to quaver, and Jerome couldn't ignore the guilt stabbing his gut. "Fine, fine," he said. "But I'm not going to mei haus." He pointed to the sofa. "I'm going to sleep right here in case they decide to come back and are bolder this time."

"I'll get you a pillow and blanket."

While Renee retrieved the items for him, he checked the windows and doors, making sure they were secure.

"Danki, Jerome," she said as she handed him the bedding.

He nodded and then watched her retreat to her room.

After sinking onto the sofa, he peered up at the ceiling. Scenarios of what could have happened to Renee and Jeannie raced through his mind while he tried to get comfortable on the worn, lumpy piece of furniture. The muscles in his shoulders and back tightened with worry, anger, and frustration.

And then there was the memory of the feel and scent of Renee's beautiful hair, and the way she held on to him. He rubbed his forehead. He was falling for her. He couldn't deny it any longer. His feelings for Renee were real, and they scared him. He didn't want to risk his heart, but she'd already managed to carve out a piece of it.

Shifting to his side, Jerome groaned. He knew one thing for sure. He wasn't going to get any sleep tonight.

Chapter Fifteen

Renee tossed and turned, but every time she closed her eyes, she saw a vision of her grandmother's smashed teapot and the threatening words written in bright red paint on the porch.

Her heart was in shambles. But tonight's events weren't the only burden on her heart. Finding out about family members she didn't remember, and the reason her father had forbidden her mother from seeing them, just added to her anguish. She rubbed her eyes and kicked off her bedsheets.

Sitting up, she turned in the direction of her closed door. Jerome was out in the den, and more than anything she wanted to sit with him and talk. At first she'd felt like a dummkopp for completely breaking down in front of him, but he'd been a balm to her fractured soul. As he held her, she realized she needed him more than ever. She reached up and touched her hair while remembering how it felt to be in his strong arms—safe and protected.

Then shame hit her like a punch to her stomach. She'd been alone with him with her head uncovered. To make matters worse, she'd held his hand during their ride home from Naomi's house. Had Jerome considered that too forward? But it had felt natural to hold his hand, and he seemed as at ease with it as she had been. Still, what would Mamm think? What would her stepfather and her bishop say about her behavior?

Renee covered her face with her hands. She prayed Jerome didn't consider her forward. She hadn't spotted any judgment in his expression. Instead, the kindness and concern in his blue eyes told her that he'd only wanted to protect her.

Still, Renee's mind swam with confusion and worry. What if the person who had vandalized her home returned? What if they brought a weapon this time? Her body shook with fear.

Should she allow Jerome to call the police? But her bishop had made it clear that they should never involve Englishers in their problems. Yet if an Englisher was the problem, didn't they need the police department's help?

Renee rubbed her eyes with the heels of her hands. She needed to get some sleep, or she'd never be able to complete all her chores when her alarm went off. She turned toward her clock. It was nearly two in the morning, and sleep was the last thing on her mind. Instead, she longed to sit in the den and share her worries with Jerome, but he could be sleeping. She shook her head. After what they'd endured tonight on the porch, he had to be as frazzled as she was.

But what would he think of her if she walked out to him? Was it inappropriate—just as inappropriate as his arms holding her and his hands caressing her hair—her *uncovered* hair?

A shiver raced through her as she recalled his touch. It was something she'd never experienced before. Yet she knew it meant nothing. He was only trying to comfort her after she'd completely broken down.

And they were friends, weren't they? Wasn't it okay for friends to talk after a stressful experience? And what happened tonight was definitely stressful.

Renee pushed herself up and flipped on the lantern on her nightstand. She had changed into a fresh nightgown before climbing into bed. She shoved her arms into a gray cotton robe and tied it over her light blue nightgown before covering her hair with a blue scarf.

She didn't want to risk waking him up if he was sleeping, so she switched off her lantern and ambled down the hallway. The room was cloaked in blackness, except for two faint streams of light sneaking past the green window shades.

Renee stilled in the doorway and nibbled her lower lip while she again debated if she should have stayed in her room.

This is so inappropriate. What would Mamm say if she knew I was alone with a man in the middle of the night? I should just go back to bed!

Hanging her head, she spun and started toward her room as more shame gripped her. When a floorboard creaked, she froze.

"Renee?" Jerome's deep voice was soft. "Is that you?"

She hugged her arms over her robe as her face heated. "I'm sorry. I thought we could talk, but I never meant to wake you up. I'll go back to my room because—"

"It's fine. I'm wide awake. Come here."

She hesitated for another moment, but something inside pushed her forward. It was like an invisible force yanking her to him. She sank down on an armchair across from the sofa and gripped the robe's cuffs.

Jerome flipped on a lantern sitting on the end table beside the sofa, and the warm yellow glow illuminated his handsome face.

"I can't sleep," she admitted.

"Neither can I."

They stared at each other for a moment, and once again part of her felt the urge to flee to her room, but another part of her wanted to unload all of the confusing emotions afflicting her heart and her head.

"When I saw you hunched over on the porch," he began, his voice raspy, "I thought something had happened to you, and I was going to lose you." He rubbed his eyes.

Her chest hitched, and something palpable expanded between them while silence overtook the room.

"What if they come back?" she finally whispered. "What if they bring a weapon this time?"

"I meant it earlier when I said I won't let anything happen to you or mei schweschder."

"Who do you think is doing this?"

His eyes flared, and his expression became fierce. "I don't know, but I promise we'll find out."

And she believed him.

"We'll get it all cleaned up tomorrow," he said.

She nodded, and her thoughts turned to her grandmother's teapot. She couldn't stand the thought of sweeping up the broken pieces, but the person harassing her wasn't capable of stealing her memories of sitting in her grandmother's kitchen and drinking tea. God had kept her and Jeannie safe. That was what mattered.

Thank You, Gott, for Your protection.

Her gaze roved over Jerome, taking in his stoic expression, his tanned arms, and his long legs, which he'd stretched out in front of him. His left trouser leg was rumpled, revealing a pink, angry, puckered scar that ran the length of his shin to the top of his bare foot. That was the leg that he favored when he walked—limped, actually. Could that scar be a result of the "old injury" on which he blamed his limp?

Then the questions she'd pondered so many times pestered her again. How had he gotten hurt? What had happened to Amanda? And was his injury in any way connected to what had happened to his late fiancée?

Could Renee be a balm to his soul like he'd been to her tonight?

Jerome tilted his head. "What's on your mind, Renee?"

She hesitated. If she questioned him, would she be crossing another line that might risk losing his friendship?

"You can talk to me." His expression was so tender that it sent warmth straight to her heart. "Go ahead and say whatever it is you're thinking."

She paused and hugged her robe tighter against her middle. "I noticed your scar," she said slowly. "What happened to you, Jerome?"

He pulled his legs toward the sofa and swiped his hand over his trouser leg, hiding the scar while his lips formed a thin line.

She held her breath as the moments ticked by.

He looked away, and his Adam's apple bobbed as he swallowed hard. Then he frowned and studied his lap.

Tension hung like a giant chasm between them, nearly choking her, and it became apparent he wasn't going to answer.

Ach, nee.

She'd managed to not only cross a line but also alienate him. Her heart began to fracture. The room suddenly felt too small. She had to get out of there.

"I'm sorry." She popped up from the chair as guilt and shame stabbed her belly. "Forgive me for being so forward and bold tonight. It's not who I am. I pray you don't think badly of me." Her words sounded thin and reedy.

She started across the room and tried to swallow back her threatening tears. "Gut nacht, Jerome. I hope you get some sleep."

Jerome scrubbed his hands over his face as Renee's soft footsteps moved toward the hallway. A sudden yearning to open up to her started deep in his gut and expanded through him.

He leaned over the back of the sofa. "Renee, stop," he managed to say, and his voice cracked. "Please. Come here. Sit with me."

She stopped in the doorway and ran her finger over the zipper on her robe. "I don't mean to intrude in your business."

"You're not intruding."

She lifted her eyebrows. "I've already been too bold tonight." She grimaced. "Mei mamm would be so disappointed in me. I'm so embarrassed." Her voice was thick.

"No, she wouldn't." He shook his head. "I'd tell her that you're a gut and caring friend."

Her eyes widened, but she remained in the doorway.

"Please, Renee." His words were hoarse.

She hesitated for a moment.

"I want to tell you."

"Okay," she whispered, and empathy replaced the worry on her face. She sat on the chair beside the sofa and folded her hands on her lap.

Memories of that day come back to him, and he fought the urge to push them down, like he had for the past two years. He studied the worn brown fabric on the arm of the sofa. "It was mid-July. It will be three years soon."

Renee remained silent.

"It was hot—*really* hot—and humid. The air felt thick. There were some clouds in the sky, but the newspaper said it wasn't supposed to rain for a few days. I can still remember the sound of the frogs croaking in mei dat's pond when I hitched up my horse and buggy." He absently moved his hand over the arm of the sofa. "I was going to start a new job the next day, and Amanda was supposed to be up early to babysit for her aenti."

He closed his eyes as a vision of Amanda rose in his mind— sunkissed blond hair, powder-blue eyes that he'd always get caught in, a smile that lit up the room, and a contagious laugh that aways cut through his murkiest of moods.

It occurred to him that Renee would have no idea who Amanda was. He'd never mentioned her name. In fact, he rarely said her name out loud since the guilt refused to allow him to find any joy in their memories.

Jerome pinched the bridge of his nose and tried to calm the raging emotions threatening to pull him under and drown him. "She was...she was my fiancée. We'd started dating right after we were baptized. I'd had a crush on her for as long as I could remember."

He slumped against the sofa and kept his eyes trained on its arm. "I was so arrogant then. I knew she liked me, and I was certain she'd date me—as long as her dat gave me permission—and I was sure she'd marry me as soon as I was making enough money to support us. We were going to get married in November and live with my folks. I was arrogant enough to believe that after a year or so of working at mei *onkel's* plumbing business that I'd be able to buy or build a haus, and we'd start a family and have the perfect Amish life." He gave a sardonic laugh. "But I managed to mess all that up in one night."

He moved his finger over a seam on the sofa cushion and avoided Renee's eyes. "We decided to sneak out that night to meet friends at a lake and swim. Stargazing and all that. We'd gotten home from youth group around ten, but we'd planned to go back out again after our folks were asleep."

His body began to vibrate as the memories pummeled him, and he crossed his arms over his middle. "I picked her up and then we started toward the lake. Everything was fine, but then a storm came out of nowhere. All of a sudden the sky opened up, and it was pouring. Thunder crashed all around us, and lightning lit up the sky. I couldn't see the road in front of us, and I had to completely rely on my horse." He sucked in air. "Amanda wanted to turn back, but we were only a few miles from the lake. I convinced her to keep going. I was certain that as fast as the storm started, it would be over just as quickly."

He cringed as a knot of anguish bloomed in his chest. "And then a truck came barreling through a red light," he croaked. "It happened so fast."

Renee slipped onto the sofa beside him and pulled his hands into hers. He stared at their threaded fingers, and her warm touch gave him the courage to continue.

"The truck T-boned us on the passenger side." He wiped his eyes and fought to get hold of his emotions.

"It's okay," Renee whispered. "If this is too hard for you, then you can stop."

Jerome finally allowed himself to meet her gaze, and he drank in the tenderness in her dark eyes. "I have to get this out." He sniffed. "I want to tell you everything."

Her lips formed a sad smile, and she gave his hand a gentle squeeze. "Take your time."

"Since the passenger side of the buggy is always the closest to the traffic, Amanda took the brunt of the crash." His voice shook. "The buggy rolled. When it stopped rolling, we were in the middle of a field." Jerome's eyes flicked to his injured leg. "The buggy was on top of me." Tears gathered in his eyes. "Amanda…" His tears broke free, and he covered his face with his hands.

"Oh, Jerome," Renee whispered while swiping his tears away with her fingertips.

He pulled tissues from a box sitting on the end table and wiped his eyes and nose.

The only sounds came from the clock ticking on the mantel and a car rumbling past in the distance.

Jerome pulled in air through his nose and forced his words out. "She was thrown several yards from the buggy. She didn't make it."

"I'm so sorry." Renee's words were soft and vibrated with grief.

He rolled his pant leg up to his knee, revealing the angry pink scar that ran the length of his leg from above his knee to his ankle, and Renee's eyes locked on it. "My leg was crushed. The doctors believed I'd never walk again. I was covered in bruises, and I have scars all over my body. I had several surgeries on my leg, and the community raised money for my medical care and rehabilitation." He pushed his pant leg down and then a frown overtook his face. "The driver was drunk," he said, and the words tasted bitter in his mouth. "He'd had at least a dozen beers before getting behind the wheel. He walked away from the accident with no injuries, but he's in prison."

"I'm so glad he can't hurt anyone else." Renee angled herself closer to Jerome. "And the Lord helped you defy the odds. You proved them all wrong by walking again."

"But I shouldn't have been the one to live. It was *my* fault." He pointed to himself. "I never should have insisted we go. Amanda told me that I needed to rest before my first day on the job, but I told her that we deserved a fun night out with friends. If I'd listened to her, then she'd still be here." His voice wavered, and he paused. "I'll never, ever forgive myself."

"It wasn't your fault," Renee whispered, linking her fingers with his again. "It was Gott's will, Jerome."

His face twisted into a scowl. "I should never have taken Amanda out that night. She didn't deserve what happened to her." He yanked his hand out of hers. "That's why I'll never get married. I don't deserve to be happy after what I did. I not only killed my fiancée, but I destroyed her family. They have to live with the grief of losing her, every day. And every time I take Jeannie or you or someone else out in my buggy, I worry that I'm going to mess up again, and they'll get hurt or worse, just like Amanda."

He paused for a moment and watched the clock ticking on the mantel across from them. "The truth is that I'm nee gut. All I do is cause people pain, and I can't allow myself to hurt anyone else."

"Nee, Jerome. That's not true."

"It is," he insisted. "That's why I'm alone. It's best for everyone in the community if I stay alone so I can't hurt anyone else."

Renee hesitated before grabbing his hand again. "Jerome," she murmured. "You're a gut man. What if Gott wants you to fall in love and have a family?"

"Nee. I'm a hazard."

She touched his bicep. "I'm thankful that you've been here for me. Danki for being my friend."

"You're better off to stay away from me." But as he said the words, he couldn't stop the cloud of sadness billowing through him.

Silence engulfed the room.

"We should try to get some sleep," he finally said. "And we should go to the police station tomorrow. We can take my horse and buggy and file a report."

"Nee. We need to leave the Englishers out of this."

He gestured toward the window. "I'll at least talk to Murray."

"What if it's him?" Worry was evident in her voice. "What if he tries to hurt you?"

"He wouldn't. Not in broad daylight. I'll ask him if he saw anything and see what he says. If he's not guilty, then he could be a witness."

"Gut point." Relief overtook her face. "Gut nacht, Jerome."

While she walked toward the hallway, he felt as if a fifty-pound weight had been lifted from his back. Although sharing what had happened didn't change his past, it was cathartic to get it off his chest and share it with someone he trusted. The sympathy in her eyes felt so welcome. Renee was a good friend, and although he felt his heart craving more, it was best that she remain his friend and only his friend.

He flipped off the lantern before trying to get comfortable on the lumpy sofa. While he stared through the darkness at the ceiling, he couldn't stop thinking about how much he cherished Renee. He would do anything to protect her and his sister.

Jerome remained awake most of the night, puzzling over who was threatening Renee and what he could do to stop the harassment.

Chapter Sixteen

Thursday, May 8

Renee yawned on her way down the hallway later that morning. She'd slept in short spurts while contemplating what Jerome had shared, wondering how she could show him that he was worthy of love, and worrying that the person who'd been threatening her would become even more bold.

When she reached the den, she peeked over at the sofa, expecting to find Jerome sleeping there. Instead, the sofa was empty, with the blanket folded neatly under the pillow.

She moved her hand over the couch and recalled how Jerome had poured his heart out to her only a few hours earlier.

Help me convince him, Lord. Show me how to heal his broken heart.

After storing the blanket and pillow in the linen closet, she tried to push down her exhaustion and focus on breakfast. She was cracking eggs into a large pan when Jeannie pranced into the kitchen.

"It's a schee day that the Lord has made," she sang. "Let us rejoice and be glad in it!" She came to stand beside Renee. "I slept like a rock last night. How about you?"

Renee slapped a hand over her mouth to shield a yawn. "Not exactly."

"Is everything okay?" Jeannie asked.

Pointing to the refrigerator, Renee said, "Please grab the bacon, and I'll tell you what happened last night."

Jeannie set the bacon in a large skillet with the eggs and started the burner, while Renee explained how someone had vandalized the porch, leaving a threatening message in red spray paint, along with the shattered remains of her grandmother's teapot.

"Thankfully, Jerome heard the vehicle drive away, and he came over and found me on the porch."

"Wait." Jeannie held her hand up like a traffic cop. "Someone spray painted the porch and smashed your grandmother's teapot?" she asked, and Renee nodded. "And you didn't think it would be a gut idea to wake me?"

"We didn't want to bother you," Renee explained. "Jerome slept on the sofa to make sure we were safe. I guess he got up earlier than usual to take care of the animals." Most likely he hadn't slept either.

Jeannie stared at Renee for a moment and then marched out of the kitchen. The front door squeaked open before a gasp sounded. Then the door closed, and Jeannie reappeared in the kitchen doorway. "Why didn't you wake me?" she demanded again.

"I told you. We didn't want to—"

"But this is serious, Renee!" Jerome's twin pointed toward the hallway. "The threats are getting worse." She rushed over to Renee. "Did you call the police?"

Renee sighed. "Nee."

"Are you going to?"

"Nee." The bacon began sizzling, and she turned the flame down slightly before using tongs to flip the pieces over in the pan.

Jeannie touched Renee's shoulder. "This isn't just a prank, Renee. This person is getting bolder. What if he had broken in and tried to hurt us?"

"You think it's a man?" Renee asked.

"Why wouldn't it be a man?" Jeannie's laugh was sardonic. "You think a woman would do this?"

"I don't know."

Jeannie's brow puckered while she worked to start the percolator. "I'm going to tell mei dat about this and see what he says. I disagree that we should sit here and not do anything to protect ourselves." She pinned Renee with a look. "And if there's a next time, you need to wake me up. I'm so sorry that you had to endure a sleepless night without me here to support you." She touched Renee's arm. "You're one of my best friends, Renee, even though you've just come back, and I want to support you."

Renee's heart squeezed. "Danki, Jeannie. I feel the same way about you, but Jerome and I thought you should get your sleep. You have to work today."

"I'll call my folks and tell them what happened. Then I'll stay here and help you clean up that mess. They'll understand." She gathered up dishes and utensils and set the table.

Renee nodded. "Danki."

The scent of coffee permeated the kitchen, and soon the meal was on the table. Renee consulted the clock. It was almost eight. Jerome should have been in the kitchen by now. Was he okay? Had he fallen and gotten hurt after a restless night?

"I'll check on him," Jeannie said, as if she could read Renee's mind.

Jeannie started toward the back of the house just as the back door opened with a squeak.

Heavy footsteps sounded before Jerome entered the kitchen. Dark circles rimmed his dull blue eyes, and a scowl clouded his face. He barely glanced at his sister or Renee on his way to the sink to scrub his hands.

Renee and Jeannie shared a concerned expression before they sat at the table.

Jerome joined them and immediately bowed his head in silent prayer. Then he began scraping eggs and bacon onto his plate.

"How are your chores going?" Renee asked.

With his eyes trained on his plate, Jerome shrugged, and her heart sank. She'd hoped that after last night they had bonded, but the way he brushed her off said otherwise. At the same time, it was clear he'd gotten very little sleep.

"Renee told me what happened last night, Jerome." Jeannie thumped her finger on the table. "You should've woken me up. This is a very serious situation, and I don't appreciate being left out."

Jerome sipped his coffee and eyed his sister over the mug. He set the mug on the table and leaned forward. "You didn't miss out on anything. Renee and I talked, and I slept on the sofa to make sure you both were safe. There was no reason to wake you up and scare you."

"I could've helped you two through it," Jeannie insisted. "I would've wanted to know what was going on."

Renee patted her hand. "We'll include you next time, Jeannie. I'm sorry." She turned toward Jerome, and he gave her an exasperated expression.

"But I hope there isn't a next time," Jerome said.

After breakfast, Renee and Jeannie cleaned up the kitchen before Jeannie hurried off to call her parents to tell them what had happened and that she planned to stay at the farm and help clean up the mess. Renee grabbed a trashcan and stepped out onto the porch.

She surveyed the bright red, spray-painted message: *GET OUT! GO BACK TO OHIO!*

An uneasy feeling danced along the length of her spine and tears flooded her eyes as she crouched and began picking up the broken pieces that had once formed her grandmother's beautiful teapot.

While she worked, she frequently glanced around, wondering if the person who had done this would return.

Please, Lord, protect us!

After collecting all the shattered pieces of porcelain, she retrieved a bucket of water mixed with baking soda to try to remove the paint. While working, she tried to hum her favorite hymns, but her mind kept replaying the anguish and guilt etched on Jerome's face while he shared the story of the accident that changed his life.

"I'll never get married. I don't deserve to be happy after what I did."

"It's best for everyone in the community if I stay alone so I can't hurt anyone else."

She yearned to prove to him that he did deserve happiness and that he needed to find a way to forgive himself. That was what Amanda would want, if she had loved him. But how could Renee get through to him?

The storm door squeaked, and she whirled around toward the front door, where Jerome stood scowling.

"Hi," she said with a smile.

He moved to stand behind her, and his eyes darted around the porch. "The baking soda isn't working?"

"Nee." She brushed her hand over her forehead. "The red paint hasn't faded a bit," she added, tapping her finger against her chin. "Do you have any lye? I could try that."

"I don't think I have any, but I'll hitch up my horse and buggy and see if Tim has something at his hardware store that might work. I'm sure he knows of something that will take it off." He jammed his hands in his pockets. "Do you need anything else?"

Only for you to believe that you deserve happiness... "Nee. Jeannie picked up groceries on her way home yesterday."

He nodded, and his gaze focused across the street.

It seemed like he was deliberately avoiding her eyes, and worry sat like a lead bar in her stomach. Had she said something that upset him last night?

"Jerome," she said, but he continued to keep his attention on Murray's house. "Jerome, please look at me."

His gorgeous blue eyes finally met hers, but his expression was unreadable.

She stood and wiped her hands down her black apron. "Have I done or said something to offend you? Because if I did, I'm sorry."

He shook his head. "You could never offend me."

His words provided a tiny sense of relief, but her insides remained clenched. "Then why are you so distant?"

"It's not you," he said, his eyes narrowing. "I'm frustrated that I don't know who's doing this." He pointed to the porch. "I'm going to talk to Murray, and then I'll hitch up my horse and buggy." He moved his hands over his suspenders.

"Gut idea. Find out if he saw anything." She walked to the end of the porch and leaned on the railing while he limped down the driveway and across the street toward Murray Robertson's house.

Jerome fought down a hot ball of frustration while he crossed the street and marched toward Murray Robertson's house. He was determined to find out who was harassing Renee and to make them stop once and for all. Whoever was doing this had gone too far, and he would do whatever it took to end the attacks *now.*

When he reached the front door, he knocked. Then he glanced around Murray's property, finding an overgrown lawn and a garden that looked as if it had once been a home for flowers but now was clogged with bright green, sprawling weeds. The two-story gray home sported peeling paint, and the faded black shutters hung at odd angles.

Jerome peeked around the side of the house to where Murray's rusty old pickup truck sat, and then he knocked again, only louder this time.

After several moments, he banged on the door. "Murray?" he called. "Murray! I know you're in there. I see your truck. Please open the door. I need to talk to you."

Jerome glanced toward Martha's house across the street and brushed a hand over his mouth. Anger boiled under his skin at the memory of Renee hunched over on the porch and sobbing last night. The thought of something happening to her pushed him to knock one last time and then raise his voice.

"Murray," he called. "It's Jerome. I can stand here and knock all day long or you can come to the door and talk to me. It's your decision."

A thump sounded inside the house, and then a slant in the blinds cracked ever so slightly before the older man's beady eyes peeked through. "What do you want?"

Finally! "Were you on Martha's property last night?"

The slants in the shade opened slightly wider. "No."

Jerome's eyes narrowed. "Someone vandalized Martha's porch." He hesitated and waited for a reaction, but the older man just watched him. Then the agitation that had been building throughout the night boiled over. "Did you do it?" he asked, his voice louder than he'd planned.

"No."

Jerome scanned the older man's property, looking for cameras. So many Englishers these days had cameras guarding their homes and possessions, and he'd heard that many pointed toward the street and their neighbors' homes. Yet he wasn't surprised not to find any. It didn't seem that Murray had the means to care for the possessions he already had. Or wasn't inclined to. "Did you *see* who did it?"

The older man hesitated. "No."

"Did you see *anything*?"

"No!"

Jerome growled out his impatience and leaned on the window casing. "Murray, this is a serious situation, and I need your help." He squeezed the back of his neck. "*Please* come out."

The slats snapped shut before footsteps retreated from the window.

Great. Just great.

Jerome went back across the street and hurried into the barn. When he saw his buggy sitting at an odd angle, he picked up his pace. He examined the buggy and gasped—someone had tampered with it! It looked as though someone had taken a sledgehammer to one of the wheels, as well as one of the axles.

Why would someone do that? He grimaced as anger rose inside him. It had to have been the same person who had vandalized the house!

He stalked out of the barn to where Jeannie and Renee stood.

Jeannie's eyes rounded. "What's wrong?"

"Someone damaged my buggy. Now I'm going to have to get it repaired."

"Damaged it?" Renee rushed over to him. "What do you mean?"

"It looks like someone took a sledgehammer or a hatchet to the left rear wheel and the axle."

"Do you think it's the same person who spray painted the porch and stole my teapot?" Renee asked.

"Ya." When she cupped her hands to her mouth, he held up his hand. "It's going to be okay, Renee. We'll get through this. Let's worry about cleaning up the porch, and then I'll get the buggy fixed." He turned to his sister. "What did Mamm and Dat say?"

Jeannie frowned. "They're very concerned. Dat said we should talk to the bishop and consider going to the police."

Jerome huffed out a breath.

"How'd it go with Murray?" Renee asked. "Did he see anything?"

"He was no help." Jerome pointed toward the phone shanty. "I'm going to call Autumn for a ride, and I'll be back soon. Make sure the house is locked up in case the person who did this comes back," he ordered before stalking off.

Jerome sat in the back seat of Autumn's van thirty minutes later. He yawned and rested his elbow on the armrest beside him. His exhaustion, anger, and worry sat heavily on him. He stared out the window and contemplated how to solve the mystery of who was threatening Renee.

"Is everything okay?" Autumn's reflection asked in the rearview mirror.

Jerome scratched his ear. He'd never been one to share his woes with strangers, especially Englishers, but the idea of unloading his burdens and receiving an objective opinion was tempting. "No, it's not."

Autumn's eyebrows shot up. "Do you want to talk about it?"

"Yeah," he said. "I do." Then he told her everything, from the threatening note that was left on the door, to the incident last night, and ending with his buggy being vandalized.

He saw her eyes go round in the rearview mirror. "Is every*one* okay?"

"Physically, yes. Emotionally, well, we're hanging in there."

Autumn stopped the van at a red light and continued to watch him in the mirror. "Would you like me to take you to the police station to file a report?"

"No, thanks." He rubbed his sore knee.

Her eyes narrowed for a fraction of a second. "Why not?"

"Renee prefers we handle our issues within our community."

"But this is a serious situation, Jerome."

"Ya, I agree, but Renee doesn't want to involve the police."

"Huh," Autumn said. "Interesting."

When they arrived at Kings' Hardware, Jerome hurried into the store. He found Tim arranging a display of painting supplies. How ironic.

Tim faced him and grinned. "Wie geht's?"

"Do you have anything that will remove spray paint from concrete?" Jerome asked.

Tim's lips twitched. "What were you painting?"

"Nothing. Someone decided to deface Renee's porch last night." He explained what had happened, including the damage to his buggy. Tim's expression darkened.

"Who would do that?" Then understanding dawned on his best friend's face. "The same person who left the threatening note is getting bolder."

"That's my fear."

"You need to tell the bishop what's going on," Tim said.

"Ya. That's what mei dat said." Jerome leaned against the wall. "I'm considering that. I told Jeannie to talk to our folks today." He glanced down the aisle and then back at Tim. "I don't understand who would do this. And why? What do they want?"

Tim shrugged. "The farm, I guess. It's got to be someone who has some sort of stake in the property. I'm sure it's worth quite a bit of money."

"That's true, and that's why I thought it could be a Realtor, but would a businessperson go that far?"

"Maybe it's not about business, Jerome. Maybe it's personal."

A chill rushed through Jerome, but he shook it off. He hadn't even considered such a thing. But Renee had been gone for twenty years, and Martha never had anything like this happen. What could anyone have against Renee? "So, about cleaning that concrete."

"I have just the thing," Tim said, snapping his fingers.

Chapter Seventeen

Friday, May 30

Renee sat at her grandmother's sewing table on Friday three weeks later, a pen poised in her hand. The open window ushered in a fresh, late spring breeze and the scent of coming rain. She chewed on the end of her pen and studied the piece of paper sitting on the desk. She'd written *Dear Mamm*, and then stopped.

Glancing around the small room, she considered the past few weeks. Thankfully, there hadn't been another incident since they'd found the broken teapot and the threat scrawled on the porch. Renee and Jeannie were able to erase the horrible words off the porch using the paint stripper that Tim had sold to Jerome, and Jerome was able to get his buggy fixed at a nearby carriage shop. Jerome's parents and his bishop suggested that they be careful and call the police if something else happened. She'd tried to remain vigilant, making sure the windows and doors were locked at night, and she was thankful for God's protection.

Renee had spent the last few weeks enjoying her hometown. She'd visited her aunts and cousins twice and cherished getting to know them better. She'd also had another sisters' day with Jeannie and her friends while they sewed, and she attended more youth group gatherings and church services. She felt more and more like a part of the community, and although she missed her parents and Anna, she felt as if something was beckoning her to stay in Bird-in-Hand, despite her parents' mandate that she return home by August.

She had settled into a comfortable routine on her grandmother's farm, cooking and cleaning and handling laundry, and sharing meals with Jerome and Jeannie. She'd also cleared out her grandmother's garden and planted colorful flowers that reminded her of her precious grandmother. Although she felt at home in Bird-in-Hand, she still hadn't solved the puzzle of why her father had insisted they leave.

She'd spent countless hours searching the farm for clues, as well as talking to her grandmother's old friends and other members of the church district, and no one knew why her father made the decision to whisk their family away to another community. August was coming quickly, and Renee was running out of time. She needed to find the answers to her questions before she had to return to Ohio.

Twirling her pen, she looked at the blank piece of paper. She had traded letters with Mamm and Anna, but she hadn't told either of them about the threatening incidents since she didn't want to worry them.

When she told her mamm about seeing Aenti Naomi and Delilah, Mamm had written back that she was angry Renee had visited her sister and rehashed the past. Mamm told Renee to stop digging around where she didn't belong and instead focus on the issue of handling her grandmother's affairs. Renee was hurt and disappointed in her mother. She prayed that the Lord would open the line of communication between her mother and her sister, as well as her mother and her former best friend, so that their relationships might be renewed.

Renee raised her pen over the paper again and considered what to write. She had visited the lawyer a couple of times during the past few weeks and spoken to him about her grandmother's accounts and the possibility of selling the farm. She needed to make a decision. Something held her back from calling a Realtor and arranging to put the farm up for sale. Yet it seemed silly to stay in Bird-in-Hand if no one had answers regarding her family's past. Her searches of the property and conversations with community members had been fruitless.

Renee frowned and rested her chin on her palm. She was beginning to wonder if maybe Mamm was right all along, and she should let her go of her curiosity and trust her father's decision.

Her eyes cut to the lemon-yellow dress sitting on the table beside her, awaiting her to finish the hem. She'd made herself several brightly colored dresses during the past few weeks. In her heart she could feel Bird-in-Hand becoming her home. Jerome and Jeannie were like members of her family.

She turned toward the window and looked out toward the barn, hoping to catch a glimpse of Jerome working. Butterflies fluttered in her belly as she imagined his attractive blue eyes and his glorious smile. His friendship had become so important to her—more important than she could put into words. She'd never been in love before, but she was certain what she felt for Jerome was different from anything she'd experienced before. If this was what love felt like, she relished the feeling.

Shooing those thoughts away, she focused on the piece of paper and the words, *Dear Mamm*. Then she began to write.

> *How are you and Ike doing? Things are good here in Bird-in-Hand. It looks like we might get some much-needed rain today.*

Renee wilted back on the chair and sighed. Why was she having such a difficult time writing a letter to her mother? She normally enjoyed writing letters. But she felt so...distracted.

She dropped her pen on the table and turned toward the bookshelf. Something along the wall behind it caught her eye. The paint was a different shade of white. The difference was subtle, but it was as if the paint there was fresher. It seemed as though the wall had been fixed.

Why hadn't she noticed this before? She'd searched this room numerous times since her arrival. Perhaps the sun was coming in at a different angle now than it did during summertime, and a ray of sunlight shone through the clouds and hit the wall in a way she hadn't seen before?

No matter what caused it, she couldn't explain, but it was there plain as day—the wall had been fixed at some point in time, and she needed to know what, if anything, was hidden by the fresh paint.

Renee removed the books from the shelf, piled them on the floor, and then, with all her might, heaved the heavy wooden shelf away from the wall. When she noticed a latch in the wall, she gasped as a bubble of shock rolled through her. Was this a secret door? Why would her grandmother need a secret hiding place?

Her hands quavered as she yanked open the door, and she found a storage area, big enough only for a small suitcase. Renee turned on her flashlight and when she pointed it toward the wall, she spotted a small wooden box.

Then with her heart pounding against her ribcage, she reached out and grabbed it.

Jerome lifted the hammer and angled a nail on the new slat for the barn door. He pulled the hammer back and swung—completely missing the nail. But he hadn't missed his hand.

He growled as pain radiated through his thumb and up his arm. He shook his hand and hopped around, furious at himself.

The dark clouds above mirrored his foul mood. He'd awoken in a cold sweat this morning. After a few weeks of relief, the nightmares had returned, but this time he couldn't remember the dream. Still the sick feeling that always accompanied those dreams had gripped his stomach and refused to leave throughout the day.

His bad mood clung to him like a second skin, and he was relieved his twin had kept up a lively conversation during breakfast. He'd managed to head out to lose himself in chores without having to explain his reticence.

When he heard someone calling his name, he swiveled toward Martha's house just as Renee sprinted toward him, holding a wooden box. She looked beautiful, clad in a dark blue dress and black apron. The Lancaster County prayer covering suited her too.

Stop it!

He tried to dismiss the thoughts. He had developed a crush on her, but it could only lead to more heartache and disappointment, and he'd already had enough to last a lifetime.

"Jerome! Jerome!" She finally reached him and worked to catch her breath. "Look at what I found!" She held up the box.

He nodded slowly, and his eyes lit up. "Where did you find that?"

"It was hidden in a secret panel in mei mammi's sewing room." She studied his expression. "You've seen this box before, haven't you?"

"Ya. I gave it to Martha about a year ago."

"What do you mean?"

"She asked me to find a good solid box in the barn but didn't say what she wanted it for." He gestured around the barn. "I found it, and when I gave it to Martha, she teared up, saying that Abner had built it."

Renee studied the box and then her dark eyes met his again. "Did you build a secret hiding spot in the wall for her?"

"No." He shook his head. "What secret hiding spot?"

She shared where she found the box, detailing how the wall was a different shade of white paint. "It looked as if it had been painted fairly recently."

"Now it makes sense."

"What does?"

"Not long after Martha said she needed a box, she asked me to buy her some paint. I told her I'd be happy to paint whatever she needed, but she insisted she'd take care of it. I didn't think much of it at the time." He shook his head. "I guess that means she moved the bookshelf to hide the box before stowing it, painted the wall, and then moved the shelf back." He chuckled. "Well, she was definitely feisty and spry for her age."

"So the hiding spot was already there," Renee said. "What do you think the hiding spot was originally for? Maybe money?" she asked.

"That makes sense. Many of the older generation of Amish didn't trust banks, and they would hide money in their walls."

"Obviously this box is important if mei mammi went through all of that trouble to hide it." She angled the box toward him. "Can you open it?"

He examined the lock. "Let's take it to my workbench."

He set the box on the bench and turned it over. Although the box was homemade, the locking mechanism and hinges were sturdy. He tried jimmying the lock with different tools, but it refused to budge.

Turning the box over, he studied the bottom, but it was solid wood just like the top. He examined the hinges and found he had the right screwdriver. He used it to try to dislodge the screws, but they wouldn't loosen.

"I could remove the hinges, but I don't want to ruin the box."

Her brown eyes were wide. "Please, Jerome. I need to see what's inside."

"Are you sure, Renee? I might break it."

"Ya, I'm sure," she insisted, her tone anxious. "I need to get inside of this. There's a reason why she hid this, and it could hold all of the answers I've been looking for."

"All right."

For the next several minutes he hammered the hinges, and this time he managed to avoid injuring himself. Finally, one of the hinges gave way, and the top of the box cracked open.

Renee touched her collarbone as her pretty face lit up with excitement.

Above, rain drummed on the barn roof. He smelled sweet wet hay. He started hammering the second hinge, and when it loosened, the box fell open.

"Danki!" Renee exclaimed while she examined the contents. She made a small noise as she pulled out a pile of letters. "They're all addressed to mei dat, and they were returned unopened." Her soulful dark eyes glistened. "Jerome," she whispered, her voice shaking, "this could be what I've been searching for."

He nodded, and his chest constricted with a swarm of emotions—hope, grief, and worry. If Renee found what she'd been seeking, would she leave sooner than August?

But why should he be concerned about when she left, when he knew to the depths of his soul that God would eventually lead her to a man who was much more deserving than he could ever be.

He started to retreat from the bench. "I need to fix the barn door," he muttered.

"Wait!" She reached for him and then pulled her hand back. "Please stay. Read this with me."

He shook his head. "I don't want to intrude on your family business."

"Intrude?" Her brow bunched. "But we're in this together, right?" She pointed to him. "You said so yourself."

He gulped. He had said those exact words to her the night they'd found the graffiti and the smashed teapot.

She lifted her chin. "You know I'm right."

The rain pounded harder on the roof. "Fine," he said. "Let's go into the haus."

"Perfect." Her smile was triumphant. "I'll make kaffi."

Renee's hands quivered as she reached into the box and lifted a stack of letters held together by a piece of twine. She studied the pile, and her thoughts swam.

Jerome set two mugs of coffee on the table before sitting beside her.

Comforting warmth permeated the kitchen while rain beat on the roof of the house. She studied the stack as confusion, followed by doubt and fear, consumed her.

"You okay?" Jerome's voice broke through the silence.

She didn't answer for a moment, then said, "What if the letters contain something that's too painful for me to process?" She sniffed. "And what if I regret finding out the truth?"

His expression became empathetic. "You've been searching for so long, Renee. Don't let your fear steal this moment from you. You're the bravest person I know. You can't give up now."

His words gave her strength, and she peeked in the box once again. She pulled out a piece of paper containing a note written in beautiful, slanted cursive.

Renee,

I hope that you're able to understand and forgive me.

Sincerely,

Martha Mast, your mammi

Tears spilled down Renee's hot cheeks. "Why would she need *my* forgiveness?"

Jerome held his hand out toward her and then set it back on the table, but his handsome face and blue eyes reflected care and sympathy.

Thumbing through the letters, Renee found that they were in order by date, and the postmarks displayed that they were twenty years old. She wiped her eyes with a paper napkin and then tried to smile. "I need to open the first one, ya?"

"Take your time." Jerome's deep voice soothed her frazzled nerves.

Renee's hands wobbled as she opened the first letter and began to read.

Dear Emmanuel,

I was able to track down your address through contacts in a nearby Amish community. I couldn't let you leave without telling you how I feel. You're my son, and you always will be. So, I'm begging you to read this with an open mind and open heart.

I know that you're angry with me. You made that abundantly clear when you announced that you were taking your family far, far away from me. I understand your pain, and

I'm sorry for not telling you the truth. But you have to understand that I love you and so does your father, Abner.

I had wanted to tell you the truth from the beginning, but Abner insisted that there was no need to. Abner wanted us to be a family, and we are a family. Even if Abner isn't your biological father, he's still the man who has loved you and raised you since the moment you were born.

I need a chance to explain what happened. I was young as you know, and it was during my rumspringa. I went to a party with friends, and I was reckless. I'd never had alcohol, and under the influence of it, I made bad decisions that I regret. But I have never, ever regretted you, Emmanuel. You are a blessing that came from a night I had otherwise wanted to forget.

When I found out I was going to have you, I was ashamed and terrified. But I knew one thing for certain—you are a gift from God. I wanted you, but I was afraid to tell my parents.

I only shared my secret with Abner. He'd been my best friend since we were children. After I confessed my secret, he confessed his—he'd always loved me, and he wanted to marry me. I was surprised and so very honored. I didn't feel worthy of his love or his proposal, but I accepted it humbly. We both were baptized and joined the church and then we were married soon after.

I had hoped that no one would ask how you came so quickly after we were married, but rumors flew throughout the community. Abner insisted that we tell our parents we had sinned. He said he would take my secret to his grave, and

I believe that he will. To this day, he hasn't told a soul the truth. He insists that you are his son, and you are—both legally and in his heart.

But I have always carried the guilt with me. In fact, I believe God punished me for my indiscretion, and that's why Abner and I couldn't have children together. I apologized to him many, many times, but he always said that he loved me no matter what, and he's happy with our little family.

Abner is a loyal and loving man to this day, and I'm convinced that's why God chose him to be our bishop. I feel as if I don't deserve his love, but I cherish it.

Emmanuel, I'm sorry that you found out the way you did. It shouldn't have taken a blood test at a hospital to tell you that your father isn't your biological father.

I'm not only writing this letter to beg for your forgiveness, but I'm also writing to tell you the truth. Your father is Raymond Wallace. He's an Englisher. He doesn't live far from here. The last I heard he lives in Soudersburg, and his family owns a construction company. I ran into him once after you were born, and I think he figured out the truth. But it doesn't matter. He has a family of his own, and I have mine.

Emmanuel, please forgive me and come home. Your father and I love you, Lovina, and Renee. We need you in our lives. Please find it in your heart to forgive as we are called to do.

Always,

Mamm

Chapter Eighteen

Renee couldn't breathe. She tried to pull in air, leaned over and gasped, but her lungs refused to work.

A strong hand touched her back. "Renee?" Jerome's voice was close to her ear. "Renee?" Worry laced his tone. "Are you okay?" He paused while she choked. "Please answer me. Breathe, Renee."

After a few long moments, she sat up and stared at Jerome with her words caught in her throat.

"Talk to me," he said. "How are you feeling?" His eyes searched hers. "Don't keep it bottled up inside. That's not healthy."

She handed him the letter. "Here. Read this."

While Jerome read the letter, she shook her head and peered down at her lap. She was unable to put the myriad of emotions swirling inside her into words. She felt as if her world had tilted, and everything was off center.

"Wow," he whispered when he was done. "That...that was a lot."

She rubbed her eyes and tried to work through the confusion that had seized her mind.

"Renee, are you okay?" Jerome asked, but she couldn't respond. "Hey. Look at me." He gently touched her shoulder. "Renee, you're scaring me. Please say something."

Her eyes snapped to his. "Everything I've ever known has been a lie." She covered her face with her hands. "No, not everything, but the man who I thought was my grandfather isn't really my grandfather." She tried to get her thoughts in order. "He is legally, but biologically, he's not." She groaned. "Nothing makes sense now, Jerome, but everything makes sense." She gave him a weak smile. "Am I making sense?"

He chuckled, and she treasured the sound. "You are. Your grandfather, who also was your bishop, and he was my bishop until he passed away, wasn't your biological grandfather. Which means that you have another grandfather out there who is an Englisher. So, you could have Englisher relatives who have no idea you exist."

"Exactly." She sat up taller. "Like you said, this is a lot." She examined the pile of letters. "I don't know if I want to read any more."

"But you do want to read them. In fact, you need to in order to understand everything that happened."

She smiled at him. How could Jerome know exactly how she was feeling without her even telling him? They had a special connection, one she'd never shared with anyone else.

"How about this?" he suggested. "You read the letters, and I'll make more kaffi."

"Deal," she said.

For the next hour, Renee read the letters, and they were all similar. Her grandmother would beg her father for forgiveness and plead with him to bring her family home to Pennsylvania.

But the last letter was different. In this letter, Renee's grandmother explained that her grandfather wasn't doing well. He'd been diagnosed with a heart condition that would most likely be fatal, and she planned to build a daadihaus for herself so that Renee's father could return to Bird-in-Hand to take over the farm and help her.

Tears flooded Renee's eyes as her grandmother's desperation poured from the letter and straight into Renee's heart. She covered her face with her hands as her emotions broke free. She tried in vain to stop herself from losing it in front of Jerome again, but she couldn't. It was too much.

"Renee." Jerome's chair scraped on the linoleum, and soon his arms were around her. "It's okay," he murmured. "You don't have to cry."

She relaxed against him and rested her cheek on his strong shoulder. Soon her tears subsided, and she sniffed and wiped her eyes with her fingertips. "I just don't understand why mei daed couldn't forgive his mamm. It doesn't make sense. She made a mistake, but she did everything she could to make it right. Why couldn't he follow Jesus's example and forgive her?"

Renee sat up and blotted her eyes and nose with a napkin. "I don't know what to do with these emotions, Jerome. It's all so much to take in." She moved her fingers over the envelopes while her thoughts spun. "Mei dat ripped mei mamm away from her family. And he stole me away from my family." She turned to Jerome. "He took me away from my friends, like you and Jeannie. And he did it because he was angry with his mamm. That's not right. It's against our beliefs to hold a grudge."

He nodded. "You're right. He was wrong," Jerome said. "But you need to give yourself time to process this."

"Oh, Jerome," she said. "Now I understand why she hid the letters in the wall."

"What do you mean?"

"Mei mammi left the letter in the china cabinet for me so that I would keep looking." She took a deep breath. "I think she wanted me to find this so that I could know the truth. But she wanted to protect this secret at all costs. She wanted to try to save her reputation and also my daadi's. She left clues only for me."

He nodded. "That makes sense." His expression radiated sympathy. "I promise I'll keep this secret for you, Renee. Martha was like my own mammi, and I would never do anything to hurt her or your family."

"Danki," she whispered as fresh tears formed. "This is a lot to process."

He paused for a moment and then said, "What if we prayed together? Would that help you feel better?"

"Ya." She studied his handsome face, and an overwhelming feeling overtook her, something that she couldn't quite comprehend. She closed her eyes as he began to pray.

"Gott, we thank You for leading Renee to the answers that she's been seeking for so long. Please help her come to terms with what she's learned and guide her while she sorts through all of the decisions she needs to make for Martha's estate. Amen."

"Amen," she whispered before covering his hand with hers, giving it a gentle squeeze, and opening her eyes. "You're such a gut man, Jerome."

His face flashed with something that resembled shock, and he pushed his chair back. "I need to get back to my chores," he mumbled before rushing out of the kitchen.

Her eyes stung as she watched him go. After all this time, Renee finally knew the truth. She was overcome with sympathy and love for Mammi and how she'd worked so hard to make things right but couldn't. Despite all of Mammi's efforts, the tragedy had destroyed their family.

Right now, the last thing Renee wanted was to be alone with her thoughts.

Jerome stalked through the driving rain to the barn, where he re-trieved his hammer and began banging it against the door. He swung the hammer with all his might, but it did nothing to cure the ache that had opened up inside him like a black hole.

He stopped hammering and slumped against the barn wall before sliding down to sit on the ground. Bending his knees, he leaned forward and let his head fall into his hands. He tried to stop the image from appearing in his mind, but he couldn't. It was the nightmare he'd endured last night. He hadn't remembered it until Renee covered his hand with hers in the kitchen and told him he was a good man.

As soon as her skin touched his, the nightmare returned in full force. Same as always, he was riding in his buggy at night and then the storm hit. He couldn't see, and then all of a sudden the pickup truck slid through the stop sign and slammed into the passenger side of the buggy.

Then the buggy was rolling and rolling and rolling, and it finally came to a stop on top of Jerome, pinning him in the mud. When he twisted his body, he saw the body of a woman lying a few yards from him in the mud, while the rain continued to drench him.

Somehow he was able to get out from under the buggy, and when he touched the woman's face, he realized it wasn't Amanda... *It was Renee!*

This time, he had killed Renee!

In the dream, he dropped to his knees and sobbed while begging God to save Renee and take him instead. And that was when he'd awakened in the darkness, drenched in a cold sweat.

Bile rose in Jerome's throat. He tried to swallow it back as the truth hit him as hard as the pickup truck had. The dream was proof of what he'd thought all along—he was no good for Renee. The best thing he could do was stay away from her. It was the only way he could protect her.

And that was why he needed to steer clear of her, no matter how much it ripped his heart apart.

Renee was better off without him.

Renee set the last dish on the table and then peered out the window toward the barn. It was after six and neither Jerome nor Jeannie had arrived for supper. She had spent the afternoon rereading the letters and trying to make sense of them, but finally set them aside and tried to drown her conflicted feelings with the familiar chore of cooking. Now a vegetable soup simmered on the stove and corn muffins cooled on the counter, both recipes she'd found in her grandmother's cookbook.

After waiting a few more moments, her worry propelled her out the back door and down the path leading to Jerome's house. The rain had stopped, but dark clouds still clogged the sky. She knocked on the door and then stuck her hands into her apron pockets.

Footsteps sounded before the door opened, revealing Jerome. His frown sent worry cascading through her.

"Is Jeannie here?" she asked.

He shook his head. "She left a message that she needed to stay late to help my folks with inventory."

"Oh." Renee tried to read his face, but it was a mask of indifference. "Why didn't you tell me?"

"I was going to."

She waited for him to elaborate but he remained silent, and the apathy in his expression and tone was slowly breaking her heart. What had changed since their last conversation? "Why haven't you come in for supper?" she asked.

"I'm going to make a sandwich."

She tried to decode his coldness. "Why?"

He pressed his lips together.

"Jerome, did I do something to offend you?" She could hear the quaver in her voice.

He shook his head. "It's better if I stay away from you."

"Why?" she asked. When he remained silent, she said, "You think you're a bad person, but you're not."

"I need to go, Renee," he said. "I'm sorry."

Then he closed the door in her face.

Renee ignored how her eyes stung and hurried over to the phone shanty. She dialed her aunt's number and then closed her eyes.

Please answer. Please answer. Please answer!

"Hello?" a voice said.

"Aenti Naomi?" she asked.

"Renee! Wie geht's?" her aunt said.

"I know it's last minute, but is there any chance I can come see you? I just made soup and corn muffins. We can eat it together. I have something important to share with you."

"That sounds wunderbaar," Naomi said. "I'd love to see you."

"Danki." Renee hung up with her aunt and dialed Autumn's number for a ride.

While Autumn drove through town toward White Horse, Renee moved her fingers over the wooden box. Her mind spun with confusion over why Jerome had rejected her, along with shock over the truth about her grandparents.

"That's a pretty box," Autumn commented from the front seat. "Did someone make it for you?"

"I found it in my grandmother's house," Renee said. She removed the top and peeked at the letters.

"It's real nice," Autumn continued. "I bet it's an heirloom, huh?"

Renee frowned. She wasn't in the mood to chat about her grandmother or anything. She just wanted to talk to her aunt. She prayed that Aenti Naomi could help her make sense of everything.

If she were at home, she'd lean on her mother or Anna when she was sad or upset, but they were miles and miles away. A sudden wave of homesickness wafted over Renee, and she did her best to tamp it down deep.

"I can't believe June will be here on Sunday," Autumn continued. "It certainly feels like summer. It's gotten hot during this past week. I don't know about you, but I love the summertime. I love to swim. Do you like the beach? I sure do."

Renee peeked out the window while Autumn continued to talk about her favorite summer activities.

When they reached her aunt's house, Renee jumped out of the van. "Could you pick me up in a couple of hours?"

"Sure thing!" Autumn said. "If you need more time, just call."

"Thanks." Renee shouldered a tote bag containing her portable casserole dish and carried the box in her hands while she went up the porch steps.

The front door opened, and Naomi ushered her into the kitchen. They prayed and then filled their bowls with soup before buttering a corn muffin each, but Renee's stomach had tied itself in a knot, and food was the last thing on her mind.

"Where's Onkel Dennis?" Renee asked.

"He's out in the barn." Naomi gave a dismissive wave. "I could tell that you want to talk, so he ate supper and then went out to work in his shop to give us some time alone." Her aunt's expression was full of concern. "What's bothering you, Renee?"

"I finally know the truth," Renee said before setting the stack of letters in front of her aunt.

Aenti Naomi's eyes were wide. "About why your dat left?"

Renee nodded, then told her everything about how her grandmother had gotten pregnant at a party and then married her best friend before they raised her father as their own. "Mei dat had somehow figured out that Abner wasn't his biological dat, and that's why my family left."

Naomi huffed out a puff of air. "I'm stunned. Abner was the bishop, and he kept that lie to himself." She sank back in her chair. "I can't believe mei schweschder didn't tell me, but if it was that upsetting to Emmanuel, then it makes sense." Her aunt's expression softened. "How are you handling all this?"

"Not great." Renee moved her fork around on her plate. "I can't wrap my head around why mei dat didn't forgive his mamm. We've all sinned and fallen short of the glory of God. Why would he go against our beliefs and allow his anger to shatter his family?" She pointed to herself. "*My* family?"

"I'm struggling to understand how this happened, and now that I know the truth, I don't know what to do with all of these feelings. I'm angry with mei dat for breaking up our family, and I'm disappointed that he made mei mamm promise not to tell me the truth. I'm also angry that mei mamm never told me. She allowed me to come here to figure it out for myself, but she could've just told me." Renee blotted her damp eyes with a napkin. "And I'm angry at myself for disrespecting my parents because I'm angry with them."

Naomi reached across the table and patted her hands. "You're allowed to go through all of these feelings, but remember to always keep your eyes on Jesus. Pray and ask Gott to heal your heart."

Renee sniffed. "Ya, I will." She held her aunt's hand and tried to settle her roaring emotions, while she and her aunt continued to talk about the news and work through their shock together.

Renee placed her tote bag, the wooden box, and her purse on the kitchen table later that evening. She yawned and set the container with the remaining vegetable soup in the refrigerator and the left-over corn muffins on the counter.

"How's your aenti?"

Renee spun toward Jeannie who stood in the doorway, watching her with a hesitant expression.

"Gut." Renee closed the refrigerator and sat at the table. "How was work?"

"Gut." Jeannie sat across from her. "Jerome said you had a rough day." She rested her hands on the table.

"What did he tell you?"

"Only that you found some letters that explain everything, but he insisted I should give you some space and wait until you're ready to share any of it."

Renee studied her. Jeannie and Jerome were twins, which meant that they were likely very close. Had Jerome possibly told her why he suddenly pushed Renee away? And if he had, would Jeannie admit it, or would she keep her twin's secrets to herself? "Is that all he told you?"

"What do you mean?" Jeannie asked, her blond brows drawing together.

"Did Jerome mention why he'd been in a bad mood all day?"

Jeannie actually snorted. "Mei bruder is grouchy sometimes, and I've gotten used to it." She tilted her head. "But I'm worried about you. What did you find out?" She held up her hands. "You don't have to tell me if you don't want to."

"I want to."

She told Jeannie about the box, the letters, and the secrets. Jeannie's blue eyes were wide with shock by the time Renee finished. "I went to mei aenti's haus to share it all with her and to get her advice on how to handle it."

"What did she say?"

"She told me to allow myself to go through my emotions and then ask Gott to help me forgive my parents, for not only keeping the secrets from me but also for taking me away from my community."

Jeannie nodded slowly. "Was that helpful?"

"Ya." She rested her elbow on the table and her cheek on her palm. But she still had no idea how she was going to get over the heartbreak of Jerome's rejection. She moved the tip of her finger along the edge of the table.

"Renee, I can tell that something else is bothering you, and if you want someone to talk to, I'm right here."

She studied Jeannie's face, and for a moment, she considered pouring her heart out and sharing her confusing feelings for Jeannie's twin brother.

Suddenly, she knew what she had to do.

Jerome had made it clear that he didn't want to have Renee in his life. She couldn't understand what she'd done to push him away, but she needed to respect him and give him his space. After all, God had led her to the answers she sought, and now she had to figure out what to do with the farm and go home to the community where she belonged. She may have felt at home in Bird-in-Hand, but it wasn't where she belonged. She would return to her mother and Anna.

And that would be that.

When Renee felt her heart start to crack, she did her best to dismiss it. She also tried to supress a sudden rush of tears. She couldn't break down in front of Jeannie. If she did, then her sweet friend would insist she open up to her. It would be awkward to tell Jeannie that Renee was falling in love with Jerome, but he didn't love her.

Love?

Oh no.

Renee feigned a yawn. "Oh, excuse me," she said, pushing back her chair to stand. "I'm wiped out after today. It's been so emotional that it's taken everything out of me."

Jeannie's pretty face pinched and then recovered. "Oh, okay. You need some gut rest."

"Gut nacht," Renee said as she stood. "I'll see you in the morning."

As she made her way to her bedroom, Renee tried to hold back a wave of tears that threatened to drown her. She'd try to find a way to get over Jerome, but she feared it would be impossible.

Chapter Nineteen

Saturday, May 31

Jerome pushed open his back door just as a fancy black car pulled up and parked. *What on earth?* He descended the porch as the Realtor exited the car.

"Hi there!" She waved at him. "I'm sure you remember me. I'm Belinda Walker."

Jerome frowned. "What do you want?"

The woman pointed toward the main house. "Is Renee home?" She started down the path. "I haven't spoken to her in a few weeks, and I wanted to check in. I have plenty of clients who would love to get their hands on this place and would pay top dollar for it." She rubbed her palms together. "Has she been inspired to sell yet?"

Been inspired to sell?

Those words lit a fire in Jerome's gut as he followed Belinda up the path toward the house. "What do you mean by 'has she been inspired to sell?'"

"Oh, you know!" Belinda's laugh sounded as fake as her long, red nails were. "Sometimes it takes a little push to get someone to make a decision. I was wondering if she'd finally done it." She rapped on the back door.

Jerome stood at the bottom of the stairs. "Did you have anything to do with *inspiring* her to make that decision?"

Belinda blinked at him. "What do you mean?"

The storm door opened with a squeak, and Jeannie stood in the doorway. "Can I help you?"

"Hi, I'm Belinda Walker." She shoved a business card in his sister's face. "Is Renee here?"

Jeannie shook her head. "She went out to run some errands with our driver and should be back soon." Her brow wrinkled. "What's going on?"

Jerome scowled. He hadn't come into Martha's house for breakfast that morning, so, prior to hearing from Jeannie, he'd had no idea where Renee was or what was going on. He wasn't surprised she'd gone shopping alone since they hadn't received any more threats. He couldn't help being protective, but he was sure she'd return soon. Most likely he'd been in the barn milking the cows and hadn't heard Renee leave. "What can we do for you, Belinda?" His words held a thread of sarcasm, but he didn't care.

"Well, you have my card, honey," she told Jeannie, before descending the stairs and shoving another card toward Jerome. "And here's one for you. Just tell Renee that I'm around if she's finally ready to sell. I'm anxious to get this place on the market so we can all get ourselves a nice offer." She stalked toward her car.

Jeannie came to stand beside Jerome. She read the card. "Realtor, huh?"

"Yeah. I still wonder if she's the one who's been threatening us."

"Why?"

"She wanted to know if Renee's been inspired to sell yet."

His sister's mouth dropped open. "She actually used those words?"

"Ya."

The fancy car backed down the driveway, and he shook his head. He couldn't stand Belinda's boldness, and if she was the one making the threats…

"Why didn't you come to breakfast?" Jeannie asked him.

He started toward the barn. "I have too much to do today, and I'm behind on my chores."

"Whoa." She rushed after him. "You can't lie to me. I'm your twin, and I know when you're lying."

He kept moving forward. His boots crunched on the hay while he grabbed a pitchfork and began mucking his mare's stall.

"What's going on with you, Jerome?" Jeannie demanded with her hands on her hips.

"Nothing." He growled out the word. "I'm busy, Jeannie. Running a farm is a lot of work, and in case you haven't noticed, I'm the only one here doing the work." He gestured around the barn. "If you'd like to help, then great. You can grab a brush and start brushing my mare. If not, then get out of my way," he snapped.

He continued working, his movements jerky, and out of the corner of his eye, he could see his twin hadn't moved.

Fantastic.

His sister was as stubborn as he was, which always made their arguments more colorful.

Jerome kept his focus on his work and hoped Jeannie would get the hint and leave. After several moments he faced her and brushed an arm over his forehead. "Don't you have chores to do?"

"I'm not leaving until you tell me what's going on with you. Both you and Renee have been acting weird, and I want to know why."

He stilled. "Renee's been acting weird?"

"Ya." Jeannie threw her arms up in the air. "She hardly said a word during breakfast. And then she ran off to take care of some secretive 'errands'"—Jeannie made air quotes with her fingers—"as soon as the kitchen was cleaned up. Did you two have an argument or something?"

"Nee." He went back to mucking the stalls.

"If you don't want to talk to me, then fine. Have it your way!" Jeannie stomped out of the barn while muttering about how aggravating twin brothers were.

Jerome kept working and tried to dismiss the aching muscles in his back and neck. Although he despised hurting his sister by not telling her the truth about his absence at breakfast, he also didn't want to open himself up. If he explained that he was avoiding Renee in order to save himself from hurting her, Jeannie would give him another lecture about how it was time to move on and find love again, and blah, blah, blah.

He didn't need a lecture. Instead, he needed everyone to leave him alone and allow him to live his life the way he saw fit. He'd checked on the farmhand job in Gordonville, and the farmer told Jerome to let him know when he was ready to start. The salary was comparable and included living quarters. The job would be similar, but the idea of leaving Martha's farm still hurt him deep in his soul. This place had become home to him, especially after meeting Renee.

Pushing those thoughts away, he brushed his mare and then walked around to his house. What was he thinking? This was never "his" house. Nothing belonged to him except his horse and buggy. Including Renee.

His stomach gurgled, signaling it was time for lunch. As soon as he reached his porch, he heard someone call his name.

Jerome turned and froze just as Murray Robertson scrambled up the dirt road leading to the farm.

The middle-aged man's beady eyes were wild, and he kept stopping to look behind him as if he expected someone or something to jump out and attack him.

"Jerome!" Murray yelled before peeking over his shoulder. "Jerome, I need to talk to you. It's urgent."

Stepping off the porch, Jerome met him at the top of the driveway. "What do you want?"

"Jerome." Murray worked to catch his breath as if he'd run a mile instead of simply crossing the street and walking up a driveway. "I need to warn you."

"Warn me?"

The older man nodded with emphasis. "You need to be careful."

"What do you mean?" Jerome's words were measured.

Murray checked over his shoulder before scanning the farm. "You need to watch your back."

"Why?" Jerome demanded as his body shuddered.

Murray shook his head and backed away from him. "That's all I can tell you!"

Before Jerome could ask him another question, the strange little man scurried down the driveway.

What was that about?

Jerome scrubbed a hand over his face and tried to figure out what had just happened. Was Murray warning him because he knew something, or was he warning him because Murray was planning something and was odd enough that he liked to warn his victims?

Nothing made sense anymore!

He turned toward his house, but the sound of an engine pulled his attention back to the driveway.

Now what?

The white van that he'd grown to know so well steered up the rock driveway and stopped in front of him.

"Hi, Jerome," Autumn called from the driver's seat.

He nodded a greeting.

The back door opened with a squeak before Renee stumbled out with her arms full.

Jerome rushed over and grabbed a container before it fell to the ground. When his hand brushed hers, heat skipped up his arm.

"Danki," she muttered. She balanced two tote bags and another container and then reached for her purse.

He held his arms out. "Let me help you."

"I'm fine," she mumbled.

Oh, he'd had it with stubborn women today! "Renee, let me help you," he repeated.

Her lips formed a thin line before she handed him the container and the tote bags. Then she paid Autumn. "Thanks for the ride."

"You're welcome." Autumn waved again. "I'm sure I'll see you soon."

"Where were you?" he asked as the van motored out of the driveway.

"I needed to run some errands."

He almost rolled his eyes, but perhaps he deserved that response. He hadn't been forthright with her either lately.

Renee took the tote bags from him.

"Want me to carry this inside for you?" he asked, holding up the container.

She shook her head. "That's for you."

He peered down at the container and then up at her. "I don't understand," he said.

"I was at the market, so I picked up supper for you." She shifted her weight on her feet. "I figured you've been avoiding meals with me, and I didn't want you to starve."

The sadness in her eyes almost tore him in two. For a moment he dreamt of telling her that he was sorry, he cared about her, and he wanted to her stay in Bird-in-Hand, run her farm with him, and build a life with her.

But that was merely a pipe dream.

Renee paused for a moment as if waiting for him to respond, but his mouth couldn't form the right words.

Finally, she turned and walked away from him.

"Wait," he called, and she spun, her dark eyes sparkling with something that looked like hope. "Belinda was here again. She's still anxious for your business."

"Oh." She nodded.

"And Murray was just here. He said he had to warn me."

"Warn you?"

"Ya. It was strange. He kept looking over his shoulder, and he didn't explain what he meant. Just make sure the doors and windows are locked."

"I will." She hesitated. "Anything else?"

He shook his head, and her face clouded with a frown before she continued toward the house.

As he watched her go, he fought the urge to run after her. But he knew one thing for sure—he wouldn't let anything happen to her.

Sunday, June 1

Renee sat at the kitchen table. Her gaze moved out toward the den, where Jeannie lounged on the sofa reading a book. A fresh breeze swept in from the nearby open window, along with the musical lilt of happy birds.

Since it was a Sunday without church service, Renee and Jeannie had planned to go to youth group, but when they'd awakened that morning, neither of them felt like going. Instead, they decided to stay home.

With her chin resting on her palm, Renee examined the letter she'd started to her mother two days ago. So much had happened since then. She'd found the answers to her questions about her family, and she'd lost her friendship with Jerome.

Renee looked out the window toward the barn. She hadn't seen or spoken to Jerome since she'd given him the food she'd picked up from the market last night, and to her surprise, Jeannie hadn't said a word about him at dinner last night or breakfast this morning. She was unusually quiet, and Renee wondered if she was up to something. It wasn't like Jeannie to not want to go to youth group. Renee also had a feeling that the twins had had a disagreement. While she was curious about what had caused their rift, she decided to stay out of it.

She also tried to ignore the ache blooming in her chest. She missed Jerome, but she was determined to find a way to evict him from her heart and mind, although it seemed impossible.

Turning her attention toward the letter to her mother, she picked up her pen. Now that she knew the truth about why her father had left the community, she was ready to tell her mother how she felt about it.

If she could only find the right words.

Renee scrutinized the words she'd written two days ago, before her world had been turned upside down.

> Dear Mamm,
>
> How are you and Ike doing? Things are good here in Bird-in-Hand. It looks like we might get some much-needed rain today.

She crumpled the paper and tossed it into the trash can. She examined a blank piece of paper and then closed her eyes and opened her heart to God.

> Lord, please help me find the right words to express to my mother how I feel about the news I've found out about my father and his past. Let me share my heart with her in the most respectful way possible.

Renee felt renewed and then began to write.

Dear Mamm,

First, I want to thank you for allowing me to come to Bird-in-Hand. While I had hoped to respectfully take care of my grandmother's estate, I also wanted to find out the truth about why my father moved us to Ohio and cut off all contact with friends and family here.

I know that you have always been a dutiful wife, and you believe it's your job to follow your husband's wishes, even after your husband has passed away. And while I respect that, I must be honest and tell you that I also resented it. I've wanted to know the truth, and now that I'm twenty-five and old enough to be a wife and mother, I believe I deserve to know the truth.

Apparently my grandmother also felt I should know what happened. She left me a box full of letters addressed to my father but returned unopened to her. She also left me a note asking me to forgive her for what happened.

I read each and every letter, and it was heartbreaking. She missed us all, and she loved us all very much. But because of my father's stubbornness, we all lost our precious family and friends.

I've been struggling for the past few days to understand how my father could hold a grudge for more than a decade. I understand why he was upset. The father who raised him was not his biological father and finding that out as an adult had to be devastating—especially when his father was the bishop and the one who is supposed to be the role model of Christ's love and forgiveness for the community.

Yet, on the other hand, my father was an adult and should've understood what a complicated situation it was. My heart is broken for both my father and my grandmother, but it's also broken because you didn't trust me with that information. But unlike my father, I'm not going to hold a grudge. I understand why you felt you had to withhold that information from me, and I'm grateful that you and Ike allowed me to come here to find out for myself.

Now that I've accomplished what I came here to do, I'm going to talk to the lawyer and discuss my next steps with the farm. I'll be in touch to let you know when I plan to come home.

Please give my love to Anna and tell everyone hello.

With love,

Renee

She folded the letter and stuffed it into an envelope. She was addressing it when a knock sounded on the back door, so she finished and set it next to the box with her grandmother's letters.

"I'll get it." Jeannie yanked the door open. "Mamm. Dat. What a surprise!"

Renee joined Jeannie and her parents in the den. She set her grandmother's box on the coffee table. "Gude mariye."

"What is the lovely smell?" Delilah asked.

"My new candle." Jeannie pointed to a jar candle on the coffee table. "It's vanilla."

Delilah chuckled. "You and your candles."

"I'll make kaffi." Renee put on the percolator while Jeannie pulled out a cheesecake and plates.

"Where's your bruder?" Harvey asked while they sat at the table.

A strange expression flickered over Jeannie's face as she stood. "I'll go get him."

Her parents shared a look when their daughter excused herself and headed out to the daadihaus.

"How have you been, Renee?" Delilah asked.

Harvey folded his hands on the table. "We know what's been going on here with the threatening notes, graffiti, and your mammi's teapot. I hope that situation has quieted."

Delilah nodded. "In fact, Jeannie has been worried about you, which is why she invited us over today."

Aha! So, Jeannie had been up to something!

"How are you doing?" Delilah asked.

Renee divided a look between the twins' parents. "I finally found out why mei dat moved our family away, and I'm doing okay."

Chapter Twenty

A loud pounding sounded on Jerome's door. He groaned and pushed himself up from the sofa. After taking care of the animals, he'd planned to read and nap all day, but, of course, someone had to decide to visit him. He hoped it was a quick visit.

"Who is it?" he called on his way to the door.

"Who do you think?"

He almost laughed. Naturally, it was his twin coming to check on him under the guise of another argument. He could depend on his sister to be predictable if nothing else. He wrenched the door open and glared at her. "What do you want?"

"Is that how you greet a guest?"

"You're not a guest. You're mei schweschder." He leaned on the doorframe. "Are you here to bicker some more?"

She folded her arms over her green dress and lifted her chin. "Maybe."

He made a sweeping gesture toward his kitchen. "Well, you might as well come in and get comfortable." He started toward the counter. "Kaffi?"

"Nee."

"Juice?" He opened the refrigerator. "Milk? Water?"

"Nee!" Impatience vibrated in his twin's voice.

He shut the refrigerator door and spun toward her. "Okay. I'll bite." He pressed his hip against the kitchen counter. "Why are you here then?"

"To talk."

He raised his hands, palms up. "So talk."

She rubbed her forehead. "You're truly aggravating, Jerome."

He slipped his hands into the pockets of his trousers.

"I can tell that you're hurting." She pointed to her chest. "I can feel it in here too. That's why I told you that you can't lie to me. We're more than just siblings." She gestured between them. "We're zwillingbopplin. We're connected. And that's why I need you to be honest with me and tell me what's wrong."

He shrugged.

"Come on, Jerome…" She dragged out his name. "Stop playing games with me. Stop egging me on and pulling me into an argument just to get me to leave. *Talk* to me." She took two steps toward him. "You haven't been the same since the accident. You can fool other people, but you can't fool me."

He turned toward the window and spotted a horse in the pasture and a buggy nearby. Was that Dat's horse? He couldn't tell from this angle. "Who's here?"

"What?" she asked.

"Who's here?" He nodded toward Martha's house. "Visiting."

"Mamm and Dat."

"Is that why you came here? You want me to come over and visit?"

"Ya." She folded her arms over her middle. "I invited them because I thought maybe they could help pull you and Renee out of your bad moods." Then she held up a hand. "But I don't want you to visit with them until you tell me the truth."

He started toward the hallway. "I'll get my hat."

"Nee!" She stomped after him. "We're not leaving this haus until you tell me what's wrong."

Ignoring her, he reached for his hat, which hung from a peg on the wall.

"This is about Renee, isn't it?" she asked.

He froze with his hand on his hat.

"Aha! I hit a nerve." She actually sounded proud of herself. "You're upset because of Renee. I could tell there was something brewing between you two. I couldn't quite put my finger on it, but there's an energy there. It's obvious that you care for each other."

"It doesn't matter how I feel because she's leaving," he said, setting his hat on his head. "She found the information she was searching for, so it's only a matter of time before she returns to Ohio." He worked to keep a stoic expression on his face, even though his words were almost painful to say.

"But what if she didn't leave?"

"Never gonna happen." His tone was flat.

"With Gott all things are possible. What if she did stay, Jerome? What if you told her that you cared about her and you wanted a future with her and you asked her to stay, and she said yes?"

He shook his head. "She'd never say yes to me."

"Why do you believe that?"

Jerome felt the wall he'd been building around his heart begin to crack. He turned and started toward his bedroom. It was best that he remain by himself today. He was too emotional for company. "I'm going to take a nap. You can let yourself out. Tell Mamm and Dat I said hello and I'll see them soon."

"Oh no you don't!" Jeannie's footsteps sounded behind him before she slipped past him and blocked the door to his bedroom. "I'm not leaving until you talk to me, and until you're honest with me." Her lower lip wavered. "Please, Bruder. Tell me what's wrong, so I can help you."

Ugh. Now his twin was playing dirty. He couldn't stand it when women cried, especially the ones he cared about the most. His sister knew this well, and she also knew exactly how to manipulate him.

"Jeannie," he began, his voice sounding thick. "I'm no gut to anyone. That's why it's better that I lay low until Renee leaves." He pointed toward the hallway. "Now I've told you the truth, and you can go."

Jeannie's blue eyes studied him. "Nee, that's not it."

He leaned his head back and groaned. "I tell you the truth, and you still don't believe me? What's the point, Jeannie?"

"Why do you think you're not gut enough for Renee?"

"I'm not gut enough for anyone."

"Why?"

"Because all I do is hurt the people I love." His voice was tremulous, and he worked to rein in his emotions.

"You love her." Jeannie's voice was soft, almost reverent.

Dipping his chin, he pressed his fingers into his eyes.

"Jerome, this is so gut. It means that Gott sent her here to help you heal."

"Nee, nee, nee." He shook his head and glowered as he met her hopeful expression. "I won't ever heal, and I don't want to. I don't deserve to."

His twin rested her hand on his shoulder. "Gott forgives you, Jerome. You need to forgive yourself."

"It's not that easy," he whispered, his voice gravelly.

"It can be, Jerome. You need to allow yourself the same grace that Gott's love gives us."

Her words struck him silent. If only he could believe her.

"Just listen to me," she began. "Gott loves you, and so do I. And so do Mamm and Dat, and I think Renee does too. She hasn't been the same since you two stopped talking. I can feel how much you love her." Her fingers pressed into her collarbone. "And I think that if you're honest with her, she might open her heart to you."

He sniffed and wiped his eyes.

"Please come over to the haus with me. You can visit with Mamm, Dat, and Renee." She looped her arm through his. "I promise you don't have to talk. I won't make you open up with your feelings."

"I'd rather be alone."

"Okay." She started down the hallway. "I'll tell Mamm and Dat that you don't want to see them. Then they'll come over here and ask you a zillion questions about what's wrong." She continued toward the door. "See ya, Jerome," she sang with a little wave.

He ground his teeth together. Oh, his sister could be impossible!

"Jeannie..." He hoped his tone held a hint of a warning.

She whirled around. "Then come on!" She beckoned him.

Ugh! She always won!

"Fine," he growled.

She grinned, and he rolled his eyes.

"I don't feel like I should share the reason since it's private," Renee said. "But I can tell you that mei dat was upset about something that happened in mei mammi's past. He found out, and he couldn't find it in his heart to forgive her."

Delilah patted Renee's arm. "You seem like you've accepted the secret, whatever it is, and I'm glad to hear that."

Harvey looked down at his mug then up again. "I can't imagine not forgiving mei mamm or dat. We're taught to forgive, and it's never an option not to."

"That's exactly how I feel. And the letters that mei mammi left for me to read are sad. She died with a broken heart. All she ever wanted was her family back." Renee tried to smile past the tears clogging her throat. "I wrote mei mamm a letter, and I told her how I feel about it. Naturally, I forgive mei dat for the pain he caused, but it still hurts."

"I'm happy that you finally found your answer. Does that mean you'll be leaving soon?" Delilah frowned.

Renee tried to gather her response just as the back door squeaked.

"Look who I found," Jeannie sang before she fluttered into the kitchen.

Jerome stood in the doorway, and Renee's heart wrenched as his gaze met hers. For a moment she felt the world slip away, and it was as if they were the only two people in the room. His bright, intelligent blue eyes were locked on hers, and the intensity in his expression urged her to grab his arm, yank him out to the porch, and force him to talk to her until they ran out of words—if that could even be possible.

But that would be inappropriate. He'd made it clear he wanted her to stay away from him, which was probably why it took Jeannie so long to bring him over for a visit.

"We were wondering where you were." Delilah's voice broke through Renee's thoughts.

Jerome said nothing, and Renee's stomach tightened. Was he going to turn and leave? Could he not stand to be in the same room with her?

"Are you going to join us, sohn?" Harvey asked. "Or do we need to force you to sit down?"

Jeannie brought another plate, fork, and mug to the table before she poured Jerome some coffee. "Sit, Jerome." His sister's tone made it sound as if she was ordering a child to follow the rules, and for a moment, Renee was certain he'd leave, but, instead, he did as he was told.

They all bowed their heads in silent prayer before Jeannie cut the cheesecake and distributed pieces. While they ate, the five of them visited, with Jeannie and her parents doing most of the talking. They discussed their fabric store, community members, and their plans for the upcoming summer.

Jerome mostly listened, and when someone spoke to him, he kept his responses short. Renee studied his expression, and she longed to know what he was thinking. She took in his stony countenance, and she tried to recall his radiant smile. She yearned to find a way to convince him to smile at her again, but she feared that she'd lost that privilege when he decided he no longer wanted or needed her to be close to him.

She knew one thing for sure—Jerome's absence had left a hole in her heart.

At that moment, she realized it was time to go home. She knew what she had to do with the farm, and now it was time to put her plan into action.

Later that afternoon, Jerome and his father walked outside to hitch up Harvey's horse and buggy.

"I'm so glad we had time to visit today," Delilah told Jeannie and Renee after they'd finished cleaning up the kitchen.

Renee felt a stitch in her chest as Delilah pulled her in for a hug. She'd be heading home to Ohio soon—possibly even before the next church service if her plan came together quickly.

Delilah rested her hand on Renee's shoulder. "I want to tell you that I'm glad you found out the truth. Don't forget that no matter what, Harvey, Jeannie, Jerome, and I are here for you. I wrote your mamm a letter, and I invited her to come visit. I'm hoping she'll write back soon and tell me she wants to come. We'll always welcome you all here, no matter what you decide to do with the farm, okay?"

Renee's eyes misted over. "Danki, Delilah."

Jeannie wrapped her arms around her mother's neck. "It was so gut seeing you, Mamm, and I'll see you again tomorrow at work."

"You'd better," Delilah teased, and they both laughed.

The three of them walked outside and joined the men standing by the horse and buggy.

"Are we ready?" Harvey asked his wife.

"Ya." Delilah hugged Jerome and whispered something in his ear.

Jerome nodded and patted her back before she sat in the buggy. Then he waved to his parents as their horse started down the driveway.

"Gut nacht," Jeannie told her twin before she scooted toward the house and disappeared inside.

With a nod at Renee, Jerome began walking toward his little house.

"Wait, Jerome." Renee's pulse zoomed as she followed him. "I need to talk to you."

He stopped and faced her, his expression blank. At that moment, he reminded her of when she'd first met him, and his coldness formed a block of ice in her chest.

"I've been doing a lot of thinking," she began. "And I've accomplished what I set out to do here, so I think it's time for me to go home." She paused and waited for a reaction. All he offered her was a stiff nod, and his apparent disinterest sent a pang spiraling through her. "I was considering putting the farm up for sale, but another thought occurred to me. What if I signed it over to you?"

His eyes widened and shock flickered over his face. "Why would you do that?"

"Because this is your home." She pointed to the daadihaus. "This is where you've lived for more than two years, right?"

He shook his head. "Renee, I'm not family."

"But you were mei mammi's family," she countered. "I could tell by how you've spoken about mei mammi that you took care of her. You were the only family she had. You deserve this place."

He shook his head again. "Nee. That's not right. It's legally yours. I heard what Belinda told you, Renee. This land is worth at least a million dollars." He scoffed. "That's *a lot* of money. I can't let you give that away. It would be life-changing for you and your parents. It's yours, Renee. I don't deserve it."

"Ya, you do, and I've already discussed it with my lawyer. All he has to do is draw up the paperwork. I'll sign everything over to you, and then I'll go home."

The words hung between them for a moment, and she linked her fingers together, waiting for him to tell her that he wanted to stay. But he only gawked at her.

Finally, he licked his lips. "Sleep on it," he said. "Don't make any hasty decisions. We can discuss it tomorrow." Then he turned and walked away.

"Gut nacht," she called after him, but he kept moving.

And her heart sank with the feeling that he was walking right out of her life forever.

Chapter Twenty-One

Jerome sat up with a start. Someone was screaming his name. A strange smell reached his nostrils. Smoke?

Fear gripped him and he jumped out of bed, yanking on trousers and a T-shirt on his way to the door.

"Jerome!" His twin's voice was frantic as she pounded on the door. "Hurry! It's an emergency! The haus is on fire!"

He pushed open the door, and Jeannie stood on his porch with tears pouring down her face. She pointed toward Martha's house, where flames licked up the side of the building, and smoke poured from the roof.

His stomach fell like a rock. He grabbed his sister by her shoulders. "Where's Renee?"

"In the haus," she managed between sobs. "I screamed for her, and I tried to get to her, but I couldn't. The flames, and the smoke…" Her voice broke.

"Call 911!" he hollered, racing toward the house.

Help me save her, God! Please!

Renee never expected to die this way...

She awoke with a gasp. Her eyes burned as soon as she opened them. She tried to suck in air, but she could only cough. And then she choked and coughed again.

What was happening? Why couldn't she breathe?

Her eyes stung and immediately watered, blurring what little she could see. She felt around on her nightstand for her battery powered lantern. Where had it gone?

A crash sounded. Was that her lantern hitting the floor?

She held up a hand in front of her face, but she couldn't see it. What was swirling around her, choking her?

Smoke?

But if there's smoke, then there must be a fire...

Is Mammi's house on fire?

Panic scratched her throat while she continued to cough. She tried to call out to Jeannie, but her voice sounded like a croak.

She had to find Jeannie and get out of this house before it was too late!

Gott, please, save us!

Coughing, she crawled out of her bed onto the floor. She swiped a hand over her eyes and tried to orient herself, but there was a cloud of smoke stealing the air and fogging her vision. Where was the door? Or the window?

A thump sounded, and she thought she heard a voice. Was that Jeannie? Or maybe Jerome?

Gott, please!

She crawled, keeping her body flush with the floor, and she bumped into her dresser. Why was the dresser in the wrong place?

Her lungs burned, and she couldn't stop coughing. She couldn't find the door, and she didn't have the strength to stand up and look for the window. All of the fight went out of her. She was just so tired.

Hugging her arms around her middle, she thought, *this is it.* She was going to die without having a chance to say goodbye to her mother.

Forgive me, Mamm!

A crash sounded. Was that glass breaking?

"Renee!" Jerome's voice rang out over her coughs. "Renee! Where are you?"

She tried to respond, but her words were choked off by another coughing fit.

"Follow the sound of my voice," he instructed. "I'm at the window. Hurry! The haus is nearly engulfed in flames. Renee! Renee!" He repeated her name while she crawled in the direction of his voice.

When she reached the wall, she slowly stood, and strong hands grabbed her arms and lifted her out of the window before carrying her across the yard.

Sirens wailed closer and closer.

A blanket was wrapped around her shoulders, and Renee shivered despite the humid June night. She kept her eyes closed while she fought against another coughing fit and worked to catch her breath.

"It's okay." Jerome's deep voice was next to her ear. "You're safe now. The paramedics are almost here, and they'll take care of you."

Renee's eyes opened. "Jeannie! Where's Jeannie?" Her voice croaked.

"She's safe," Jerome said. "She got out of the haus and ran over and woke me up. Then she called 911 from the phone shanty while I came for you."

Renee turned to where Jeannie stood with neighbors just as a fire engine rolled up the driveway, followed by two ambulances.

Her eyes focused on her grandmother's house, which was completely engulfed in flames, and her heart began to break. Then she gasped and stood.

"Sit, Renee," he instructed, gently tugging on her arm.

"Mei mammi's wooden box," she said. "Where is it?"

He shook his head. "I don't know."

"But—"

"Shh." He took her hand and led her toward the ambulance. "You need to be seen by the EMTs. We'll worry about your mammi's wooden box later."

She glanced down and cried out in surprise at the sight of a bloody gash on his hand. "You're bleeding, Jerome!"

"I'm fine." He shook his head, but she took a corner of the blanket and wrapped it around his injured palm. "I cut my hand on glass after I broke the window with a rock."

Her heart swelled as she looked up at him. "Jerome," she whispered. "You saved my life."

He ran a finger down her cheek, and she leaned into his touch. Then he tilted her chin up. "Renee, I'm so sorry," he began, his voice sounding husky. "I'm...I'm—" His eyes locked on her mouth and then he dipped his chin. His lips were a breath away from her.

Renee was overcome with a heady rush of emotions, and her legs felt like cooked noodles. She grasped Jerome's muscular shoulders to hold herself upright.

Suddenly the piercing screams of sirens were closer, and lights flashed around them.

"Jerome! Jerome!" a man hollered.

Jerome dropped the blanket and stepped away from her, and his face twisted up in a ferocious glower. "Murray!" he bellowed as the neighbor rushed over. "Did you do this?" He pointed to the house. "Is that why you said I needed to watch my back, Murray? Is it because you planned this and you almost killed Renee and my sister?" His hands were balled into fists, and the small, older man backed away from him.

Renee's mouth dropped open. She'd never seen or heard such fury erupt from Jerome.

"No, no!" Murray yelled, holding up his hands. "I didn't do it, but I called the police." He pointed a shaky finger toward a squad car parked beside an ambulance and the fire engines. "I called the police because I saw who did it."

Renee sucked in a startled breath as a pair of arms wrapped around her.

"Let's get you to the ambulance," Jeannie said, steering her toward the waiting EMTs.

Renee leaned against her friend. "I was so worried about you." Her words broke and sobs erupted from her throat.

"I know," Jeannie said as her own tears began to fall. "And I was worried about you too."

Jerome's right leg vibrated as a police officer wrote on his notepad and then looked across the picnic table at him and Murray. Behind him, the house continued to burn while firefighters worked to put it out.

"Now, Mr. Robertson," the officer began, "you're telling me that you saw who started the fire?"

Murray nodded his head. "The person was wearing all black, including a black hoodie, which is strange since it's almost seventy-five degrees. I saw the person running from the house and then I saw a small sedan drive away. And I heard a boom, saw smoke, and I called 911."

Jerome felt like he was going to come right out of his skin. He didn't want to sit at this table and discuss what happened. No, he wanted to run out to the ambulance and hold Renee. He glanced over to where an EMT spoke to her. She was wrapped in a blanket, and she wore an oxygen mask on her face. Jeannie sat beside her, also wrapped in a blanket and wearing an oxygen mask.

He could feel adrenaline rushing through his veins. He wanted to run, wanted to scream, and wanted to find the person who had done this.

He rubbed a hand over his face as the events of the night rushed through his mind. He'd almost kissed Renee. That was the moment when he finally admitted to himself that he was crazy about her and angry with himself for pushing her away.

But how could they even have a relationship? She was leaving. She'd already told him that she wanted to give him the farm before she left, but he didn't want the farm. At the moment he realized that all he wanted was *her*, but he didn't know how to make that work without ruining her life.

"Excuse me, Mr. Graber?"

Jerome's eyes slid to the police officer who seemed to be around his age. "Yes?"

"What do you remember?"

"Officer Franklin," one of the EMTs said as she walked over. "Um, Miss Mast is insisting that I check Mr. Graber's hand."

She pointed to Jerome, and he held up his bloodied right hand. He'd wrapped it in the white T-shirt that he'd worn to bed, and now his shirt was covered with blood. His hand throbbed. But he'd been so consumed with everything else going on around him that he hadn't even noticed how badly he'd cut it up when he used a rock to break Renee's window and then swept away the glass with his hand.

Officer Franklin nodded toward the EMT. "We can talk while you bandage it. What do you remember about tonight?"

"My sister, Jeannie, is staying in the house with Renee, and she woke me up screaming that the house was on fire. I think the same person who did this is the person who has been harassing us since mid-April." He nodded toward the house, which continued to burn.

Officer Franklin stopped writing and leveled his gaze on Jerome. "Harassing you since mid-April?"

Jerome nodded and winced while the EMT cleaned out his wounds. The scent of burning wood was still strong.

"Tell me about this harassment," Officer Franklin said.

For the next several minutes, Jerome explained the threatening letter, break-in, graffiti, and smashed teapot incidents. He answered questions and explained that he didn't have any evidence since the letter was most likely burning along with the house. Firefighters called to each other while working to get the blaze under control.

"Why didn't you call the police?" Officer Franklin asked.

"That's not our way in this community," Jerome said, and the officer shook his head while he took more notes.

Officer Franklin then turned to Murray again. "You said you saw the car tonight?"

"I did," Murray said. "It was a black sedan."

"That's what Belinda Walker drives," Jerome said.

"Who?" the officer asked.

While the EMT finished cleaning out Jerome's wounds and bandaged his hand, Jerome explained who Belinda was and how aggressive she'd been.

"I'll interview her," Officer Franklin said.

Jerome nodded before continuing to answer more questions. He silently prayed that God would help the police get to the bottom of this. It was time for the harassment to stop and the assailant to face punishment for their crimes.

Renee rested on a gurney and examined her grandmother's house while she sucked in oxygen through a mask. The fire department continued to work diligently to put out the flames, but Renee already knew the house was a total loss. Her heart began to fracture as her family's legacy literally went up in smoke before her. Where would she stay now? And what about her clothes? And where were her grandmother's letters? Had they been destroyed in the fire too?

Tears built up in her eyes, but she'd done enough crying. It was time for her to be strong. She scanned the area, taking in all the firefighters, rescue vehicles, and police officers, until she finally found Jerome sitting at a picnic table. He spoke to a police officer and to Murray while one of the EMTs bandaged his hand.

Her pulse skittered as she recalled how he'd rescued her and then nearly kissed her. Her thoughts churned while she tried to make heads or tails of what happened between them. Did that mean he cared for her? Nothing made sense right now.

"Jeannie! Renee!" a familiar voice called.

"Mamm!" Jeannie yelled from the gurney beside her. "Dat!"

Jeannie's parents rushed over to the ambulance, and Jeannie jumped into her father's arms. "I called you right after I called 911. I'm so glad you heard the phone ringing."

"Ya, me too." Harvey touched her shoulder. "We called our driver and thankfully he was able to bring us right over. We wanted to get here as quickly as we could."

"Ach, nee!" Delilah cupped a hand to her mouth while she took in the fire. "This is just terrible. I'm so relieved you're both okay." She handed both Jeannie and Renee robes, which they pulled on over their nightgowns, and also gave them each a scarf to cover their hair. Once Jeannie was properly covered, Delilah pulled her daughter in for a tight hug.

Tears flowed from Jeannie's eyes. "Jerome broke a window and saved Renee. If he hadn't been here..."

Delilah turned to Renee and opened her arms. Renee allowed Delilah to pull her in for a warm hug and more tears broke free. Renee held on and sobbed into her shoulder as all the fear and grief poured out.

"It's okay, mei liewe," Delilah murmured. "Let it all out."

Renee worked to get control of her emotions.

"Excuse me, I'm Officer Smith." A female police officer, who looked to be in her early thirties, approached. "I'd like to interview Ms. Graber and Ms. Mast about what happened here tonight." She pointed toward Jerome's house. "Officer Franklin and I would like us to talk in Mr. Graber's home."

Delilah handed Renee a tissue, and she blotted her eyes and nose.

After the EMTs checked their vitals one last time, Renee and Jeannie walked arm in arm toward the house and took a seat at the kitchen table across from Jerome and the other officer. Jeannie held Renee's hand while they went over what they remembered from each of the incidents, starting with the threatening letter, missing teapot, and graffiti, and ending with the fire.

While she shared her point of view, Renee frequently glanced over at Jerome and found him wiping his eyes and sniffing. Her lungs constricted for him, and she longed to cradle his injured hand in hers and thank him for being her hero. When his eyes finally met hers, he gave her a watery smile that made her heart dance.

They went through every detail over and over again until Renee was tired of talking. It was obvious that they had no idea who had done this. Talking until they were blue in the face felt like a waste of time.

By the time they finished their interviews, it was after two in the morning, and Renee had a difficult time keeping her eyes open.

"I think we're done here," Officer Franklin said. "My partner and I will interview the folks you've mentioned. We'll be in touch." He slapped his business card onto the table.

Officer Smith smiled. "Thank you for your time. I'm so glad you all got out safe. If you think of something you forgot, please give me a call." She handed her business card to Jeannie.

The two officers headed for the door, and Jeannie followed them.

"I'm going to find Mamm and Dat," she said before hurrying outside.

Chapter Twenty-Two

Renee scooted around the table, sat beside Jerome, and took his injured hand in hers. She moved her fingers over his, and her soft touch sent happy tingles floating up his arm despite his painful wounds. "Are you okay?"

Jerome nodded, and a heavy ball of anguish formed in his gut. His eyes roved over her face, taking in the soot peppering her cheeks, and he tried to hold back his emotions. Why couldn't he stop his tears? He felt like a dummkopp. He needed to get himself together.

But he knew the answer to that—it was guilt. He should've protected her. The person who did this should've never gotten that close. He needed to find this person and make sure that the police locked them up and threw away the key so that they could never hurt Renee or his sister again.

Renee touched his cheek. "Jerome, talk to me," she said. "Are you okay?"

"Yeah." His voice was scratchy. "You?"

She nodded, but he spotted tears in her eyes, and his lungs compressed.

The door opened, and Dat came into the kitchen. "The fire captain said that you're okay to stay here tonight, Jerome. The fire is out. I checked on the animals, and they're all fine. The other buildings are safe," he told Jerome before looking at Renee. "You can come with us." He pointed to the clock. "It's after two. You need to get some rest."

Renee stood, and her eyes lingered on Jerome. He could feel her prodding him to walk with her.

Jerome pushed himself up from the table and followed them outside, where the entire farm was illuminated by lights from the fire trucks. The smell of smoke overwhelmed him as he glanced around the farm. Martha's house was reduced to a pile of ash, and once again shame assaulted him.

I'm sorry I couldn't protect your granddaughter or your home, Martha. Forgive me.

Renee sniffed beside him. "The letters. They're all gone," she said. "I have nothing left from mei mammi. Nothing that connects me to the past and my family."

Jeannie looped her arm around Renee's shoulder. "What matters is that we're all here." She looked up at Jerome and then back at Renee. "The three of us. We have each other. Gott protected us." She touched Jerome's arm. "I'm so thankful. We're all blessed."

Renee nodded. "You're right."

"Who do you think did this?" Dat asked as he came to stand beside Jerome.

"The police are going to check into the Realtor, but why would she burn down the haus?"

Dat shrugged. "Well, if she wants to give Renee a reason to sell, destroying a haus would do it. And a developer would only have to clear the land before building apartments, a neighborhood, or retail space."

"That's true, but it just doesn't feel right." Jerome's eyes moved toward the road and Murray's house. "Murray seemed so eager to help. He's odd, but I don't think he'd be willing to cooperate if he was involved."

"Unless he likes the attention," Dat said. "Some people act badly because they want the focus to be on them."

"I don't know…" Jerome shook his head. "Something's bugging me, but I can't put my finger on what it is."

Dat patted his shoulder. "You need to leave that to the police. Let them do their job."

Jerome examined his injured hand. "I don't know how I'm going to take care of my chores."

"Don't worry about it. You get some rest, and I'll be back here in a few hours to take care of the animals."

"You don't have to do that, Dat. I'll figure it out."

"Nee, sohn. It's time you let someone help you for once." Dat indicated the fire truck. "I also talked to the fire captain, and he said their investigation will be over by noon tomorrow. I'm going to call around and get folks out here to help us clear the land and start rebuilding."

Jerome nodded and once again felt overwhelmed. His eyes started to sting, and he rubbed the bridge of his nose. Why was he so quick to tears? It had to be the exhaustion.

Dat turned toward Mamm, Jeannie, and Renee, who were discussing sharing clothes until they had time to make new dresses. "Let's get these two home so they can rest."

Renee nodded, and he could see the exhaustion etched on her beautiful face.

Jerome said good night to his family, and Dat ushered Mamm and Jeannie toward the driveway, where a green van, owned by Dat's driver, waited for them.

Renee's eyes focused on Jerome and then she threw her arms around his waist and pulled him against her. "Danki for rescuing me, Jerome," she said, before she released him and hurried after his family.

He gulped as she disappeared past a fire truck.

"Here's a clean nightgown," Delilah told Renee while they stood in the spare room across the hallway from Jeannie's room. She hung the nightgown on a wall peg. "And here are a couple of Jeannie's dresses. I'm so glad she didn't take all of them over to your haus."

Jeannie stood by the doorway. "I think my shoes will fit you too, and I have an extra prayer covering."

Renee's eyes brimmed with tears. "I can't thank you enough."

"Don't be silly." Delilah sat on the bed beside Renee. "That's what we do in our community—we take care of each other." She touched Renee's cheek. "You're like a second dochder to me. If you need something, then tell us. We'll help you. And Harvey is going to organize a rebuild. He's going to see if they can start clearing the land tomorrow."

"Really?" Renee's voice came out in a squeak.

"Ya." Delilah stood. "Now you get cleaned up and go to bed. Don't worry about getting up early tomorrow." She chuckled. "What am I saying? It's already Monday. Sleep in and rest." She looked at

Jeannie. "You and Dat can go over to the farm with Renee this week. I'll worry about the store. Mei schweschder will come and help." She moved to the hallway. "Get some sleep." Then she closed the door gently behind her.

Renee turned her gaze on Jeannie, who stood by the door. "Will you stay in here with me?"

"Ya, I was going to offer since it's a queen-sized bed."

"I don't want to be alone. I know when I close my eyes, I'll see those flames."

"I understand." Jeannie sniffed. "I woke up when I heard a crash."

"A crash?" Renee sat up taller.

"Ya, I told Officer Franklin while you were talking to the EMTs. It was like a window smashing and then I thought I heard footsteps. It sounded like they were in the family room, but I don't know. Maybe I heard the footsteps before the crash?" She shook off the memory. "It's all a blur now, but I think someone was in the house before they started the fire."

"They were in the family room?" Renee hugged her arms around her middle. "I put the wooden box on the coffee table when your folks came to visit." She pushed herself back on the bed and leaned against the headboard. "Do you think whoever broke in took mei mammi's box?"

Jeannie's brow puckered. "Why would they take your box?"

"I don't know. It seems silly when I say it. Never mind."

Jeannie climbed onto the bed beside her. "Is everything okay between you and mei bruder?"

Renee moved her hands over the hem of her nightgown while her mind replayed how Jerome had rescued her, injuring himself in the process, almost kissed her, and the way he looked at her before she left tonight. Her chest felt heavy with grief over losing her grandmother's house and possibly also losing his precious friendship.

"I can tell you two like each other."

Renee hugged her legs to her chest. "I care for him. In fact, I might even love him, but he rejected me." She explained how he pushed her away the day she found the letters. "I thought he might care for me, but now I'm not sure." She decided to keep the detail about him almost kissing her close to her heart. It felt too personal to share.

Jeannie frowned, and her blue eyes glistened. "It's not you, Renee. He can't forgive himself for what happened with Amanda."

"He told me about the accident, that night that the porch was graffitied. We sat in the family room and talked for more than an hour, and he finally opened up to me about it."

Jeannie sniffed. "Amanda was one of my dearest friends, and when she died, it was horrific. Devastating. And Jerome…" She dabbed a tissue on her eyes. "Mei bruder was broken, and he's been broken ever since. He can't forgive himself for her death. He carries that guilt with him always. It's like it's permanently imprinted on his heart." Then her pretty face brightened a bit. "But I believe you can help him move past the guilt. You can teach him how to love again, and you can show him that he's worthy of love."

Renee sighed. "I don't think so. I had believed I might be able help him, but after he told me he wanted me to stay away, I realized that I was wrong. I thought maybe Gott led me here to make a difference in Jerome's life, but I realized that was prideful. Instead, I think I was only supposed to take care of mei mammi's estate and find out the truth in order to settle my own curiosity and help me better understand mei daed."

She moved her fingers over the beautiful log-cabin-patterned quilt covering the bed. "I made a decision yesterday. I'm going to sign the farm over to Jerome and return home to Ohio." Her words wavered. "I might even go home later this week after everything is settled."

"Nee." Jeannie's expression was fierce, reminding Renee of when Jerome had interrogated Murray earlier in the evening. "You can't leave."

"I have to leave. I promised my parents I'd be home by August. Now that I know the truth, it's better if I go back now." Renee wrapped her arms around her middle again, as if doing so would stop her heart from breaking.

Jeannie angled her body toward Renee. "Just listen to me," she began. "Jerome and I have a connection. We're zwillingbopplin. I know when he's feeling something overwhelming, and he feels things with me too. And when it comes to you, he has some very strong feelings."

Renee swallowed a gasp as a fluttering sensation filled her chest.

"I understand that you feel Gott leading you back to Ohio, but please don't leave before asking mei bruder to open up to you. I think you're the person Gott is calling to break down the wall he's built about his heart."

Jeannie's words settled in Renee's soul.

"Promise me you'll try to talk to him," Jeannie added.

Renee nodded. "Okay."

"Gut." Jeannie stood. "I'm going to get cleaned up and put on a fresh nightgown. You should do the same." She disappeared through the doorway.

Renee stared after her friend and then opened her heart to God.

Lord, please lead me to the path You've chosen for me. If I'm supposed to be the one who helps Jerome's heart heal, then please give me the opportunity and the words to reach him.

Then she pushed herself up from the bed and changed into the fresh nightgown before snuggling under the quilt. Her mind spun with everything that had happened that night, and she waited for sleep to find her.

Monday, June 2

Jerome found his father in the barn with the cows later that morning. The milkers were hooked up and working while Dat stood nearby. Jerome limped over to him, and he was certain every single muscle in his body screamed in pain—not to mention the throbbing gashes in his right hand. He'd truly overdone it when he flew into action to rescue Renee, but he was grateful he'd managed to save her. He'd do it again in a heartbeat.

Thank You, Gott.

"Gude mariye." Dat grinned. "Or should I say good afternoon?"

Jerome slowly sidled up to him. Even his good leg was on fire. "I didn't realize you enjoyed milking cows."

"Didn't I tell you I worked on mei daadi's farm when I was a teenager?"

"You may have mentioned it once or twice." Jerome lowered himself onto a few bales of hay, hoping to soothe his nagging body parts.

"I fed the horses and chickens too," Dat said before sitting on a bale beside him. "You like working here?"

"Ya. That's why I took the job."

Dat rubbed his graying light brown beard. "Why did you turn down your onkel's offer to work as his plumbing apprentice after the accident?"

Jerome was so stunned by the question that he flinched as if his father had slapped him. "Why are you asking me about that now?"

"Because we've never talked about it, but I've always wondered why you gave up on everything after the crash."

Jerome gawked at his father. "Amanda *died*, Dat."

"I know, sohn." Dat's expression was full of empathy. "But you didn't."

Jerome opened and closed his mouth like a fish stuck out of water.

"Sohn, I know that you blame yourself for what happened, but you didn't kill Amanda. That other driver did, and no matter what, it was Gott's will."

Jerome shook his head. "It's not that simple. We weren't supposed to be out that night. It was my fault." He jammed a finger against his chest. "I'm the reason why she's dead, and I have to live with that."

"But you're *not* living. You gave up all of your dreams after that night, and it's painful for your mamm and me to watch you walk around in a daze, like your life is over. That's not what we want for you, and it's not what Gott wants for you. You're here, Jerome, and you're *alive*. You need to start acting like it."

Jerome shook his head. Dat was wrong.

"If you want to pursue a career as a plumber, then you should go for it."

Jerome pointed to his leg. "I'm injured."

"Nee, you're not." Dat smiled. "You saved Renee from a fire last night, Jerome. You care for these animals every day. If you want to be a plumber, then you need to call your onkel and ask him to make room for you. I know he'd do it."

"I like it here." Jerome scanned the barn and the herd to avoid his father's sympathetic face.

"Because you work alone."

Jerome's eyes snapped to his father's.

"Ya, I know you, sohn. You've been hiding here for more than two years. Farming is gut and important work. It's hard work. I learned that when I worked for mei daadi, but you've talked about becoming a plumber since you were six years old, and you went out on a job with your onkel. Don't give up on life, sohn. You're young, and if you want to change professions, you should do it now while you can."

Jerome tried to swallow against his dry throat. "Renee wants to sign the farm over to me."

Dat's eyebrows shot up. "She does?"

He nodded. "She told me yesterday before the fire. She said that she wants me to have it, and she's going back to Ohio."

"How do you feel about that?"

He shrugged despite the pain radiating inside.

Dat opened his mouth to speak but was cut off by another voice.

"Jerome!" Tim jogged over to him. "I heard about the fire. I'm so glad you're okay." He pointed toward the barn door. "There's at least two dozen men here to help, and a dumpster will be delivered soon."

Dat shook Tim's hand. "Your dat got my message."

"Ya. We're ready to start the cleanup." Tim shook Jerome's hand next. "Mei dat and I started calling members of the district as soon as we got word."

Jerome and Dat walked out of the barn with Tim. A line of buggies moved up the driveway toward the building, and Jerome's chest constricted. He didn't know what he'd do without his community.

Tim rubbed his hands together. "Let's get to work."

Chapter Twenty-Three

Renee and Jeannie got into the back of Autumn's van, and Renee covered her mouth to hide a yawn. She'd barely gotten three hours of sleep before she forced herself to get out of bed at ten that morning.

Since Jeannie was asleep beside her, she took a shower, dressed, and quietly padded downstairs to make breakfast. By the time Jeannie came down, the eggs, bacon, home fries, and toast were ready. It seemed that Renee had worked up an appetite after last night, but her heart and her body ached after the fire. She was anxious to get to the farm to see if there was anything left that she could salvage—particularly her grandmother's wooden box full of letters—but she was certain everything had been reduced to ashes.

"I heard there was a fire at a farm in Bird-in-Hand last night," Autumn said while she steered the van onto Old Philadelphia Highway. She peeked at them in the mirror. "Did you hear anything about it?"

Jeannie lifted her chin. "It was at Renee's farm."

"Oh no," Autumn said. "I'm so sorry to hear that."

Renee studied her driver's expression. Something seemed…off. But maybe it was her exhaustion making her overly emotional.

They drove on in silence for a while.

"Are you going to rebuild?" Autumn suddenly asked.

Renee peered up at the woman's reflection in the mirror and tried to decipher her expression. "Ya. Why?"

"Just wondering." She was quiet for a few moments. "Do you know what started the fire?"

"It was arson," Jeannie chimed in.

"Are you sure?"

"Ya, I'm sure. I heard someone prowling around inside the house, followed by a crash," Jeannie said. "It was arson for sure, and the police are investigating."

"Interesting," Autumn quipped. Her eyes met Renee's in the mirror. "Such a tragedy."

But her tone held no sympathy. Instead, it was flat and void of emotion.

Was Renee imagining the driver's strange reaction?

When they arrived at her grandmother's farm, the rancid scent of smoke and ash choked Renee's lungs. She and Jeannie disembarked the van before Jeannie paid Autumn.

"Thanks for the ride," Renee told the driver.

Jeannie rushed off toward the group of men working to clean up the pile of debris that had once been Renee's grandmother's precious home.

"Renee," Autumn said.

She spun toward the Englisher. "Ya?"

"Maybe you should consider going back to Ohio, since it's obvious someone doesn't want you here," Autumn said, before pushing her sunglasses farther up the bridge of her nose and backing the van out of the driveway.

Renee gaped at her while the comment echoed through her mind. The words had stung like an ice pick to her chest.

What exactly did Autumn mean, and why would she make such a cruel statement to someone who had lost her ancestral home?

She tried to file the comment away while she headed toward the knot of people working. Amish men yelled to each other in Pennsylvania Dutch while they loaded the debris into a large dumpster.

Moving closer to the concrete pad that had once been her grandmother's home, she didn't spot anything that could be salvaged, and she didn't see anything resembling the precious wooden box.

Had the box gone up in flames?

She searched the sea of people for Jerome and found him talking to an Amish man near the barn. She started toward him, taking in the large bandage on his right hand and the dark circles rimming his gorgeous blue eyes.

When his gaze tangled with hers, his lips lifted in a faint smile, sending a happy glow through her. And at that moment she knew two things for sure—she was in love with Jerome Graber, and she had no idea what to do about it.

Conversations buzzed around the farm later that afternoon while the men continued to work, cleaning up the debris. Tables set up near the barn held a variety of food that the women in the community had prepared. Jerome stood nearby while men moved down the line filling their plates, with Renee and Jeannie pitching in to help serve them.

Renee was beautiful in a dark green dress and apron, which were slightly too long for her. Most likely they belonged to his sister, who was a couple of inches taller than Renee. He had tried to talk to her earlier, but he kept getting interrupted by men who needed his help on various tasks. He'd already helped Melvin Yoder put in an order for supplies, which would be delivered Wednesday.

He turned his attention back to the worksite and tried to tamp down the frustration burning through him while he watched the men continue to work on cleaning up the remnants of the fire. He yearned to help. He wanted to do something to contribute, but instead, all he could do was watch from the sidelines. He glared at his injured right hand, which was the source of his disability.

His best friend sidled up to him. "Arson, right?"

"Huh?" Jerome studied Tim's expression.

"I said it was arson, right?"

"Possibly." He shared the details that his sister had told him last night. "Jeannie actually heard someone in the haus before the crash."

Tim gave a low whistle. "That's serious." He glanced toward the debris and then back at Jerome. "Who do you think did this?"

"I don't..." Jerome stopped speaking when he spotted Murray headed toward him. What was he doing here?

"Jerome! Jerome!" His neighbor rushed over, holding up his phone. "I need to show you something." The older man joined him and Tim. "I found something on my camera."

"Your camera?" Jerome squinted his eyes. "I thought you didn't have one."

"It's kinda hidden on the eaves of my house, but it's pointed at Martha's farm."

Jerome's posture stiffened as Murray moved his finger over his phone and then held the screen up in front of him and Tim.

"Watch this," Murray instructed.

Jerome's pulse rocketed while he watched a small sedan park in the driveway. A hooded figure climbed out of the car. A few moments later, smoke and flames shot up from the house. Then the figure returned to the car, and the vehicle sped out of the driveway.

"Have you given this to the police?" Jerome asked Murray.

"Yeah," the man insisted. "They just left my house. I sent them all of the files from my camera, including what I had the day that the other incidents happened here."

"The other incidents?" Jerome asked. "You have footage from the day the person left the letter and the day they damaged my buggy and graffitied Martha's porch?" When Murray nodded, Jerome's anger boiled over. "Why didn't you tell me you had a camera when I came to talk to you, and you refused to open the door?"

Murray's face fell. "I didn't want to get involved, but when I saw the fire, I knew that I'd been wrong." He paused and shook his head. "I should've been a good neighbor back then, but I'll do better from now on."

Jerome exhaled. He had to give the man credit for coming forward, even it was late. "That car," he began, pointing to the video, "it's on the other videos too?"

Murray nodded. "But I can't read the plate number. The police are going to try to use some of their fancy software to decipher it. It's obviously a small, dark-colored sedan. Possibly a Ford."

"And that means it's not the Realtor," Jerome muttered.

"What?" Tim asked.

"I'll explain later," he told his best friend, before addressing Murray again. "Thank you."

"You're welcome." Murray pointed toward the cleanup. "Would it be all right if I pitch in?"

Jerome smiled and held up his right hand. "That'd be great since I'm no help."

Murray nodded, pushed his cell phone into his back pocket, and then joined the men working on the cleanup.

"What were you saying about the Realtor?" Tim asked once the older man was gone.

"That car wasn't hers. Unless she has another car that she uses outside of her business appointments, it can't be her."

"Then who did this?"

"I don't know, but we're going to find out," Jerome said.

"We got the debris all cleaned up today," Tim said later that evening while they sat at Jerome's kitchen table. "As soon as the supplies arrive, we can start building you a new haus, Renee."

"Danki," Renee managed to say, fighting back the emotion that had gnawed at her all day long. She'd been so overwhelmed with appreciation for the members of the community who had come out to help her and Jerome. She was certain her grandmother would be just as thankful.

Jerome ate a bite of the hamburger casserole that one of the women had given them for supper and sipped from his glass of water. "I've been thinking all day about what Murray shared." He explained the videos he'd seen and described the small, dark-colored sedan. "I don't think the Realtor did it, and I'm convinced now that it wasn't Murray. So, what are we missing?"

Renee turned to Jeannie beside her. "Didn't you think Autumn was behaving strangely in the car this morning?"

"Ya," Jeannie said. "She asked about the fire, and it was like she already knew about it. Then she sounded sarcastic when she called it 'such a tragedy.'" She made air quotes with her hands.

"But she was even ruder after she dropped us off, and you walked away," Renee added.

"What did she say?" Jerome leaned forward, his expression full of curiosity.

"She said, 'Maybe you should consider going back to Ohio, since it's obvious someone doesn't want you here.'" Renee's stomach turned as she repeated the words. "I saw hate in her eyes."

A strange expression flickered over Jerome's face.

"Lately she's given me a strange feeling," Jeannie said. "She's been nosier than other Englishers."

"And she showed up out of nowhere," Tim added. "She has no family. She just appeared one day and said she wanted to drive for the Amish."

"You know her too?" Jeannie asked.

"Ya, she lives on the same street as my folks. She's renting a small haus over there."

Jerome tapped the table. "I realized something. She was listening that day at the hardware store when I told you about the threatening letter," he said. "And she gave me a ride the day that I asked for your help with the graffiti on the porch. I told her about it."

Renee inhaled sharply. "I told her about the letters and the wooden box."

Jeannie crossed to Jerome's counter and returned with a business card. "But why would Autumn want to hurt Renee and us?" She set the business card next to Jerome.

He glanced at it, and then his eyebrows lifted as he met Renee's stare. "What was your biological grandfather's name?"

"Raymond Wallace," she said. "Why?"

Jerome pushed the card over to Renee, and she read it:

Autumn Wallace Martin

Wallace!

Renee's body vibrated with shock. "Do you think...?"

"Ya, I do." Jerome nodded. "I think we found her motive."

"Hold on." Tim held up his hands. "Stop speaking in code and explain. Please."

Renee took a deep breath and then said, "My biological grandfather was an Englisher named Raymond Wallace. According to this business card, Autumn's maiden name was Wallace, and Jerome and I think that maybe Autumn and I could be related somehow."

"And that's why she's targeting you," Jeannie said, finishing her thought. "She knows that you're related, and she thinks she's entitled to something."

"Maybe," Renee said.

Jerome pushed back his chair and stood. "Let's find out." He started toward the door.

"Where are you going?" Renee trailed after him while her heart pounded in her chest.

Jerome frowned. "To call her."

"And say what?" Tim asked.

"I'm going to ask her to come over here and talk to us," Jerome said. "When she gets here, we'll ask her if she's the one who's been harassing us all along."

"Nee," Renee said. "What if she's dangerous?"

"We won't know if she's the one unless we ask," Jerome insisted.

Jeannie threw her hands up in the air. "What if she doesn't admit it? Then we're wasting our time."

A mixture of anger and determination flashed over Jerome's countenance. "If she's arrogant enough to tell Renee to go back to Ohio, then she's arrogant enough to come over here and talk to us."

Renee tried to swallow past the lump of apprehension in her throat. "Jerome, I have a bad feeling," she said.

Jerome's eyes locked on Renee's. "We need to figure out who's trying to hurt you before it's too late." He extended his left hand toward her. "Do you trust me?"

She threaded her fingers with his, and his warm skin caressed hers. "Ya, I trust you."

"Gut. Then I'll call her." He let his hand drop to his side.

Renee whispered a prayer of protection as he hurried out the door.

Jerome returned a few minutes later. "Autumn's on her way over."

Renee wrung her hands. "What did you say to her?"

"I told her that we wanted to talk to her about something, and she said she'd be right over." He absently moved his left hand over the bandage on his right. "She seemed eager to talk to us too."

Renee shared a worried look with Jeannie while a pit expanded in her stomach.

Tim shook his head. "We need to be careful, Jerome. She could be narrisch."

"She most likely *is* crazy, and that's what I'm worried about," Jeannie added. "She's already threatened Renee and vandalized her porch. We should call the police *now*."

"Nee." Jerome crossed the small room and peeked out the window. The sun had begun to set, sending a rainbow of colors cascading across the sky. "Let's see what she has to say first."

A tense silence wafted over Jerome's kitchen while they waited for their visitor to arrive. Renee's mind buzzed with questions about Autumn. Could she be the person who had been harassing her since she'd arrived from Ohio?

And could she *actually* be Renee's relative—possibly her cousin? Would her blood relative deliberately treat her so badly and threaten her?

Renee rubbed her temples where a headache brewed. It seemed as if the world around her was spinning out of control.

Several minutes later, headlights swept across the small house as an engine motored up the driveway.

Jerome glanced out the window. "It's a small, dark sedan," he said. "This one is different from the van she uses when she drives us around. That means she has more than one vehicle. It looks like the car Murray's camera captured each time something sinister happened on the farm."

"So it *is* Autumn?" Jeannie asked, and her face clouded with worry.

"Looks that way." Jerome turned toward Renee. "I'm going outside to meet her."

"Nee. I will." Renee stalked toward the door.

He grabbed her hand. "Let me do the talking." He gave her hand a gentle squeeze. "I've told you more than once that I refuse to let anything happen to you."

The concern in Jerome's eyes sent warmth radiating through Renee, but she needed to stand up for herself and her grandmother's farm.

"I appreciate that, but I have to do this." She shook off his grip and marched toward the door just as a loud knock sounded. Her pulse drummed as she yanked the door open and found Autumn standing on the small porch. "Autumn," she said, her voice sounding strange to her own ears.

"Oh, hi, Renee." Autumn glanced past her. "Jerome called. Said he wanted to talk."

Renee eyed Autumn as a wave of confidence bubbled up inside of her. "Have you been harassing me since I came to Ohio?"

Something unreadable raced over Autumn's features. "What do you mean?"

"Did you leave a threatening note on my door?" she asked. When Autumn stared at her blankly, Renee continued, counting the offenses off on her fingers. "Did you break into my house, steal mei mammi's teapot, vandalize my porch, damage Jerome's buggy, and then burn down my house?" Her voice and her hands shook.

Autumn sneered. "Why would I do that?" she asked.

"Just tell the truth," Jerome's voice boomed. "Did you do it?"

Autumn glanced around the room. "Is this an interrogation?"

"Ya, it is." Tim took a step toward her. "Now, tell us the truth."

"Please," Renee added.

Seconds ticked by, punctuated by a clock ticking somewhere in Jerome's house. Renee held her breath, waiting for the woman to speak and admit to everything she'd done to terrorize Renee and her friends.

"Autumn," Renee began slowly, "are we related?"

The woman threw her arms up in the air. "Fine, fine. It's about time the truth came out anyway. Yes, we are related." She moved closer to Renee and then pointed between them. "You're my cousin. We have the same grandfather."

Renee nodded. "Raymond Wallace is your grandfather."

"*Was*," Autumn corrected. "He died a few years ago, and I got nothing. Absolutely nothing. Then my good-for-nothing husband left me, and he gave me nothing too." Her lips formed a thin line. "That's why, when I heard that you were coming here to take over the farm, I thought to myself—How is it fair that she gets *everything* while I get *nothing*. No job. No home. No family. Just *nothing*." She dropped her large purse on the floor with a thud, and it spilled open. "That's why I decided to have a little fun." She shrugged. "If I have to suffer, then someone else should too."

"You're saying you targeted Renee because you're unhappy?" Jerome asked, and his words were measured.

Jeannie scowled. "You wanted to spread around your sadness?"

"That's right." Autumn had the nerve to smile and actually appeared proud of herself.

"That's why you tried to kill me?" Renee asked. Despite trying to sound confident, she could hear the thickness in her voice. "You wanted me dead to fill some hole you have in your life?"

"No." Autumn shook her head, sadness flickering over her face. "I never meant to kill you."

"But the fire," Jeannie exclaimed, pointing in the direction of where Renee's mammi's house had once stood. "You almost killed both of us!"

"That—that was a mistake. There was a candle on the coffee table in the den, and I knocked it over by accident," Autumn said.

"Oh nee. My candle," Jeannie whispered.

Renee shook a finger at Autumn. "Then why were you in my house if you didn't want to hurt us?"

"I wanted to take something that meant a lot to you."

Renee let those words roll through her mind. "Like the teapot?"

"That old teapot?" Autumn asked with a derisive snort. "That was the first thing I saw, so I grabbed it."

Renee seethed. "That belonged to mei mammi. It meant a lot to me."

"And it made you sad that I broke it, right?" Autumn demanded. "That's what I wanted—for you to be as miserable as I am."

Renee shared a shocked expression with Jeannie and then focused on Autumn again. "You wanted to take something important to me," she repeated, before understanding lit in her mind. "Did you take my box of letters?"

"Maybe," Autumn quipped.

"You did, didn't you?" Renee demanded, her voice rising, but when Autumn only shrugged again, Renee's chest burned with anger. "And if you only meant to make me miserable, then I'm going to ask you again why you tried to kill Jeannie and me?"

Autumn frowned. "I already told you that I never meant to hurt you—only *scare* you enough so that you'd leave. I didn't want to have to see you living your happy life here on the farm every day."

"Did you even bother to call for help when the fire started?" Tim asked.

"No." Autumn shook her head.

"That proves you really didn't care what happened to Renee and Jeannie, did you?" Tim challenged her.

Jerome slipped closer to Autumn while she kept her eyes trained on Tim.

"Look, I wanted to make sure Renee was as miserable as I am. That's all." Autumn held up her hands.

"Then tell me where you've taken my box of letters," Renee said, her voice quavering.

Autumn shook her head.

"Give them to me," Renee pleaded with her. "Please, Autumn."

"No." Autumn turned and reached for her purse, but Jerome grabbed it and held it up. "Hey! That's mine!" She tried to jump for it, but Jerome was a least six inches taller than she was.

"She has a gun," Jerome announced, holding the purse up higher.

She has a gun?

Renee's insides twisted. *Gott, please protect us!*

Tim stepped in front of Renee and Jeannie and motioned for them to stay behind him.

Autumn jumped up and down, reaching for her purse. "Give it to me!" she yelled.

Jerome glanced over at Tim, handed him the purse, and then grabbed Autumn's arms and held them behind her back. "You need to calm down, Autumn," he ordered. "You're done making our lives miserable, and it stops *now*."

Suddenly, red and blue lights reflected off the walls as sirens sounded.

"Autumn, the police are here," Jerome told her. "You need to give yourself up."

Renee rested her hand on Jeannie's shoulder and breathed a deep sigh of relief.

Danki for protecting us, Gott!

Chapter Twenty-Four

Conversations buzzed, and the lights from the police cars reflected off the side of the small daadihaus while a team of officers took photos and made notes. Jeannie and Tim stood by the line of vehicles talking to an officer, while another hauled Autumn Martin away in handcuffs.

Officer Franklin wrote on his notepad and then studied Jerome. "You have good instincts, but you should have called me," he said. "It was a dangerous move inviting Autumn over here to talk to you without me present, especially since she brought a gun with her. Thankfully, she's agreed to confess to everything. She said something about a box of letters that belongs to Renee. One of our officers is searching Autumn's car. If you find anything that belongs to you or Renee, let me know."

"I will, but how did you even know she was here?"

The officer pointed toward the driveway, where Murray Robertson hurried toward them. "Your neighbor called me when he saw the car pull up."

"Jerome!" Murray raced over to them, huffing and puffing while trying to catch his breath. "When I saw the sedan pull into your driveway, I called the police right away." He glanced around the scene. Nearby, an officer was talking to Autumn while she sat in the back of a squad car. Another was busy searching her vehicle. "Is everything all right?"

Jerome shook his neighbor's hand. "Ya, thanks to you. The culprit was our driver." He quickly explained how he'd called Autumn, and she came to the farm and admitted everything, also bringing a gun with her. Then he scanned the area for Renee, who stood by Autumn's car. "Excuse me," he said before joining her at the back.

The female officer lifted Renee's grandmother's box out of the trunk of the car, and Renee took it.

Jerome sidled up to her. "You got your box of letters back."

"Jerome!" She turned toward him, and her teary smile pinched his heart. She set the box on the ground. "I can't believe it was Autumn who did all this."

"Ya, I know. I'm so glad it's over finally."

She rested her hand on his. "I saw an officer take Autumn away in handcuffs." She pointed to the cruiser where Autumn sat in the back.

"She admitted everything," he said. "And Officer Franklin told me we can take the box of letters home, since Autumn explained that she stole them before setting your haus on fire."

Jerome rested his hand on Renee's shoulder. "Are you okay?"

"Ya." She turned toward the police cruiser. "I want to talk to her."

"You sure?"

She nodded and threaded her fingers with his. "Come with me." She gave his hand a tug and then steered him over to the police car, where Autumn stared at them.

"Have you come to gloat?" Autumn asked, her expression stony.

Renee shook her head. "I wanted to tell you that I forgive you," she said. "And I'm sorry you're so lonely and sad."

Autumn's eyes narrowed.

"Gott loves you, Autumn," Renee told her.

Autumn's frown relaxed slightly.

"Would it be okay if I prayed with you?" Renee asked.

"Whatever makes you happy," Autumn muttered.

Renee closed her eyes. "Lord, we ask You to please bless Autumn. Help her on her journey to find happiness, and show her that no matter what, You love her, and You forgive her sins. In Jesus's name. Amen."

Jerome gave Renee's hand a gentle squeeze. He was overwhelmed by Renee's loving heart.

The female officer returned to the car. "We need to take you down to the station, Ms. Martin."

"Autumn, don't forget that Gott loves you," Renee told her.

The officer nodded at Jerome and Renee and then placed her hand on the door and started to push it closed.

"Wait. Please," Autumn said, and the officer held the door open. Then she turned to Renee, and her eyes sparkled with tears. "Thanks," she whispered.

Renee held on to Jerome's hand while the police cruiser backed out of the driveway, and the taillights disappeared into the dark.

"I think you got through to Autumn. That was pretty amazing, Renee," Jerome told her. The warm yellow light from his lanterns poured out of his kitchen windows, highlighting her lovely face.

"Despite everything she did to us, I could feel her sadness." She touched his cheek, and her lip quivered. "When you said she had a gun, I was so afraid she was going to kill you in order to hurt me." Her eyes glittered with unshed tears. "I couldn't stand the thought of losing you."

He traced the lines of her palm with his finger, and the warmth of her skin gave his rattled nerves comfort. "I saw the gun in her purse, and I was afraid she'd hurt *you*." His eyes searched hers. "Renee, I care about you, deeply, but I'm so afraid of hurting you like I hurt Amanda. At the same time, the idea of you leaving and going back to Ohio is killing me." His voice was raspy.

"Oh, Jerome." She clucked her tongue. "I care about you too." She touched his chest. "Mei dat died with bitterness on his heart. Don't let your grief consume you. Gott has forgiven you, and you need to forgive yourself."

He sniffed. "That's what mei dat told me earlier today. He said that I've been acting like I died in the accident. I put my entire life on hold, and when I thought I'd lost you today, I realized that he's right. I've been stuck in a holding pattern since that day, but I'm tired of it. I want to start living again, and I want to live my life with *you*, Renee."

She laughed. "That's music to my ears, Jerome. Because…because I love you."

His heart felt like it was going to explode. "*Ich liebe dich*," he whispered. "I love you with my entire heart, Renee. Please tell me that you'll stay in Pennsylvania, and if you don't want to, then let me come to Ohio with you. I'll join your community. I can't be without you. Tell me that we can work this out."

"That's what I want—a life with you." She moved her hand across his cheek, and he leaned into her touch. "Let's run the farm here together, Jerome. Let's build a life here on mei mammi's farm."

"Ya, that's what I want." He leaned down and kissed her. Then as he held her close, he closed his eyes and silently thanked God for bringing Renee into his life and for healing his heart.

Epilogue

Wednesday, August 6

"This is the kitchen." Renee gestured around the room.

Mamm ran her finger along the counter. "It looks similar to Martha's original haus. What do you think? It's nice, ya?" She turned toward Ike.

"It's schee." Ike glanced around the small room. "Definitely functional."

Renee pointed to a wall of windows overlooking the barn and pasture. "I love that I can peek out here and see Jerome walking in from the barn."

"What she's really saying is that she likes to check on me and make sure I'm doing my chores instead of just standing around day-dreaming," Jerome quipped.

Renee turned, and Jerome winked at her while leaning in the doorway.

Her heart felt light as she considered how much had happened during the last few months. Jerome had recovered from his wounds following the night of the fire, and the gashes on his hand quickly healed, leaving light-colored scars.

A week after the fire, Renee returned home to Ohio to tell her parents what had happened, and then she convinced them that she wanted to move to Pennsylvania permanently to start a new life. While she was sad to say goodbye to her friends in Holmes County, they understood. Anna continued to work with Renee's mother in the basket shop. She was disappointed to see Renee leave, but Renee promised to return for her wedding and already had the trip planned for October.

Two weeks later, she moved back to Pennsylvania and stayed with Jeannie and her parents. The deacon from her church district in Ohio wrote a letter to the deacon in the Graber family's church district stating that she was a member in good standing, and after that, she was considered an official member of the Graber family's church district.

Renee quickly felt like a part of the community, and she cherished getting to know the other members. She also enjoyed going to youth group every week with Jeannie, and she was thrilled when Jerome decided to join them. Each Sunday she had a blast playing volleyball and singing hymns with Jerome, Jeannie, and their friends.

After the new house was ready, Renee and Jeannie moved in, and Jerome reached out to Ike for permission before asking Renee to date him. She had cherished every moment of getting to know him better. They talked about everything, and they never seemed to run out of words. Renee had never been happier in her life.

And now that her parents had finally come to visit, things were even better.

"Let's move on to the bedrooms," Renee said, leading her parents down the hallway, past where Jerome stood smiling. "This is Jeannie's room," she said, pointing to the first bedroom. "And this is where you'll stay." She opened the second bedroom door, and Ike carried their bags into it.

"Where's your bedroom?" Mamm asked.

Renee led her across the hall. "It's here."

Once inside, Mamm took her hands in hers. "Renee, I haven't had a chance to tell you how proud I am of you." She touched Renee's cheek. "You're so strong and brave." She frowned. "I'm sorry I never told you the truth about what happened between your dat and your mammi. I believed I had to guard that secret for your dat, but looking back now, I realize I was hurting you by not telling you what happened."

"It's okay. I've come to grips with that, and I'm not angry with you or with Dat." Renee paused for a moment. "But I still have one question."

"What?"

"Why did Dat insist we join a stricter community?"

Mamm sank down onto the corner of the bed. "After he found out that Abner wasn't his biological daed, he felt betrayed, and he said that it hurt even more since Abner was the bishop. He believed that if the bishop could lie like that, then he shouldn't be considered a man of Gott."

Mamm seemed lost in thought while she moved her fingers over Renee's pink and grey nine-patch-patterned quilt, which Renee had stitched herself during one of her sisters' days with Jeannie and their friends. "By joining a more conservative community, your dat thought we'd be living a life that was closer to what Gott wants for us. He said that he couldn't go to church and listen to a man who was chosen to be bishop but had lied to his sohn."

Renee considered that. "I honestly believe Mammi wanted to tell Dat the truth, but Daadi thought he was saving Dat from hurt by not admitting he wasn't his biological daed. I don't think they ever meant to harm anyone."

Mamm nodded. "I agree, but your dat was devastated." She frowned. "I always hoped he would forgive his parents, but he was a stubborn man."

"That's true."

"Where did you find the letters?" Mamm asked.

"There was a hiding place in the wall."

"Do you know why Martha put them there?"

"Ya, I think I do," Renee began. "When I told the lawyer I decided to keep the farm, he asked me if I'd found the letters. I was surprised he knew about them. I asked him what would've happened to them if I hadn't found them or kept the farm. He said that Mammi left a contingency plan for the letters."

Mamm's brow pinched. "What do you mean?"

"Mammi asked the lawyer not to tell me about the letters until I made a decision about the farm. If the property was going to someone else, the lawyer had instructions to retrieve and destroy some personal items, but he said that what Mammi prayed for was for me to return to Bird-In-Hand." Renee's eyes misted with tears, and she swiped them away. "The truth is that I felt Gott leading me here and also Mammi calling me too. Deep in my heart, I'm sure I'm supposed to be here." She paused and took a deep breath. "I'm grateful that you understand."

"I'm glad that you know the truth, and I'm also happy that you found a home here. As difficult as it is to be away from you, I understand why you want to stay." Mamm sniffed. "But I'll miss you."

"I'll miss you too." Renee's heart clenched. "But I promise I'll visit you. And you need to come and visit more often. I know Delilah and Aenti Naomi can't wait to see you." She touched her mother's arm. "You're finally ready to see Aenti Naomi, right?"

"Ya, I am. She and I have a lot to discuss." Mamm pulled her in for a hug. "It's so gut to be back here. I'm glad you led me home too." Renee sniffed and held on to her mother.

She could hear Jerome and Ike talking softly in the next room as they moved to the hallway. "Why don't you and Ike get settled, and I'll start supper?"

Mamm nodded. "Perfect."

Jerome joined them in the hallway and took Renee's hand. "Can we talk for a minute?"

"Ya."

Jerome led her out to the porch. "Your folks are great."

"Of course they are. They raised me," she joked with a cheeky grin.

He laughed, and she enjoyed the sound. She was so thankful that he had finally opened up to her, and he smiled more than he frowned these days. His happy expression faded, and her stomach pitched.

"Is everything okay?" she asked.

"Ya." He scratched a spot on his cheek. "Um, I wanted to thank you."

"For what?"

"For being you." He touched her nose. "You've taught me so much since I met you in April, and I believe that Gott sent you here not only to find out why your dat moved, but also to help me come through the darkness and into the light again." He took her hands in his. "You've shown me how to live again, and more importantly, you've taught me not only to love but that I'm worthy of love."

He moved his thumb over her palm, leaving shivers in its wake. "Renee, I love you, and I'm so glad that Gott led me to you." He paused for a moment. "When I was a child, I dreamt of becoming a plumber and working for mei onkel. In fact, that was my plan before the accident. But after the accident, I took the job here because I thought I was better off working alone."

Jerome rubbed his elbow. "The funny thing is, I came here so that I could be alone, but working here led me to you. Now I know what I want, and I don't want to be a plumber. Instead, I want to build a future with you here, on this farm. Would you consider that?"

She nodded. "Ya, I thought that's what we planned."

"What I'm trying to say is..." He hesitated. "I just asked your dat's permission, and I'd be honored if you would be mei *fraa*."

Her stomach flipped. "Oh, Jerome, yes! I'd love to be your wife."

"Whew!" He laughed. "I was worried for a second." He ran his finger down her cheek. "Danki for bringing my heart back to life, Renee." Then he leaned down and brushed his lips over hers before resting his hands on her shoulders. "Ich liebe dich."

"Ich liebe dich, Jerome," she said. "Now kiss me again."

"Gladly," he said with a grin.

Closing her eyes, Renee savored the feel of his lips. She couldn't wait to see what God had planned for her future with Jerome in her new home of Bird-in-Hand.

From the Author

Dear Reader,

I met my Amish friend Ruth (fictional name to protect her privacy) when I was researching my very first book, *A Gift of Grace*. We visited for the first time for two hours in her kitchen in Gordonville, Pennsylvania, and she was the most soft-spoken, warm, and patient person I'd ever met. She never lost her patience with her children, and, since she has seven, I was impressed. I knew I could learn to be a better person by following her example.

My friendship with Ruth has grown tremendously since that day in 2008. We moved from occasional phone calls and visits to more regular calls. She and one of her daughters read my early manuscripts and helped me with the details and accuracy of my books.

We've also been on many adventures together. Not only have we gone shopping and met for lunch, but I also helped with suppers she hosted in her home. One beautiful summer day, I took her, her three boys, my two boys, my mother, and a friend to a lake where we enjoyed each other's company. When we're together, we're simply two women having fun, and it doesn't matter that she's Amish and I'm "English."

My greatest honor, however, was when Ruth invited me to attend a church service hosted at her place. I'll never forget sitting in her barn and listening to the ministers while observing the folks in her congregation. I knew that this was a once in a lifetime experience that I would cherish forever.

Although I've never lived in Lancaster County, Pennsylvania, whenever I visit it feels like home to me. Just seeing the rolling patchwork of farmland and the horses and buggies gives me a feeling that I can't quite describe. After writing dozens of Amish fiction books, it has become a part of me, thanks to Ruth's special friendship. She has generously shared her culture with me, and I'm forever grateful.

I'm honored to share *A Heart Set Free* with you. I hope you enjoyed reading the story as much as I enjoyed writing it. And I hope that the story fills your heart and inspires you the way the Amish culture inspires me.

Signed,
Amy Clipston

Acknowledgments

As always, I'm thankful for my loving family, including my mother, Lola Goebelbecker; my husband, Joe; my sons, Zac and Matt; our five spoiled indoor cats and our precocious outdoor cat. I'm blessed to have such an awesome, amazing, supportive, and purring family. Special thanks to my mother who graciously read a draft of this book to check for typos.

To my critique partner, Kathleen Fuller, thank you for your help plotting this book. I've learned so much from you, and I look forward to working together on our future projects.

I'm also grateful to my special Amish friend, who patiently answers my endless stream of questions.

Thank you to my wonderful church family at Morning Star Lutheran in Matthews, North Carolina, for your encouragement, prayers, love, and friendship. You all mean so much to my family and me.

Thank you, Zac Weikal, for your help with my social media plans, my website, my online bookstore, and all the other amazing things you do to help with marketing. I would be lost without you!

I would also like to thank my literary agent, Nalini Akolekar, for her guidance and advice. I'm so grateful we can work together.

Thank you to my amazing editors, Jane Haertel and Sabrina Diaz, for your friendship and guidance. I'm so excited to work with you, and I hope we have a chance to work together again in the future.

I'm grateful to each and every person at Guideposts who helped make this book a reality.

To my readers—thank you for choosing my novels. My books are a blessing in my life for many reasons, including the special friendships I've formed with my readers. Thank you for your email messages, Facebook notes, and letters.

Thank you most of all to God—for giving me the inspiration and the words to glorify You. I'm grateful and humbled You've chosen this path for me.

Discussion Questions

1. Jerome's fiancée died in a crash two years before the story started. Think of a time when you felt lost and alone. Where did you find your strength? What Bible verses helped?

2. When Jerome meets Renee, he feels an instant connection with her. As he gets to know her, he fears he's not good enough for her due to the accident that changed his life. Can you relate to how he feels? If so, how did you overcome those feelings of inadequacy?

3. At the beginning of the story, Renee dreams of finding out the truth about why her father left Pennsylvania and took her and her mother to Ohio. Even though her father passed away, her mother still refuses to share the truth with her. What do you think inspires her to go to Pennsylvania and search for the answers she's seeking?

4. What has Jerome learned about himself by the end of the novel? How does that influence his thoughts about a future with Renee?

5. Autumn Martin is the person who harasses and threatens Renee in order to get her farmland. What do you think of Autumn and

her behavior throughout the book? If you were Renee, how would you have handled that stressful situation?

6. Renee finds out that her father, Emmanuel, moved his family away from Bird-in-Hand because he refused to forgive his mother for lying about who his biological father was. Instead of healing that rift, he and his mother both passed away without making amends. What do you think about Emmanuel's decision not to forgive his mother? Do you believe that as a Christian, he should have forgiven her?

7. Have you ever visited Amish Country in Ohio or Pennsylvania? If you could go anywhere for vacation this weekend, where would you choose to go?

8. What role did Jeannie play in Jerome and Renee's relationship? How did she bring them together throughout the story?

9. Jerome is close to his sister, Jeannie. Do you have a special relative with whom you're close? If so, who is that relative and how did he or she influence you and your life?

10. Renee realizes throughout the book that Bird-in-Hand is where she wants to make a home with Jerome. She decides not to return to Ohio to be with her family. Do you agree with her choice to stay in Bird-in-Hand and start a life with Jerome?

About the Author

Amy Clipston is an award-winning and bestselling author and has been writing for as long as she can remember. Her fiction writing "career" began in elementary school when she and a close friend wrote and shared silly stories. She has a degree in communications from Virginia Wesleyan University and is a member of the Authors Guild, American Christian Fiction Writers, and Romance Writers of America. Amy works full-time for the City of Charlotte, North Carolina, and lives in North Carolina with her husband, two sons, mother, and six spoiled rotten cats.

Amy loves to hear from her readers. You can find her at AmyClipston.com, on Facebook at www.facebook.com/AmyClipstonBooks, and on Instagram at @Amy_Clipston.

A Note from the Editors

We hope you enjoyed *A Heart Set Free*, published by Guideposts. For over seventy-five years, Guideposts, a nonprofit organization, has been driven by a vision of a world filled with hope. We aspire to be the voice of a trusted friend, a friend who makes you feel more hopeful and connected.

By making a purchase from Guideposts, you join our community in touching millions of lives, inspiring them to believe that all things are possible through faith, hope, and prayer. Your continued support allows us to provide uplifting resources to those in need. Whether through our communities, websites, apps, or publications, we inspire our audiences, bring them together, and comfort, uplift, entertain, and guide them. Visit us at guideposts.org to learn more.

We would love to hear from you. Write us at Guideposts, P.O. Box 5815, Harlan, Iowa 51593 or call us at (800) 932-2145. Did you love *A Heart Set Free*? Leave a review for this product on guideposts.org/shop. Your feedback helps others in our community find relevant products.

Find inspiration, find faith, find Guideposts.

Shop our best sellers and favorites
at **guideposts.org/shop**

Or scan the QR code to go directly to our Shop.

Printed in the United States
by Baker & Taylor Publisher Services